Shadow of Life

G.A. Stratton

To Regina, my pseudo-twin
and my son, Thomas

CHAPTER I

HE LEANS OVER *the edge of the palace balcony, scanning the capital with its sprawling buildings, jumble of streets, markets, and gardens. It is a collage of raw sienna houses, translucent green flax, and a pop of red roses—all interwoven by tawny alleys. The azure sky peaks over the top of a massive ziggurat and obscures the horizon. He wipes away the sweat creeping down his cheek and watches the slaves lay their neat rows of mud bricks to bake in the midday sun. The heat is no respecter of persons, whether king or slave—it roasts them all.*

The king shades his eyes, glancing at the afternoon sun scorching the city of Akkad in southern Mesopotamia. Its citizens scramble to escape the blistering temperatures. Workers rest under the meager shade of the date palms. Grandparents nap in the blissful cool of their brick homes as their grandchildren frolic in the muddy waters of the Euphrates.

The Euphrates, the mother of life, offers an errant breeze, siphoned into the palace courtyard. The Akkadian monarch lifts his face, luxuriating in the cool wind ruffling his hair, grateful it is not a Shamal, the dust storms a nuisance that plagues the city this time of the year. He cocks his head to the side, listening anxiously for any sound from the birthing chamber. The only audible noise is the rhythmic clicking of the weavers' looms and the muffled songs of the masons.

A feeling of doom plays havoc with his nerves. Strange, he thinks, that doubt does not grip in him in battle, but the birth of his sixth child inflames his superstitions. Most royal marriages are callous political arrangements, but he is fortunate to have found love. He fears for his beloved queen. She bore five healthy sons, but the perils of childbirth are beyond his comprehension. So, he bows his head, offering a silent prayer to Inanna for her safety . . . and his secret wish for a daughter.

His heart fills with pride as he gazes over his city. His grand-sire built this empire with blood and sweat, and through military conquests, he extended its boundaries, a testament to the fact that any-thing is possible—a comforting thought that lessens his trepidation.

At last, he hears the sound of a baby's welcoming cry, and a smile lights his face at the thought of another successor to their dynasty. The king suppresses the urge to join his wife; men are not welcome during labor, the domain of women and bad luck, so he waits patiently. He does not have to wait long.

The head midwife scurries along the great hall, weaving among the forest of columns and bearing her precious cargo. The massive corridor is impressive, but now its length is a curse, allowing him time to study her blood-splattered gown. His heart sinks. She kneels *before him, anxious for his approval, and offers him the swaddled newborn. "A girl, sire." She is unsure if a female child is acceptable.*

"The queen?" The king stares down at her bloody apron, afraid of the answer. He hesitates before meeting her eyes.

"An easy birth. She rests in comfort," she answers proudly and presents the latest member of the royal family.

He exhales audibly, not realizing he was holding his breath. "I prayed for a daughter." He takes the baby from her, cradling it close to his chest. Inanna was merciful, so tonight, there will be sacrifices to her. "A princess." The new father beams.

"She is the most beautiful child, Your Majesty," the midwife boasts.

He unwraps the swaddling, inspecting his daughter for flaws. The midwife spoke true: his daughter is perfect, with ivory skin, wavy ebony hair, and the blackest eyes. Her eyes catch his attention. He thought newborns, like kittens, could not see after birth, but this one seems to study him. Her face is so serious it makes him laugh aloud, which startles her. Instinctively, she stretches out her tiny arms. To pacify her, he hums a lullaby, and she coos with pleasure. He touches her tiny fingers, which curl around his.

The midwife is enchanted with this picture of paternal love: The mighty king enthralled by his tiny daughter.

"You shall be Nadira, which means precious and rare," he whispers to her.

The baby smiles and captures his heart. He grins back and promises, "And I shall love you forever."

Forever is a long time.

It's one of those dreary nights when it's better to hide inside than to venture out, the weather soggy and miserable. Rain pummels the restaurant's windows. Nadira studies the spectacular view of the glistening skyline. The harbor twinkles in the distance, resembling an erratic set of Christmas lights. New York City is her chosen sanctuary, a seething mass of humanity, vibrant and always in motion, the perfect place for her to disappear. She lives here unnoticed among the other eight million inhabitants.

A thud at the window startles her as a pigeon hits the pane before spiraling lifeless to the pavement below. She stares down at the people scurrying about and trying to dodge raindrops, drowning in the futility of the task. Her view offers a sense of disconnection from the world, like a snow globe where the action is encapsulated but very separate from the observer.

She slumps back in her chair. The privacy of her table offers a panoramic view of the diners. Her dusky eyes study them, envying their ignorance. She dwells among them but is not one of them, a daily balancing act between inclusion and deception. She is a visitor to their world, a refuge from her own, belonging to neither. Her self-imposed exile affords her a unique perspective on human society. Her ability to hear all their thoughts is a definite advantage but also maddening. Humans use too many words to express the simplest of ideas, but the silliness of their banter does amuse her. She surveys the wine list in an attempt to ignore their chaotic thoughts and senseless conversations.

She prefers to remain detached, but the diners steal glances at her. Her appearance attracts their interest. "Stunning" best describes her, with porcelain skin, expressive eyes, and a cascade of ebony hair, a combination that demands a second glance. Hers is not a soft beauty born of leisure but one forged by tribulation. Her whole life, beauty has been both her blessing and curse; it has made her the object of desire and hatred, each with devastating consequences. Her own father, possessive of her beauty, sacrificed her life. However, that was a long, long time ago and is rarely remembered.

Her eyes dart to the entrance as she senses his presence. Damn, he found her again. She can't escape him, bound by time and blood. Gregor's ability to locate her is uncanny. It's as though his sole occupation is to monitor her, which irritates her to no end. On cue, a tall, distinguished man enters the room, scans the crowd, spots her, and then strides up to the table. Nadira glances up, annoyed at the interruption.

His handsome features never fail to impress. The high cheekbones, aquiline nose, and obsidian green eyes remind her of a bird of prey, beautiful but lethal. An expensive black business suit extenuates his athletic build, combined with his quick intelligence and powerful sensuality, making it almost impossible for most women to resist him. Well, except for her.

"It didn't take you long to find me," she says.

Gregor slides onto the seat across from her. His dark eyes sparkle with childlike pleasure, as though he found her in a game of hide and seek. "Not when you know where to look," he replies.

A lock of his raven black hair tumbles across his forehead. His provocative smile could melt any woman's reserve, but Nadira's defenses are formidable. The innocence of his response touches her, and his concern is flattering, but she resists the temptation to brush that errant hair off his face.

Her companion for centuries, he is the most exasperating being she has ever known. Their relationship is a battle of strong wills, a game of words with hidden meanings, veiled truths, and secrets they guard from each other. Physical intimacy is not part of the deal.

"Am I that predictable?" she asks.

"Today, I knew where you would be: among people and expensive liqueur" is his response.

Their species exists side by side with humans—dependent on them, interwoven like the threads of fabric. Though no longer hunted for food, human hemoglobin is still an integral part of their diet. The lure of blood is potent but not the reason she seeks their company tonight. Her motivation is premeditated and more elusive.

A fleeting look of pain contorts her lovely features. "Yes, an anniversary I would rather forget," she confesses.

She gazes out the window, trying to shake off this ancient sorrow. The pain does not cleave her heart as it once did. Most of the year it is tolerable . . . except for this day, when she exposes the wound, hemorrhaging her grief. She has yet to cauterize this ulcer on her soul.

They sit in silence until he takes her hand in his. "Nadira, you become so morose and withdrawn during this time. I struggle every year with new ways to cheer you. Please, come to the club with me. We will dance and lighten your heart." He flashes his most engaging smile.

She studies him, wondering why he keeps trying when it would be easier to forget her. She sighs as she glances down at her hand in his. "I don't approve of some of the clubs you frequent.

The wave of women throwing themselves at you becomes tedious," she complains.

"Are you jealous?" he asks. It would be better if she admitted the truth, but she never does. It is true: human women are drawn to him like moths to a flame, but can he help it?

"Why would I be jealous? The attention is distracting, that's all," she says, shooting back with a half-truth, but it is a lie nonetheless. A smile crosses his face as he realizes that she is not being honest. She peers into his eyes, unfathomable green pools drawing her in, and struggles to regain her composure.

"We don't have to go to a club. We can go anywhere you want. You work too hard," he begs, his eyes pleading with her.

Distracted, they fail to notice a presence near the table. She silently curses; it is dangerous to be so preoccupied that you lose track of your surroundings. Gregor has that effect on her. In public, they must safeguard their identities.

The waiter stands silently beside the table and awaits acknowledgement. Begrudgingly, Nadira glances at him with a look so cool that he visibly shrinks. He realizes that he interrupted his clients prematurely, a rookie mistake that could cost him a sizable tip.

"Madam." He smiles, eager to please and rectify his error.

"I would like to speak to the sommelier, please." Her voice is icy, more annoyed with herself for dropping her guard than at the waiter.

"Right away, madam," he answers. The waiter scurries away to retrieve the restaurant's wine expert.

Gregor teases Nadira. "You certainly know how to take the starch out of a man."

Her sharp retort dies on the tip of her tongue with the arrival of the haughty sommelier.

"How may we serve you, madam?" the sommelier asks.

Nadira scans the wine list. "What is the oldest red you have?"

"An 1865 Chateau Lafite, madam," he answers proudly. The restaurant's wine cellar is the best in New York.

She closes the list. "Good. I'll take the bottle."

The sommelier, a seasoned wine aficionado, is stunned. He lowers his voice to a whisper. "Madam, the Chateau Lafite is sold by the glass. The bottle is offered at one hundred and fifty thousand dollars." He knows only a select clientele can afford this precious wine. He is unfamiliar with this particular client, and his condescending response infuriates her.

Nadira impales him with a cold stare. "Perfect. I'll take the *whole* bottle."

Her emphasis on the word "whole" makes the sommelier nervous. He fidgets with the wine list as beads of sweat form on his forehead. "Very well, madam," the sommelier concedes. He hurries from the table, unable to believe his blunder. Heaven forbid he offend a special client, especially one who can afford such an expensive wine.

Gregor watches the sommelier's retreating back.

"He picked the wrong night to cross you." He smiles condescendingly.

Nadira's temper flares. "Why do you torment me like this?" Gregor knows how to push her buttons.

"Pardon me, I forgot. You use moral principles and civic duty as criteria for your yearly forays." His reply strikes a nerve.

She eyes him, knowing what verbal sparring awaits her tonight. "Gregor, why argue? Grant me some peace on this one night that gives me a little pleasure," she pleads, hoping he will cease his badgering.

Gregor softens his tone in response to her tortured look. "I cannot be false. Tonight will give you pleasure because it is our nature." He confronts her with the truth, striking at her Achilles's heel, her conscience.

Nadira studies Gregor, but his expression is unreadable. She decides that being on the offensive is less painful. "Aren't you being a hypocrite? You have no qualms about your excursions."

His response is unexpected. He laughs. "No, I don't. I admit what I am and make no excuses. I do not pretend to be something else. *Esto quod es.*"

She sighs. Latin, the ancient language—Gregor reverts to it whenever he wants to make a point. Nadira rivets him with a spiteful look. "'Be what you are.' I prefer *veritas odium paret.* 'Truth creates hatred.' Are we to continue this conversation in Latin?" she asks. She rarely wins their arguments or pierces his emotional armor, so she resorts to glaring at him across the table. He grins back smugly.

The sommelier's return interrupts them. With great ceremony, he uncorks the bottle and pours the wine with a practiced grace into her glass. He waits for her approval.

Nadira swirls the ruby liquid and sniffs the bouquet, its earthy aroma perfuming the air. "A beautiful nose," she comments, using the wine terminology for a pleasant smell. She lifts the glass to her lips, sliding the sparkling fluid between her full lips. The action is so graceful and sensual that it catches the sommelier by surprise. She graces him with a dazzling smile. He stares at her, captivated. "A wonderful finish," she tells the sommelier, who flushes with pride.

"Thank you, madam." He bows and leaves.

Nadira glances at Gregor, who is studying her like a cat.

A slow smile plays across his face. "Glad to see you sheathed your claws. I am relieved that no human was hurt during the tasting of the one-hundred-and-fifty-thousand-dollar bottle of Chateau Lafite." Gregor's eyes shimmer with laughter.

Try as she might, Nadira cannot resist their charm, and her anger drains away.

"Shall I pour?" he asks. He lifts the wine bottle from its bucket. She nods, watching as he deftly fills their glasses, beginning their annual tradition, a tradition she dreads, but like the ocean tides, it is inevitable and predictable. He glances around the room at the other diners, engrossed in their meals. He catches a wink or two from admiring women, their desire painted on their faces like their makeup. Modern women are so liberal sexually that he yearns for the old days when flirtation was a game of anticipation rather than just about the sex. He stalls until Nadira is ready to commence.

She stares at her wine glass, gathering courage. "A toast to my husband, Cristo."

"To Cristo," he toasts.

They raise their glasses, savoring the ancient elixir, a look of satisfaction affixed to their faces. He holds the glass to the light, illuminating the liquid within, turning it a blood-red color.

"Every year, I sit beside you, drinking some premium vintage liquor. 1865 was a very good year." He pauses, inhaling its rich aroma before continuing. "The Civil War ended, man finally reached the summit of the Matterhorn, and *Alice's Adventures in Wonderland* was published." Gregor twirls the glass as the wine dances within its crystal confines.

"I remember. It was an especially good year. Do you remember Charles? Poor man used that horrible pseudonym, Lewis Carroll. His stories were fantastic. His Hatter is my favorite—reminds me of my milliner in Paris. He was very mad, indeed," she reminisces.

"Yes, but he designed fantastic hats. You looked fetching in them," he adds.

Nadira smiles at the compliment. The wine warms with their memories. Gregor eyes her over the rim of his glass. She seems relaxed, so he decides to ask the question she never answers. Maybe this year, his luck will change.

"Nadira, what was Cristo like?" He immediately regrets his decision as her face hardens into a rigid mask.

"You know I do not talk about him," she replies curtly.

Gregor is unsure of his footing but decides to press on. "You never do, but never is a long time to remain silent about someone you loved." He probes at the root of her pain. "I know the subject is taboo. You withdraw every time I ask, but I continue to hope you will trust me with your secretive past."

"My *past*, as you refer to it, spans over four millennia. I evolved with human civilization and traveled its circuitous path through history. I was ancient when your mother birthed you.

You have only scratched the surface of my existence. There is much you do not know about me, Gregor," she responds.

She delivers her testimonial with such calm authority that his question seems foolish. She is right: it is as though she did not exist before that fateful day when she rescued him. Destiny threw them together, but her past is an impenetrable void.

A flood of painful memories assaults her psyche, threatening to overwhelm her. She struggles to wrestle them back into her subconscious, hidden away and forgotten. She feels trapped and eager to flee his incessant interrogation.

"Thank you for caring, but it's time for me to go," she says. She jumps up, pushing away from the table.

Impulsively, Gregor grabs her arm. "Nadira, there is no honor in these meaningless acts. With each victim, a piece of your soul withers," he admonishes her.

She peers down at his hand. Their eyes meet. He has ensnared her with his arguments but can't hope to hold her, so he releases her arm.

Her voice wavers. "What soul? These acts as you call them are not meaningless to me."

His tone is somber. "What significance can they hold after all these centuries? It is the same every year: swift violence followed by weeks of regret. Violence begets violence. Only you can put an end to this madness."

Stunned speechless, she stares at him with an expression akin to a caged animal. His rhetoric paints her into an intellectual corner that she can't escape.

He adds, "If you have no soul, then why do you care so much? We are not beasts without laws or a conscience," he reminds her, but the conversation is not going as he expected as she distances herself from him.

She studies Gregor's earnest face and then drains the last of her wine. "Everything on this earth dies except regret. I live with my regret and my lost love. Love transcends time and space, but hatred burns brighter than any other emotion. In eight centuries, my hatred has not lessened toward his murderers, these humans. I cannot forgive or forget," she says.

"Cannot or will not?" he queries.

He rivets her with a look filled with a silent plea for resolution, but she will not concede. She glances at the room filled with people, all unaware of the threat in their midst.

"Tonight, I will unleash that hatred." She hisses her warning.

Gregor shakes his head. "Hate humans? I think not. You live as one all year . . . except tonight. No, Nadira, you can deceive yourself but not me. Make no mistake: it's not vengeance you seek, but rather you satisfy the bloodlust. It reminds you of what you really are, but tread carefully, lest you embrace our darker nature," he warns her, but she is beyond reason.

She hesitates for a moment as her mind grasps the logic of his argument, but the hunger is stronger and wins her over. The time for debate is over. Her whisper stings the air. "I am Akhkhazu. Tonight, there will be blood." She gives him one last tormented glance and then storms out of the restaurant, the black cocktail dress clinging to her lush body, her ebony locks swinging with each forceful stride. Every man's eyes follow her fleeing form. The dining room is dead silent. Politely, the diners try not to stare at him.

Surrounded by humans, Gregor shrugs his shoulders and jokes, "Women!"

CHAPTER II

THE IMAGE STARING back at Nadira in the polished elevator doors startles her. The blazing eyes and scarlet cheeks are not the only evidence of her fury. Her mind is a scrambled mess, unable to untangle her raging emotions. She appreciates Gregor's honesty but despises him for exposing her weakness. He infuriates her tremendously. They are similar to combustible chemicals—when mixed, the resulting explosions are inevitable. *Why does he have such sway over me?*

The elevator doors open to a cavernous lobby, empty this time of night. Grateful for the solitude, it offers her a brief reprieve to gather her wits. Tonight is special; her senses must be sharp and her mind clear, with no distractions.

She hurries outside, steps onto the sidewalk, and pauses to allow the cool night air to steady her nerves. The rain has stopped, washing away a thin layer of the city's grime and giving everything a slick look. The misty air forms halos around the streetlights and the puddles reflect an urban rainbow, creating a surreal landscape. She takes a deep breath, drinking in the beauty of the night. Her black stretch limo waits at the curb.

The burly, no-neck chauffeur approaches her. "Where to, my lady?" he asks. He always addresses her with a formal title. All the years in her employ, he has never, that she can remember, ever referred to her as Nadira.

She shakes her head. Where *is* she going? "Hans, I think I will walk home tonight," she answers.

He looks concerned for a split second. "Are you sure?" he asks.

Nadira condescendingly smiles at him.

"Sorry, I forgot," he adds awkwardly. She doesn't really need his protection.

"Go home. I'll be fine," she tells him.

"Good night, my lady."

"Good night, Hans."

She watches as the car disappears from view before turning on her heel and briskly striding down the empty sidewalk. The neighborhood is upscale, with little pedestrian traffic. She glances up at the humans silhouetted behind their lit windows, each secure in the safety of their four walls that make up the building blocks of this neighborhood. But these pillars of the community are not the humans she seeks. She craves something rancid and foul.

Her stilettos make a rapid clicking sound on the concrete. The sound echoes down the empty alleys. She increases her pace, leaving the exclusive area behind, and makes her way toward East Harlem. She hones her senses for danger, relying on her night vision. Light fades and images sharpen. Graffiti camouflages the derelict architecture. Litter blankets the landscape. The dregs of humanity populate this nocturnal terrain; it is the perfect habitat for her quarry. Violence breaks free from the bonds of daylight as the denizens of the night come forth.

Prostitutes are the midnight street vendors alongside the drug dealers hawking PCP or crack—pick your poison. She can hear their heartbeats, smell their desperation, and feel the brutality of their short lives. She weaves through the gauntlet of grime, seemingly oblivious to her surroundings. Here she will cauterize her festering heart.

A hand reaches out of the darkness to touch her. She focuses on the interloper, assessing what she has snagged. A male prostitute no more than seventeen years old stares at her with haunted eyes. It is always the same expression on their faces as they cling helplessly to their most precious possession: life. She studies this man-child, a good-looking kid with tousled hair and a waif-like appearance—the type preferred by fashion magazines.

He produces a rehearsed smile. "I can show you a good time."

He offers her the only thing he possesses: his body. The oldest profession obtains most of its recruits by circumstance and not choice. His story is no different. He chews his lower lip while waiting for her answer; this childish habit strikes a sad chord within her. Mesmerized by this beautiful creature, emboldened by her silence, he slides closer and cups her breast with a practiced grace.

Instinctively, she takes his face in her hands, turning it toward the light and exposing his neck, his carotid artery pulsing beneath her hand. The warmth of his skin, his youth, and his vulnerability arouse her. However, she doesn't seek a prostitute. She stares into his eyes, reading his thoughts. His dreams are of freedom, home, and his mother.

Nadira smiles. "Not tonight, handsome."

She takes his hand, slides something in it, and closes his fist. She caresses his face before turning and vanishing. Unable to move, he watches her disappear into the night. He closes his eyes, slowly opens them, and wonders if she was real or just a vision.

He peers down at his shaking hands, opens his fist, and stares at the contents. Cupped in his palm is an exquisite diamond ring, brilliant under the dim streetlight. It is the largest diamond he has ever seen. He glances in the direction of his patron and wonders why she gave it to him. Then, he realizes with this windfall that he can escape this life and make a new one. He closes his fist, protecting his treasure, glances around to make sure no one is watching, and begins to run.

Propelled forward by some internal force, Nadira's pace quickens. Her sadness for the prostitute dissipates. Instead, she focuses on attracting a special type of human. Three urban predators size her up, an expensively dressed woman alone on the wrong side of town. Like lions hunting an antelope, they silently communicate their intent, trailing behind her and spreading out on both sides of the street, just waiting to spring their trap.

Nadira catches her quarries' scent. Excellent, let them believe she is the prey. She plays the part of hapless victim: self-absorbed, oblivious of the impending danger, and fearfully glancing over her shoulder. The darkness distorts the structures; humanoid buildings with broken windows become the jagged teeth of yawning giants. The neighborhood is the backdrop for her macabre play.

She spurs onward, wandering deeper into this wasteland, until she smells the harbor. Zigzagging across alleys and back streets, she prolongs the game, making them work for their prize. In her peripheral vision, something catches her eye: a dank alley. She swiftly turns down it. Her pursuers cannot believe their good fortune and converge on the alley.

Nadira walks to the end of the blind alleyway and inspects her arena. It opens onto a three-sided courtyard, has one dim streetlight, and has only one exit, with no windows facing inward. Trash litters the pavement. The aroma of garbage, mold, and urine sours the air. It is a fitting place for a confrontation—private, dark, and vile. She backs into a murky corner, kicks off her shoes, turns toward the entrance, and waits.

Her stalkers lope into the courtyard. The dim light distorts their hard faces. They hesitate while their eyes focus in the shadowy surroundings. *Only three*, she thinks. *This shouldn't take long.*

A tall brute with a missing front tooth offers kind assistance. "Are you lost, sweetheart? I can help you if you come out," he says.

One of his comrades sniggers; taunting victims adds spice to the game, a skill they developed with practice. Their first robberies were quick, messy affairs, but they discovered that prolonging their victim's pain intensified their sadistic pleasure.

His sniggering cohort rubs his filthy head. "I'll be glad to help you, pretty lady." He grabs his crotch obscenely.

The last mugger, an addict overdue for his fix, is pissed off and in no mood for chitchat. He growls, "Cut the crap. Listen, bitch, stop hiding. Get your ass out here." He kicks over a trashcan that makes a loud clatter, startling them all.

"You scared the shit out of me," baldy barks.

The tall one squints and scans the darkness. "All we want is your money. We won't hurt you." A clear lie.

She instinctively backs away from the men, accidentally knocking over an empty beer bottle. The click of the glass draws their attention. She inches backward, drawing out the anticipation.

"Damn, get out here!" the addict bellows.

Shrouded in darkness, she inches toward the muggers. The dirty streetlight silhouettes her form.

The addict snaps, "That's a good girl!"

The bald man whistles. "Today is our lucky day. I told you she was a looker. When we're done with the cash, I want to have some fun," he says, making obscene hand gestures.

The three men surround Nadira, assessing their prize. The tall brute agrees. "You're right. We'll all have a turn or two at her before we do her."

Nadira steps under the grimy light, illuminating her pale skin and crimson lips. She seems to glow, sensually gliding toward them while smiling seductively. Her lips part slowly, exposing ghostly white fangs. Her voice caresses and lulls them into a false calm as the hunters become the prey.

"Gentleman, you picked the wrong victim," she whispers.

She savors the delicious sense of confusion. Bewildered, the men stand transfixed by the beautiful fiend before them. Drawn to her like the sirens of old, they sense potential danger but are helpless to resist. Slowly, her attackers realize something is amiss and fear grips them. Human terror is her catalyst.

She strikes lightning fast, her form a blur. She springs on the tall brute, tearing out his windpipe. A fountain of pulsating blood sprays his horrified companions. He grasps his throat, futilely tries to staunch the flow, and crashes to his knees. Her next action renders them mute. She seizes his body— over twice her size—heaves it overhead, and positions his gushing throat over her beautiful mouth. She drinks deeply until her thirst slackens, licks her luscious lips, and discards his carcass onto the filthy concrete. There is a shocked silence punctuated by the gurgling sound of the brute drowning in his blood.

She licks her fingers. "Delicious."

"You killed Mike," the addict exclaims.

"Was that his name?" she responds.

The addict picks up a discarded pipe. Adrenaline pumping, he lunges at Nadira and swings his weapon in a wide arch, trying to strike her. She easily steps out of his way and darts around him. He can't track her rapid movements but instead staggers around, blindly swinging at a constantly vanishing target. Tiring of the charade, she seizes his arm and snaps it like a twig. He shrieks in pain, cradles his arm, and staggers toward her.

Enraged beyond reason, he screeches, sending spittle flying in all directions. "You're history, bitch," he threatens.

"Really?" Nadira asks. She grabs his neck, lifts him off the ground, sniffs his face, her lips curling back in a disgusted snarl, and hurls him against the building. His body plummets to the pavement, reduced to human garbage. Nadira strides over to his inert form, prodding it with her toe. She leans over and sticks her finger in the spreading puddle of blood oozing from his crushed skull. She hesitantly tastes it. "Nasty."

Nadira stares at the bald man shaking in his sneakers. The pungent smell of ammonia emanates from his wet pants, the noxious odor polluting the surrounding air. She wrinkles her nose.

"Are we having fun yet?" She licks her lips. "What was it you wanted to do to me?" She beckons him with a finger. "Your friend was an addict. His blood was tainted, but you look tasty. I'll show you a good time, lover." She steps toward him.

He backs up quickly, trips over his own feet, and falls flat on his ass. He stares up at this vision from hell and pleads with her. "Don't hurt me," he begs.

Nadira glares down at the criminal cowering before her. "How many times have you heard that plea from your victims? Did you show mercy? No, I think not. Tonight, they will have justice and so will I."

"What the hell are you?" he asks. He crawls backward crablike until he regains his footing, jumps up, and runs for his life. The sound of his footsteps grows faint until there is silence.

Nadira glances at her handiwork, relishing the smell of fear, the metallic taste of blood, but her pleasure is short-lived. The extent of her cruelty sickens her. She steps over the lifeless bodies, ready to pursue her last victim, but a familiar scent captures her attention.

Gregor strides into view holding the bald man in the air by his throat. The man dangles helplessly, making gurgling sounds as Gregor tightens his grip. "You missed one," he taunts. Gregor plunges his fangs into the hapless dupe until he goes limp and then tosses the flaccid corpse on top of his cronies. "Well, if it isn't my favorite vigilante vampire cleaning the Gotham streets of scum. I thought that was Batman's job."

"Very funny. I didn't need your help," she tells him. She glances at the bald corpse, relieved she did not taste his rancid flesh. Previously, her annual purge of criminals afforded her a twisted solace, but now, the act leaves her empty. A wave of nausea grips her, and she grapples with the churning in the pit of her stomach. Gregor is right: slaughtering criminals does nothing to honor the memory of her husband.

He watches her in the dim light. "I beg to differ with you. This one almost got away. You are getting rusty. Out of practice, I think." He outwardly teases her but secretly watches her inner turmoil.

"Unlike you." Her head aches with the thought of more debate with Gregor.

He shakes his head. "I rarely hunt. We both agree that is outdated, but I am no hypocrite about it. I do not need moral pretenses to kill. Vampires are predators."

Nadira hangs her head. "This discussion again. Will you never stop haranguing me?"

"Not unless you admit the truth about tonight," he challenges her.

Gregor's eyes bore into hers. His strong will compels her to confess what they already know. Abashed, she glances away. His words sting her conscience.

"I hate it when you are right," she confesses.

"You do realize that you cannot clear the streets of criminals in one night." This path leads to her ultimate annihilation, and he will not stand by and watch her self-destruct.

Nadira wavers, defeated, at a loss for words. She hangs her head and closes her eyes to avoid eye contact with him, her desperation clearly chiseled on her blood-spattered features.

Moved to compassion, he wraps his arm around her slumping shoulders. "Nadira, I am worried. You live as a human all year except for today. On this day, you are what nature intended you to be: a vampire. Not the proud vampire I know but a savage executioner driven by a misdirected sense of justice and the lust for blood." He drives straight to the heart of the matter. "Disguised as a human, the rest of the year you grow weaker, more isolated, and despondent."

Nadira objects. "I am not isolated. I am surrounded by people."

"Humans. You avoid all contact with our kind," he says.

"I interact with you." She knows her response is pathetic, but she is too exhausted to argue.

Gregor frowns. "Besides me. What about your father, Amon? Last time we saw him was more than seventy years ago. After the *disagreement*, we fled to America. You withdrew from life as a vampire and embraced humanity."

"You don't understand. There are valid reasons I can't see Amon or be around vampires."

"What possible explanation can there be to avoid your father and your own kind and to hide what you are?"

Nadira struggles to explain. "Humans have no expectations of me other than hard work and kindness."

They study each other. The burden of carrying her secret is destroying her. "Nadira, what are you running from?"

Agony racks her exquisite face. Her voice is tremulous when she speaks. "After Cristo's death, I did something so horrific that it is unspeakable. I can endure the guilt only with strict discipline. If you knew the truth, you would leave me." Her confession cracks her emotional shell, releasing a flood of blood-tinged tears.

Gregor is stunned. He has never seen her cry. He glances down at the human carcasses. The extermination of criminals acts as a balm on her wounded heart and vents the pressure of a life devoid of emotion. He takes her face in his hands, brushing away the crimson tears with his fingers. He smiles reassuringly. "Remember my brutality when you found me? I was a mindless beast, savaging any humans that I laid hands on. My only purpose was to satisfy the thirst. You found me and taught me another life." He enfolds her in his arms. "Nothing you do can change how I feel about you."

His words are her lifeline to absolution. She sobs quietly in his arms, releasing her anguish, slowly drawing strength from his embrace. Her misery pierces his heart, and he plants a chaste kiss on her forehead.

"This is probably not the best place for philosophic discussion. It has been a long night. Go home. I'll tidy up," he tells her.

She smiles weakly. "Thank you."

Disheveled and disheartened, she reluctantly steps out of his embrace and weaves unsteadily, stumbling down the alley until she disappears. He watches her leave for the second time tonight. A faint moan escapes from the pile of bodies. His nostrils flare in this blood-charged atmosphere. His heart burns with unrequited love, its rhythmic beats hammering in his ears. He unleashes the predator within, allowing a sinister scowl to creep across his handsome features.

"Good dessert."

Chapter III

NADIRA LANDS SOFTLY on the balcony of her penthouse apartment. She pauses to drink in the sights and sounds of the city. The wail of an ambulance, the barking of a dog, muffled club music—a symphony of noises that crescendos with the screeching of police sirens. She closes her eyes. The salty tang of the Atlantic Ocean stings her nose, and a random breeze whips her hair. She concentrates on the sound of her heart, the blood pulsing through her veins, willing it to slow to an ebb.

She clears her mind of everything but tonight's events. Her annual criminal rout was a dismal failure and her role as executioner a sham, nothing more than an excuse to satisfy her thirst. The bloodshed does not fill the void; instead, it leaves the bitter aftertaste of death. Nothing will bring her husband back to life. The reason for her crusade has been lost over time, and her vengeance slowly devours her morality.

She longs for something else, a half-remembered feeling, the golden glow of ecstasy and sheltered peace. Love is the elusive brass ring that escapes her grasp, but if she cannot fill her heart with love, violence makes a poor substitute.

She gazes up at the night sky filled with stars and locates her talisman, the North Star. For thousands of years, it was her only compass and her astrolabe her only guide. The moon's gentle glow softens the darkness, and the stars embody her longing for continuity. Tonight, the heavens offer no solace.

Her outburst unnerves her. Her tight control is unraveling, and with it, her emotional dam is cracking, leaking a flood of tears. She is relieved that her breakdown was not public—her only witness was Gregor, whose gentleness was both surprising and uplifting. He is mercurial—one minute quarrelsome, the next supportive, as though coordinating his responses to her frame of mind. Releasing him from his feral existence was the best decision she ever made.

She enters her apartment, which is startlingly modern: all sleek lines and angular edges. Like the glossy photos in a high-fashion magazine, it's a study in contrasts, like the owner. The interior is a blank white canvas, with splashes of color from the objects on display. African masks share their space with Greek sculptures and Asian textiles. It is an eclectic mix of styles and eras. The decor is a perfect reflection of Nadira's duality, clinging to the past while grappling with the future.

Positioned by the window overlooking the city is an eighteenth-century elegant fortepiano, an early version of the modern piano—a gift from Gregor. She runs her fingers over the keys. The instrument affords her a creative release for her inner voice. She sits down, closes her eyes, and excises her sorrow on the keys. She coaxes the hauntingly beautiful notes of Chopin's "Nocturne in C minor" from the ebony and ivory. Her fingers excise her pain, transforming it into music. The sound of music draws a solitary audience.

Haseem, her *Abd*, the Arabic word for "slave," listens to his mistress as she purges her grief. The anniversary of the count's death is always a sad time for the staff and doubly so for her. She loved her husband more than life itself. His death almost destroyed her. The aftermath of his murder tested them all. It took centuries for her to recuperate, but total recovery was never an option. Her music is a testament to that fact.

"I remember when Chopin dedicated this piece to his sister," she says.

She opens her eyes and stares at him, the old pain a buoy on new tears. Her eyes close, staunching the flow, and she continues to play. He waits patiently for her to finish this cathartic cleansing. She completes the composition and opens her eyes, focusing on Haseem. "Loyal Haseem, you have been with me since Barbastro."

"Since, the night you danced for the caliph . . ." he replies.

"And he gave you to me as a gift," she says, completing his sentence. "I never understood why you did not escape."

"*Sahiba,*" he responds.

Sahib is Arabic for "master." In private, he addresses her with the title. They both understand the significance of its other meaning: "prince of the blood."

"I was twelve when the raiders attacked my village, killed my parents, and sold all the children at the slave market. My first master schooled me in worldly pleasures and loved me well, but his violent death forced me to the auction block. Many of my masters were brutal. I endured their cruelty until the last of my tormentors castrated me, then I prayed for death. However, Allah denied me paradise. So, I accepted my destiny."

His story always moves her. She ponders the injustice done to him, first made a eunuch by the caliph and then a vampire by her. Haseem is a rare commodity in this turbulent world, a gentle soul undisturbed by the violent forces shaping his life.

"I granted you freedom that first night and many times afterward. But still you remain with me." She studies his tranquil androgynous face.

A slight smile plays on his lips. "It is more than a piece of paper or title that binds me to you."

"I gave you a letter of emancipation." She peers up at him.

"I remember. I tore it up, tossing the pieces on the floor." He smiles at the memory of her outrage. "Fate is a twisted path. Allah placed me in your household, where I found kindness, a position of respect, and, eventually, love. My paradise is here with you."

She taps a few keys on the fortepiano, producing a hollow sound. She cannot imagine her life without him, her trusted confident and friend. She looks away, lost in thought and questioning her motives for his continued servitude. Tonight, her need for self-reproach is overpowering.

She scrutinizes Haseem. "You pleaded with me to make you a vampire. Do you regret your decision?" Her voice filled with such melancholy that it dismays him.

"I do not lament a day spent with you. 'Regret' is a useless word and has no positive purpose." He pauses, waiting for her to respond, but she remains silent. "Some, like me, are destined for a small life and others for greatness. *Sahiba*, your destiny is etched in the sands of time." He has devoted his life to this complex vampire. She is an enigma, a vampire who embraces her humanity despite its vulnerabilities. She brings together both worlds with a grace that astounds him. "Service to you is my destiny. Our fates are entwined. I would gladly offer my life for you, *Sahiba*," he reassures her.

She is touched and perplexed. *What does he see in me to warrant such devotion?* "Your devotion humbles me. Adrian is a fortunate vampire," she says.

She refers to his vampire mate. Haseem smiles at the thought of his partner. Adrian is a freelance filmmaker with an upbeat nature. They met in 1907 at a French art gallery opening of Picasso's paintings. Adrian was one of his promising disciples. It was love at first sight for both of them. Together, they share a life of laughter and contentment.

"It is not devotion that cleaves me to you—it is the love of a friend," he confesses.

"Not friends, but family," Nadira says, and they both smile in agreement.

"*Asr be kheyr, Sahiba*. Will you need anything else tonight?" he asks, but he already knows her answer.

"Tonight, I require solitude," she responds.

He bows slightly and then vanishes.

She rises from the fortepiano, wanders to the library doors, and slides them open. The library is a stark contrast to the rest of the apartment. The rich wood panels glow, lined with bookcases filled with ancient volumes, oils from the masters, and treasures collected over centuries. This is her sanctuary, filled with things most precious to her. She clicks a remote control and the room glows.

Over the massive stone fireplace, a gallery light illuminates a large oil painting of a conquistador. He wears the same suit of armor that occupies a place of honor in the corner. The portrait dominates the space, as does the man. The artist captured the subject's raw power, laughing eyes, and sensual mouth. A face one does not forget.

One light in particular focuses on the eleventh-century suit of armor. She wanders over to it and runs her hand over a shoulder plate. She remembers him astride his warhorse wearing this armor and shining in the sunlight, his bearing proud and his powerful body draped in the colors of his king. Her Cristo, the human she wed.

He was the love of her life, her soulmate, no matter how cliché the term. No one, vampire or human, captured her heart as he did. She abandoned herself to his love. Theirs was a life of blissful happiness . . . until his sudden death. In his absence, her heart withered, she renounced emotion, and she sanctioned her annual acts of vengeance. Instead of redemption, those murders became the insidious path to her corruption. Shame torments her consciousness. *What would my father say?* She must relinquish this self-destructive behavior and reclaim her integrity.

She walks to the wall of bookcases and presses a lever, revealing a hidden safe. She enters a code on the keypad, and the safe door springs open. Rifling through the contents, she removes an ancient leather volume and a small velvet box. She puts the book down and stares at the box. She has not touched it in seventy years, preferring to forget its importance.

She opens this Pandora's Box and fingers the contents: a pair of heavy gold earrings set with large rubies circled by diamonds. The design is ancient and priceless. She lifts an earring out of the box, dangling it toward the light. The stones are prisms, catching the light and refracting a rainbow of colors onto the walls. The rubies gleam blood red—the effect is dazzling, mesmerizing her with their beauty.

Amon gave her the earrings during their last meeting. He offered her ultimate power, but his price was exorbitant. She disobeyed him, and an ugly argument ensued, ending with neither conceding their position. He gave her the earrings as a reminder of her duty. She fled her home and family and has remained in a self-imposed exile for almost a century. She can never return home or do what he demands. Never.

She replaces the earrings, closes the box, and places it back in the safe. Nadira stares up at the painting and gently runs her fingertip across the frame, caressing it. Trance-like, she gazes at the portrait.

"Cristo, beloved husband."

Lost in thought, she does not hear Gregor enter the study. He watches her from the doorway, the love for her late husband clearly etched on her exquisite features. Tonight was the first time she allowed him to glimpse her empty heart. It gave him hope that she might feel more than friendship for him.

He whispers, "Nadira."

She looks past him as though gazing at an apparition and tries to focus, to remember what she wanted to tell him. Her past enslaves her, making it hard to break free. They stare at each other for what seems an eternity.

"I was worried and came to check on you," he tells her.

She closes the gap between them, taking his hands in hers. "I am sorry for my outburst." Uncomfortable, she looks away.

Gregor is surprised by her apology. "You always wear a mask to hide your true feelings. Don't apologize for revealing your inner self. Vampires experience life like no other creature. We feel emotions more intensely. Love and hate are magnified tenfold." He looks at Cristo's painting, and her eyes follow his gaze. "We love for an eternity." Gregor gazes into her eyes. "But you already know this about our species."

She notices his eyes change color—an unusual dark green— and begin to glow with an inner passion. He studies her with those extraordinary eyes. She feels their magnetic pull but breaks eye contact, severing his hold on her. He understands her better than she understands herself and knows how to ease her angst.

"I admire your control and discipline necessary to keep your dark secret, but over the centuries, it's taken an enormous toll on you. You must let someone share your burden. If you do no trust me, then maybe your father?" he suggests.

She is touched by his heartfelt plead, which softens her resolve. She drops his hands, strides over to the bookcase, and picks up the ancient leather volume. Nadira lovingly strokes it, as though trying to decide something. He is surprised by her rapid retreat, afraid he has overstepped his bounds, and unsure what is about to happen. She returns to his side and hands him the book. Bewildered, he peers at her.

"I am ready to trust you. This is one of my journals. I think it will furnish some of the answers you deserve," she reveals.

The look on his face rewards her faith. Joy radiates from his handsome features, but she feels vulnerable, as though giving him a piece of her.

Gregor glances down at the journal. "I am honored you would trust me with this. I will guard it with my life. Thank you, Nadira."

His husky tone elicits a delicious skip in her heart. Her instinctive response startles her. Their relationship has been one of mentor and student, companions, not lovers. This is uncharted territory for them.

She kisses his cheek, and his masculine scent embraces her. She whispers in his ear, "I know you will, my *ami*."

Her silken voice caresses his heart, and his full lips respond with a provocative smile. She feels lightheaded. Too much has happened tonight, and she does not trust herself this close to him. She retreats hastily from the room. He watches her leave him for the third time.

Abandoned, Gregor studies the portrait of Cristo and ponders the contents of the journal. *After all these centuries, I will finally know the truth. What horrendous secret has Nadira kept hidden all these years?*

He picks up the remote, clicks off the lights, and closes the library doors.

CHAPTER IV

G REGOR SLIDES HIS key into the door of a handsome brownstone and steps into the comfort of his home. The rooms are decidedly masculine, awash in a sea of grays and brown, populated with familiar furniture, photos, and possessions that elicit a lifetime of memories. Vampires are defined by their past, clutching it tightly to their hearts. He relishes his history, displaying it proudly throughout the townhouse.

The painting in his living room, the first thing you see when you enter the room, is of Nadira dressed in a seventeenth-century blue ball gown. Her elaborate pearl-studded coiffure matches the twin baroques dangling from her ears. It is his favorite painting of her. He pours himself a Scotch, settles into his favorite leather chair, and flips on the brass floor lamp. Cradling the journal in his lap, he glances down at the unopened book. He has waited centuries to step into Nadira's past and meet his rival for her love. The specter of her dead husband will haunt him no more. His trepidation lessens, and he opens the journal.

The writing on the page is Nadira's fine copperplate calligraphy.

Barbastro, Al-Andalusia, anno Domini 1064

Barbastro was my home for the past thirty years. There Muslims, Christians, and Jews existed with a practiced harmony. It was an island of unsteady peace in a savage world. But peace was a fleeting concept that rarely lasts. So it was with this utopia.

The Reconquista reached our city. The pope decreed that his army would reclaim our land for Christianity. His followers rushed madly to pluck this jewel in the crown of Al-Andalusia. The predictable motives of greed, religion, and power drove the destruction.

Resistance was futile, for they came as a tide which could not be held. Fires painted the night sky with a palette of persimmon, scarlet, and saffron. Screams of women and children shattered the stillness. The pungent smell of burnt wood and flesh bit the nostrils. An insidious blanket of smoke crept across the landscape. It stung my eyes and brought tears. The loathsome perfume of sweating horses, burnt flesh, and death permeated my psyche. Our fertile soil was churned into a corrupt slime of tears, manure, and blood. The air was pregnant with fear. Water, the giver of life, was putrid and tainted with disease.

So, I waited for the inevitable. It would not be long. I heard the pounding of the battering ram on my outside wall. I had the power to end this senseless destruction, but I had to play their game. Our laws strictly forbid interference in human affairs so we could coexist with them. Vampires were forgotten in human history, but we were an integral part of it.

In Egypt, Amon and I were living gods. My fall from divinity was complete as I sat impotent. Once again, I manipulated my enemy with cunning and ingenuity and used only the strategies learned from the game my mentor taught me.

The outside door shattered, scattering my household. The invaders flooded my reception hall. Christian knights held my servants captive, their orders strewn about by their leader. I expected a simpleton of base brutality, but that was not what stood before me.

He was a powerful figure of man, handsome of feature, and fully in command of the situation. His eyes widened when he saw me. They sparkled with intelligence. I felt his desire but not his lust. We scrutinized each other. He informed me that their army had taken the city and we were his captives. Foolhardy man. I allowed no human to dominate me. I sensed pride and arrogance were his weaknesses. I attacked his Achilles's heel.

I answered him in his own tongue, which surprised him. I asked if he planned to plunder my house, rape the servants, or just kill us all. His answer surprised me. Astonished that I defied him, he was indignant and declared that they were not savages but Christians. I mocked him, declaring that the noise outside these walls proved otherwise. His face flamed at my accusation, and I felt his shame. Again, he amazed me. He gave me his promise of safety.

I underestimated my opponent, so I changed my tactics and welcomed them as guests, which is the Muslim custom. I instructed my servants to see to our captors' needs. His suspicion aroused, he sarcastically thanked me for my generosity. I delivered my final thrust to his pride. I quoted from his Christian Bible: "If your enemy is hungry, feed him; if he is thirsty, give him drink, for by doing so you heap burning coals upon his head."

Deflated, he replied, "You used my own holy scripture to chastise me." Satisfied that I made my point, I capitulated. Now we understood each other.

He asked my name.

I bowed politely. "I am Nadira Naram-Sin."

He whistled and called me by my other name, the Persian Rose. He had heard rumors of the beautiful woman that caliphs and kings worshipped. I had heard them too—fairy tales like the stories of Scheherazade.

He recited part of an Al-Mu'tamid poem. "Her piercing eyes cut my heart in two, and my eyes wept with longing for her, and I would kiss the lips behind the veil."

His honeyed compliments lessened my reserve. He was obviously a man of letters and knowledge, as well as a paradox. What a surprise to hear a Christian soldier recite Muslim poetry. Very few humans could read, let alone quote the words of an infidel. I was intrigued and wished to know more about this human.

I asked, "Do you quote love poems to your wife?"

Sadness clouded his face as he spoke of a wife taken in childbirth. He changed the subject and delivered his message of freedom. Amused, I inquired as to what they were to free us from. Naively, he believed us enslaved and wished restoration to the true faith. I laughed, which puzzled him. I told him that was the same reason the Muslims used when they conquered this land. The citizens of Barbastro were not oppressed, just the opposite. His mind was in turmoil, racing to understand this new information. He stammered for a retort.

I noticed he looked haggard. The toll of battle showed on his human form. I instructed the servants to take him to his quarters. I inquired after his name. He was embarrassed that he had not introduced himself, which was a blunder in etiquette.

He proclaimed, "I am Count Cristo Mendez de Oviedo, knight to the infante, my lady." He bowed and left the room.

Count Cristo Mendez de Oviedo, knight to the infante. This human perplexed me, but my thoughts regarding the count fled, driven out by the screams and noises outside the walls of my safe haven. The misery human beings heaped upon each other made the stones cry. My soul was vexed. I wept for my neighbors, mankind, and my illusion of peace.

I dreaded the morning of the new day. Haseem and I ventured outside amidst the carnage of last night. Stepping into the street was a shock to one's senses. The streets were strewn with wreckage, the dead, and the dying. The buildings were broken like the rancid teeth of an ancient harpy. The devastation was unimaginable. The air was heavy with smoke, stench, and blood. The urge to gorge *myself was almost unbearable. I silently thanked my mentor for my years of training and suppressed my hunger.*

I heard a muffled sob. I turned to see Haseem weep for his people. He apologized for his tears. I would have wept too if I had any tears left. There was much work to do before purification devoured the city.

We checked the bodies for life. I turned over a corpse. It was the poetry master who wrote the most beautiful lyrics, transforming words into precious jewels. I had several of his books. No further gems would flow from his lips, his throat slashed from ear to ear—a precious resource crushed under the boot of oppression.

I scanned the surrounding area for his family. Sadly, his wife and children would accompany him in the afterlife. Human life is so fragile, extinguished in an instant. I heard a disturbance and glanced up to see Count Cristo and his knights marching toward me. A rage swept over me at the sight of these barbarians. They halted in the middle of the carnage, shocked by the scene before them.

I was past politeness and strode up to the Count, took him by surprise, and repeatedly slapped his face. He stood rock still and endured my punishment. His face was scarlet from the force of my blows. His men were confused by their commander's response to my abuse. He did nothing but stare into my furious eyes.

I screamed, "These are my neighbors, my friends, and you have made them widows and orphans! Is this what you call a military campaign?" I reminded the count that he said they were Christians, followers of Jesus. "I do not remember Jesus teaching men to slaughter your neighbor. He said to love your neighbor as yourself." The soldiers shifted nervously and lowered their eyes.

He offered a feeble excuse. "We are but vassals of the pope and my king and must do as we are bid."

I could tolerate no more. I reached to slap him again, but he grabbed my hand.

"Cease. The sight of slaughtered innocent women and children was punishment enough."

I peered into his eyes, the gateway to his soul, saw his anguish, and realized there was more to this human than meets the eye.

I could not remain silent. My parting insult: "A dog does as he is told but not men. Men have free will and a conscience to guide them. Men make the wars, and women mend the chaos."

I felt his confusion. He was perplexed and uncertain what to do next. This was a new situation for this commander of men: enlightenment from a woman. He told his men, "Behold, a Persian Rose forged of Toledo steel." His compliment pleased my vanity and diminished my indignation.

The count advised me that it was unsafe to remain in the open. I told him that I must stay and aid my brethren. No sooner said when a group of drunken soldiers approached us. They mocked me as a harem slut. What happened next astonished me.

The count delivered a powerful blow to a soldier's jaw. He sailed through the air, landing in an undignified heap at my feet. His comrades drew their swords and came toward us. The count's men rapidly formed a defensive line to protect us.

The count unsheathed his sword and threatened, "Withdraw or prepare to meet your maker this very hour."

One of their own protecting a Muslim woman and her slave baffled the soldiers. They sheathed their swords, gathered their comrade, and retreated like whipped dogs.

I acknowledged my debt to the count. He bade me call him Cristo and offered protection and assistance. He asked what he could do, and I advised that they dispose of the dead or there would be pestilence. He instructed his men to follow my orders and left to find his commander.

I heard a faint heartbeat in a pile of bodies covered with rats, the harbingers of death, scampering over the corpses. I probed the bodies, extracted a small boy, and held him to my bosom to comfort his sobs. Occupied with the child, I failed to notice someone watching me.

The count stood at a distance, staring at me. The poor man, he did not realize I could read his thoughts, and they amazed me. He pondered if a woman like me could ever love someone like him. I sensed that beneath his rough exterior beat the heart of a great man.

What a strange twist of fate. Could a vampire love a human? I did not know, but I graced him with a radiant smile. His eyes met mine, and he returned my smile.

Amor Vincit Omnia (Love Conquers All)

The weeks that followed were a kaleidoscope of hard work, discovery, and pleasure. The count and his knights remained behind with the garrison, quartered at my home, a reprieve from their military life and the opportunity to learn our customs. Our days focused on returning the city to normal, disposing of the dead, tending the injured, and returning the essentials of life: water and food. The Reconquista's aftermath was a daily reminder of humankind's blind prejudice.

I discovered the count's voracious appetite for my library as few books were available to him. I introduced him to algebra, which tangled his reason. His quick mind was a fertile ground for new ideas. Our discussions on philosophy and politics occasionally ended in a standoff. We both were of a stubborn nature—unwilling to concede.

However, evening meals were a time of companionship with our captors. The sharing of ideas and beliefs gradually changed our enemies to allies, both sides wiser. Storytelling from Muslims and Christians filled the house with laughter. Music and song sweetened the night air.

The first night I danced for the count altered the course of my life. I performed an intricate court dance. I abandoned myself to the melody that manipulated by body. My silks moved about me as though a breath of air. The count's eyes never left my form. Desire was etched on his countenance. My passion ignited, spurring me to intensify the sensuousness of my dance. I finished breathless. The sound of his hammering heart rang in my ears. His husky voice complimented my dance. We stared at each other, speechless. A few feet divided us, but that space was a chasm of etiquette, culture, and species. He jumped up, excused himself, and retreated to his quarters.

I was perplexed. His thoughts were of desire and love, but he fled. My heart ached for fulfillment. Love is the lifeblood of the heart. My heart was devoid of love, but my blood burned red hot. I weighed my options: accept human love or remain alone. I made my choice.

I entered the count's quarters, concealed myself behind a lattice screen, and spied on my guest. He was sprawled naked on the bed, reading one of my books. I remained hidden in the shadows, admiring his physique; it reminded me of the gilded statue of Hercules, muscular and strong.

I stepped out of the darkness. He was startled and pulled the silks over his nakedness. He asked if I required something.

I boldly answered, "You."

Desire flooded his face and stirred his body. I had to know the reason for his escape. Did he not find me attractive? He confessed that his oath as a knight prevented him from compromising my virtue.

I quoted Buddha, "Virtue is persecuted more by the wicked than it is loved by the good."

I released the clasps of my silk kaftan, and it slid to the floor, my nakedness proudly exposed. I heard his sharp intake of breath. He sprang to his feet, lifted me as though I were a feather, and carried me to the bed.

Our first kiss was not sweet or gentle but rather one of fire. His passion exploded. I matched his furor move for move until our rapture rocked the pillars of the earth. Our blistering heat was slow to burn out. We were not sated until the first fingers of dawn stroked the room.

"My lady, you are a wanton wench," he jested. "Nadira." His voice was a caress that stirred my dead heart. He tucked his hand under my chin and tilted my face to see me better. "What would become of us?"

I did not have an answer to his query. One should not examine happiness too closely lest it disappear altogether. Instead, I kissed him ardently, ignited a spark, and fanned the flames of passion again.

So, for forty days and nights, I embraced my slice of happiness . . . until our final night.

A stray breeze blew the silk curtains and caressed my skin. My body was languorous, as though drained of all function. The moonlight silhouetted my lover. I studied his strong jaw and ran my hand across his rippling thigh muscles, whose powerful thrusts sent me into a climatic frenzy that robbed me of both reason and strength. I listened to the steady beat of his human heart. The feelings he stirred in mine were indescribable.

His mere touch set my skin on fire and melted my loins. His very look made my cold heart leap for joy. My self-control vanished with his kiss. That was what total abandonment felt like.

It was not just the physical attraction. His agile mind, generous heart, and passion for any task he undertook delighted me. I was well pleased with my choice. Our only obstacle was that he was human and did not know what I was.

His eyes embraced me. We kissed and shared lovers' compliments. He confessed his love had flowered as I quoted the Bible verse. My heart had melted with the last slap of his face. We laughed with the silliness of lovers. For the first time, my beauty did not inspire love, but rather I was the inspiration. What a heady experience.

I shared my concern about Al-Mugtadir's army. It approached the city. The Muslims sought vengeance on the Christian garrison. I warned him to flee. He put his finger to my lips, kissed my body that he had come to know so well, and drove away any thoughts of Al-Mugtadir.

Vitus (Courage)

The horses nervously paced and pawed the ground. They sensed the coming danger. His mounted knights awaited the order to flee. I reminded Cristo that the Muslim army advanced. He was hesitant to leave me. He said that I was his heart and life. I insisted he leave if, for nothing else, his knights' safety. Concern for his men dominated his passion. He would send a messenger to me when he was safe. I promised to join him. He bent down and kissed me. We exchanged our love. He signaled his men, and they galloped out of the city.

I watched the night swallow them. Haseem asked if I thought they would escape. "No," I answered. "They will not escape."

I waited throughout the night for the tragic end to our love story. My endless pacing did nothing to lessen my apprehension. I wandered to my quarters, collapsing on the bed still fresh from our love. I buried my face in the pillow infused with his scent. I concentrated on the ceramic wall tiles, spending the seconds, minutes, and hours until the sunrise illuminated their hues.

My vigil was at its end. A furious knock at my outer gate disturbed the dawn. I dreaded the news that awaited me. The servants opened the gate. Four of Cristo's knights rushed inside. They carried a blood-drenched litter. My heart stopped.

My beloved was sprawled on the stretcher, a makeshift bandage wound tight across his midsection. The bandage saturated with blood dripped onto the floor. Haseem looked at a knight, who shook his head.

The knight relayed the count's final command: "Bear me to my Persian Rose before the Reaper claims my soul."

I knelt by the litter and unwound the bandage. My beloved was mortally wounded—a horrific gash from shoulder to hip, his entrails exposed and hemorrhaging. He grabbed my hand and vowed he would not die before he saw me again.

I signaled a servant to fetch the surgeon, but Cristo shook his head. He did not fear death but rather feared the loss of me. He said the very words I longed to hear. He would give his soul to remain with me.

I asked, "Do you mean what you said?" Aye, he did.

I instructed his men to carry the litter to my bedchamber. I told them that I would nurse the count back to health. They gazed at me with pity, but they did as I bid. Alone, I whispered my secret into my lover's ear. He eyes flew open. Dazed and dying, he stared at me. A weak smile crept across his ashen face.

His dying words: "Our life was a Greek tragedy. My heart belonged to a vampire. Destiny has chosen my fate. Nadira, seal our love with your eternal kiss. Make haste, my love, for my soul escapes me."

I brushed his lips with mine and then sealed our fates with a single bite.

Biron, Dordogne, France, anno Domini 1184

The wild flowers this season overflowed the meadow. I gathered bouquets to fill the castle with color and scent. The sight of so many flowers reminded me of my wedding day. Amon performed the ceremony filled with its ancient verse. It was a perfect day, much like today, when I joined for eternity with my beloved, who offered me more happiness than a heart can contain. Our love had intensified over the past century.

I gazed at the sky. The blazing sun warmed my flesh. A wave of exhilaration washed over me. I twirled around until I fell to the ground and stared up at the clouds. I wished I could share this simple pleasure with Cristo, but he was still unable to tolerate the sun.

His continued intolerance to sunlight was strange. Usually, vampires outgrew this barrier in fifty or so years. More fortunate was the fact that his lust for blood had dissipated to a weekly need, whether human or animal, which is a close substitute for human blood—it suffices but does not empower. As time passed, he would require sustenance only once a month. Guiding Cristo in the ways of a vampire was a challenge. A man of action accustomed to being in the thick of things, he grew restless easily with his outings limited to night. I reminded him that young vampires were vulnerable and easily destroyed. The first century of a vampire's life was a perilous period. They had not learned to focus their minds and senses. The ability to harness our strength, speed, and special gifts was an art that took decades to master.

I gathered my floral treasure and skipped to the castle. The quiet of country life appealed to my need for peace and stability. The turmoil of centuries made me crave tranquility. The very concepts I treasured chafed my husband's desire for adventure and evaporated with the Inquisition's growing power. Paranoia ran rampart. These were dangerous times for vampires, but I refused to allow a sense of doom to take hold.

I entered the castle's great hall, an impressive sight with its tapestry-lined walls. The lit candles made it look especially appealing. I laid my basket of flowers on the massive trestle table. Strong arms circled my waist. A rough face nuzzled my neck, and a throaty voice declared that I smelt good enough to eat. I giggled, and Cristo swept me into his arms. Rake. My laughter made him smile, so he teased me senseless. He declared me delicious. The sun had warmed my blood.

He was jealous of my ability to go out in the sunlight and said something unusual. "When I was human, the sun drove the cobwebs from my soul."

No matter how long I lived with Cristo, he constantly surprised me with the depth of his passion. He promised when he could venture into the light that he would take me to our wheat field, with only the blazing sun for our witness, and make love to me until I cried for release. He kissed me with gusto and teased that the night has its pleasures too. I playfully slapped his chest. In mock gentility, I exclaimed, "What will the servants think?"

He laughed lustily and replied, "They would think the master loves his good wife so much that they would scold their partners for their lack."

He carried me to the master's chair and held me in his lap. I laid my head on his chest. He seemed restless, grew serious, and admitted this serenity wore on his temper. I told him that we must be prudent and fail to attract attention. I promised that once the Inquisition dissipated, we would move somewhere exciting. I pleaded with him to exercise restraint.

Patience is a virtue every vampire must possess. My husband lacked this trait, and an impetuous human resulted in a reckless vampire. The shackles of vampirism vexed his hunger for freedom. He craved the excitement and dangers of knighthood that he could not duplicate in his present state. He fed only on humans, a lethal but vulnerable predator. A solitary hunter, he scoured the countryside for victims, leaving a trail of corpses for the Inquisition.

He ran his hand through my hair, but his thoughts were far away. Cristo promised he would try, but his assurances lacked conviction. My pleas for moderation ignored, my sense of doom returned and, thus, became my constant companion. I waited patiently for the inevitable outcome of my tenuous grasp on happiness.

Mors (Death)

Cristo's second-in-command, Jean Louis, and I, disguised as peasants, stood in the shadows of the courtroom balcony. Secreted in the corner, I awaited my husband's trial for vampirism. Cristo bid me to stay away, but I did not. He feared they would ensnare me in their web of injustice. A cruel jest on our vampire laws of noninterference, I delivered my beloved's destiny to the Inquisition.

Noisy spectators filled the room. The white-robed ecclesiastic judges occupied a raised dais. The chief inquisitor entered the room. A hush fell over the crowd—the pope's judicial representative held great sway over humans. Fear saturated the room—its stringent smell was overpowering.

Two gigantic guards entered with Cristo bound in heavy silver chains. The guards struggled to lock him in the defendant's box and secured his bonds. Silver does not bind a mature vampire, and they are not easily caught. However, my husband was young and brash. As I feared, his arrogance was his downfall.

So began this travesty of justice. They called the first witness, the local tavern keeper. The inquisitor interrogated him. The tavern keeper spun his tale of Cristo and his men sharing mead and enjoying a hale and hearty good night until insulted by drunkards. Honor was at stake for both sides. A brawl ensued, ending with the tavern in ruins. Cristo paid for the damages, but the irate keeper tossed the lot out. The inquisitor, satisfied with the tavern keeper's testimony, dismissed him.

He called the next witness to the stand. This witness's story was more damning. A simpleton farmer looking for his lost cow in the forest stumbled upon highwaymen intent on robbery. He hid from the villains in the bushes, waiting for them to leave, but the sound of a solitary rider caught their attention. They ambushed the rider.

"Who was the rider?" the inquisitor inquired.

The farmer pointed to Cristo. "'Twas him, my lord."

He continued with his condemning evidence. The villains pulled Cristo from his horse, but instead of being the victim, he turned the tables and attacked them. He ripped his assailants into pieces and drank his fill, scattering their remains over the road. The silence in the courtroom was deafening—the crowd hung on every word.

The inquisitor bade the witness to continue. The simpleton's voice wavered, barely a whisper. The inquisitor demanded he speak louder. The farmer crossed himself and sobbed as he retold his frightening yarn of Cristo glowing in the moonlight and drenched in blood, emitting a blood-curdling sort of laugh, the kind that chills a man's soul. A murmur ran through the courtroom. The inquisitor released the farmer.

The chief inquisitor returned to the dais and faced the accused. He delivered his swift verdict. "Count Cristo deMendez, you are accused of vampirism, murder, and unholy acts. Witnesses have presented the evidence. How do you plead?"

I prayed he would lie or defend himself. We might have arranged an escape. Anything was possible, but I knew he would not. His enormous pride prevented him.

Cristo pulled himself to his full height. He proudly faced the inquisitor and said, "Guilty except for the unholy acts."

The inquisitor added, "We wish to be merciful. If you revealed your accomplices, your fellow vampires, we would behead you rather than burn you at the stake. What say you?"

Cristo stonily replied, "I was alone." My heart burst. He would die to protect me.

The inquisitor studied Cristo, consulted with the other judges, who all nodded, and then pronounced, "So be it. Count Cristo de Mendez, we declare you guilty and sentence you to be burned at the stake. Do you have anything to declare?"

Cristo bared his fangs. "Yes. Damn you all to hell."

My beautiful husband sentenced to burn. My mind screamed, "This was a nightmare! It cannot be real."

The chief inquisitor made the sign of the cross and proclaimed, "Take the prisoner to the site of execution. May the Lord have mercy on your soul!"

Cristo growled and lunged at the chief inquisitor. The guards struggled to subdue him and dragged their prisoner away. These humans would not rob me of my mate, my happiness. My anger simmered like a witch's cauldron. If it boiled over, nothing could hinder me.

Gregor turns the page, but the next pages of the journal are gone, torn from the binding. He turns to the final page, which is jagged and missing the top half. The writing is erratic and barely legible.

> *It was finished.*
> *What have I done? What have I become?*
> *A monster.*
> *With my last ounce of sanity, I begged a boon of Jean-Louis. I pleaded with him take me to Amon in Cathay. Reluctantly, he promised me.*
> *The threads of my mind began to unravel as the last of my strength escaped my grasp. Darkness overwhelmed me. I fell into the deep chasm of my conscience, willingly gave myself over to the horror, and blindly rushed toward oblivion. I prayed for death to be swift.*

There is nothing after this last sentence except a line where the quill dragged across the page, ending in a large ink spot. Gregor stares at the ink spot for a moment before closing the journal.

Questions churn in the pit of his stomach. *What is written on those missing pages? So many more things are left unsaid. I must know what happened. Nadira will not yield those secrets sealed in her heart for centuries. Who then?* He racks his mind for an answer.

Gregor walks out onto his rooftop terrace and looks out at the brown harbor filled with ships churning past the Statue of Liberty.

Amon knows.

CHAPTER V

Nadira climbs out of the limo in front of an impressive office building. The sight of her corporate headquarters always fills her with pride. The architect did an excellent job blending the best of historic and modern Manhattan. Its handsome architecture has an understated elegance, nothing flashy or grandiose. She hurries through the granite lobby to catch the elevator. A businessman holds the doors for her, and she nods her appreciation. He admires this new passenger; her dark navy business suit hides none of her curves. She smiles to herself when she reads his thoughts.

"What floor?" he asks.

Nadira answers, "All the way to the top."

She smiles at the euphemism for her rise in business. The wealth generated from oil production on her ancestral lands provided the means but not the satisfaction she craved. Industry has always fascinated her, its intricacies offering the challenges necessary to fill the void in her life. However, men dominated the world of business in the early twentieth century. They tried to pigeonhole her into the role of secretary or sexual conquest, but they quickly discovered Nadira was neither.

During World War II, she purchased a small pharmaceutical company whose sole product was the new drug penicillin. The lucrative market for antibiotics fueled her company's rapid expansion. She hired the brightest researchers, diversified its product line, and became an innovator in the field of medical products.

She acquired additional companies until she built a corporate empire with stakes in shipping, technology, and numerous subsidiaries. She is the CEO of a multinational conglomerate, and the top of the business world is her domain.

However, the true challenge has always been hiding her identity. She appoints trusted humans to manage the day-to-day operations, does not allow interviews or photo sessions, and constantly travels between her offices. Her companies are her sanctuary. Here she remains camouflaged as a human. She lives in the moment, forgets her past, and escapes her future. She knows that she must eventually pay the price for her sins. But not today.

The elevator doors slide open to a spacious reception area. A large brass sign identifies this floor as the headquarters of the Innamorati Corporation. She chose the name from the commedia dell'arte, which appeared in sixteenth-century Italy. It was a silly comedy with caricature lovers, but she adored the ending: the lovers are always united. In her heart of hearts, she is a hopeless romantic.

A pretty receptionist greets her. "Good morning. Jerry has all your messages."

Nadira smiles. "Thanks. Pretty dress."

The receptionist beams. Nadira continues down the hall to the double doors of her large corner office. Her assistant, Jerry, is waiting with a stack of mail and a vase of white lilies. The sight of him always makes her smile.

His job interview was unforgettable. Fresh from college, his self-confidence, exuberance, and zest for life were so refreshing that she hired him on the spot. A gorgeous human, his looks sealed the deal. She thought a little eye candy never hurt office moral. She quickly discovered that Jerry is not just a pretty face. He is extremely intelligent and maddeningly efficient, with a razor sharp wit that occasionally surprises her. He radiates a careless charm, apparent by the "Vampires Suck" pin in his lapel. As her friend, he is one of a few humans that knows her secret. He hands her the bouquet of lilies.

Nadira comments, "A little morose giving lilies to a vampire."

Jerry looks abashed. "This is a tough time for you."

She smells the flowers. "Thank you."

"What do want first, mail or appointments?" he asks.

"Appointments." She puts the flowers in a vase and then sits at her desk.

Jerry rattles off the list of appointments. "Financials at 3:00 p.m. in the conference room. Slatter from PR at 4:00 p.m. in here. Herr Dr. Graetz, the mad scientist from special research, called all excited. He said something about a breakthrough. I set up a video conference with him tomorrow at 1:30 p.m. EST."

"Did he say what kind of breakthrough?" she asks.

She focuses her full attention on him. A breakthrough could change everything in her life. Dr. Graetz is head of her Zurich special research division. A hematologist and geneticist, he and his team are developing artificial plasma. The successful creation of a blood substitute would revolutionize the landscape of vampire–human codependence.

Jerry shakes his head. "Nope. I know his research is top secret, so I didn't ask."

They begin to go through the mail, but the phone interrupts them. Jerry answers it. He nods and then hands Nadira the phone. "It's your boyfriend."

Nadira frowns. She hates it when he baits her. "Good morning, Gregor." She nods a couple of times, and Jerry makes a face. "What time?" She gives Jerry a stern look. "It's in the garage. No problem. I will let the captain know. See you then." She hangs up, and Jerry taps his pencil on the desk. "I told you, he is not my boyfriend as you define the term. He is my companion. Vampires' companions are their best friends, usually without romantic or physical love. Monogamous love is reserved for a mate. Our lives are eternal, and it is a rare vampire who lives alone. Loneliness is our kryptonite. How many times do I have to tell you this?"

"Every time I call Gregor your boyfriend."

Nadira frowns. "Will you stop teasing me?" This subject always irritates her, but she is uncertain why.

"So you say, but that is one man that wants to be more than your companion." Jerry loses the grin. "I'm serious. He feels more than simple friendship for you."

"How do you know?" she fires back.

"I am a man, that's how I know." She perplexes him with her lack of insight. A blind person could not miss the chemistry between the two of them.

"Gregor is not a man," she snaps back, uncomfortable discussing her relationship with Gregor. She has mixed feelings about the nature of it herself.

"Vampire or man, it makes no difference. Even a vampire needs love. I've watched how he acts around you. His eyes never leave you." Their conversations about Gregor always end the same: a pointless debate.

"I never noticed." In a way, it is true. She has difficulty reading Gregor's thoughts, rendering her perpetually confused about his actions.

"Of course not. He hides it from you. I am a human, so he does not bother with me. I have been around you both for five years. He is waiting for you to stop mourning your husband. Remember, an eternity is a long time to wait for someone," he cautions her.

"I do not like the direction of this conversation." Nadira studies Jerry, who smiles sheepishly. "Let's get back to work," she orders.

"You're the boss." They go through the mail, but Jerry is nothing if not persistent. "Boss, you've never told me how you two met," he says innocently.

She studies her assistant. He will not give it up without a fight. Very well, she will give him something else to occupy his attention. "Do you really want to hear this?" she asks.

"Yes. Please," he eagerly replies. He puts down his papers and gives her his absolute attention.

She closes her eyes, rummages through her vast storehouse of memories, and begins her story.

"It was the year of our Lord 1396. The Middle Ages were a turbulent time—land changing hands at the end of a sword. It was safer to reside under the protection of a nobleman, so I held a small keep in the kingdom of Hungry or rather northern Croatia. The ruling palatine had a beloved son who foolishly joined the ill-fated crusade led by King Sigismund. The army was routed at the Battle of Nicopolis. The baron's son survived the battle, but highwaymen mortally wounded him on the journey home. His yeoman bore him home to his mother." She pauses for effect. "The son died, but he returned to life the next day."

"A vampire." Jerry hangs on every word.

Nadira nods. "Some proclaimed it a miracle, others the work of Lucifer. These were medieval times. Superstition, ignorance, and the church ruled people's hearts. The mob dragged him from the castle and forced him to run the gauntlet of fervent peasants and priests, who flogged him with crosses, rocks, and excrement. He escaped into the neighboring forest."

"An outcast," Jerry adds.

"A tragic end for a nobleman exiled to the fringes of civilization, living as an animal, killing to survive. The unfortunate hunter or lost soul stumbled into his woodland, where he dispatched them with ruthless efficiency. He was so lethal that the area was called *silva gravida est sanguinis*."

"The Forest of Blood," Jerry translates. "The Baron's son. It was Gregor?"

"Yes."

Nadira's voice is ethereal and her expression frightening, instinctually raising goosebumps on his arms. Jerry rarely glimpses this side of his employer and often forgets she is a vampire.

"Go on," he prompts.

"Eventually, the villages banded together to remove this scourge from their lands. They hired mercenaries to eliminate their demon, but Gregor eluded them. I decided to intervene and began scouring the nocturnal forest. The scent of blood drew me to him, and I found him feasting on his latest victim. My first impression was of a wretched animal, nothing more. I peered down from my horse at this young predator, and I was overwhelmed with pity."

Jerry interrupts, "Pity?"

"Yes, pity. He stared at me with those extraordinary eyes filled with savagery, terror, and intelligence. He had no idea what he had become and teetered on the brink of madness. He was a monster, but his soul cried for redemption."

She abruptly stops speaking and stares at him. Her look is intense and unsettling. Her eyes are very black, hard, and unyielding, similar to a piece of volcanic glass. He squirms in his seat, withering under her gaze, unsure of what to do next.

"Boss," he says.

The word drags her back to the present. She continues her story. "Someone helped me during a desperate time of my life. I was compelled to do the same for him. We could hear the baying hounds and the shouts of the trackers as their bobbing lanterns drew closer. I told him that if he wanted to live to follow me. I spurred my horse and fled the hunters, Gregor at my side. We barely eluded capture and eventually escaped to Vienna. I was his mentor. We have been together ever since," Nadira finishes and closes her eyes.

"What a story!" Jerry exclaims. "No wonder he loves you. You saved his life."

Nadira sits motionless, reading her assistant's thoughts. *He contemplates her tale, more like a fairy tale than reality, igniting his imagination. Vampires experience history in a way that humans can only dream of and her story conveys a sense of timelessness he will never know. No human can ever fully understand a vampire.* She slowly opens her eyes. "So you keep telling me," she replies, gracing him with an enigmatic smile.

CHAPTER VI

G REGOR TINKERS WITH a red Suzuki motorcycle parked at the curb of his brownstone. Engines have intrigued him since their invention in the late eighteenth century. Engineering is his passion. It satisfies his innovative nature and has resulted in several lucrative patents. He peers over the tank toward the sound of an approaching motorcycle. A black Suzuki pulls up to the curb, and the rider hops off the bike, removing her helmet and releasing a cascade of ebony hair. Molded to her body, her black leather shows her figure to an advantage, and she preens for him, fishing for a compliment.

He obliges her. "Damn, you're smokin' hot. It's a good look for a vampire." He stands back to admire her.

Nadira grins and curtsies. "Thank you, kind sir. Nice bike."

They laugh. Both motorcycles are Suzuki Hayabusas, the fastest street-legal bikes.

"I've made the engine modifications," he tells her.

"How fast?"

Gregor puts on his helmet. "There's only one way to find out. Are you ready to wind out these crotch rockets?"

Nadira asks saucily, "Are you talking about the motorcycle or yourself?"

Gregor enjoys the double entendre. "Both," he says, lowering his face shield.

Nadira springs onto her motorcycle and replaces her helmet. Gregor dumps the clutch, lays rubber, and is gone, leaving a cloud of smoke in his wake.

"Damn," she curses. Nadira drops her face shield. The motorcycle launches forward at warp speed. She flogs it to catch up and spots him at a red light. *He wants to play, so let's play.* She zooms past him, runs the light, and barely misses another car.

Gregor shakes his head, dumps the clutch, and is in hot pursuit. The ride becomes a game of chicken. They weave in out of traffic, run red lights, and head into oncoming traffic, at times on the sidewalk. Pedestrians jump out of their way. Nadira never slows, occasionally glancing back at Gregor. He is right on her tail.

They clear the city traffic and move onto the highway, where the real race begins. Gregor accelerates alongside Nadira. The high-performance engines roar as the tachometers redline. The highway seems to recede and then disappear as they blur into a glimpse of red and black, almost too fast for the human eye to discern.

Vampires do not fear death, which makes them natural adrenaline junkies. Fast is never fast enough. They push the envelope with any activity. Their ability to fly often satisfies this mad lust for speed, with earth-hopping a common mode of transportation.

They do not slow down until they reach their destination, a large marina. They park the bikes, remove their helmets, and both grin ear to ear.

Gregor exclaims, "Now *that* will get your heart pumping."

"Even if you're already dead." Nadira winks.

They head to the largest yacht in the marina, over three hundred feet of impressive luxury moored at its own private dock.

Gregor teases, "Could you find a larger boat?"

Nadira smiles. "No, had to have this one built. It is not the *Olympic*, but it will do."

The *RMS Olympic*, the lead ship of the White Star Line in 1911, was a transatlantic ocean liner, a luxurious ship, whose facilities were comparable to her more famous sister, the *Titanic*.

"Now *there* was a ship. Do you remember her maiden voyage to New York?"

Nadira nods. "I am glad we chose her instead of waiting for the launch of the *Titanic*."

Gregor laughs. "Me too."

A white-uniformed captain waits at the gangway to greet them. Nadira addresses him. "Good evening, Captain. Take us out to deep water."

"Very good, ma'am," he answers.

The crew casts off lines, and the yacht gets underway. It clears the harbor and heads out to sea. Gregor and Nadira go below deck to change. The yacht anchors out on an empty, black ocean. The running lights switch off. The only illumination emanates from the portals and the moon. Nadira stands on the deck, basking in the brisk ocean breeze, which ruffles her hair. Gregor lounges on a deck chair, watching her.

Nadira's curiosity wins out. "Gregor, why did you want to go out tonight?"

Gregor admires the soft glow of her silhouette bathed in moonlight. "I brought back your journal," he replies.

Surprised, Nadira asks, "You finished it?" Her apprehension grows.

"Yes, last night. Did you know that the last pages are missing?"

"Yes."

"What happened to them?"

Her expression goes flat. "I burned them."

He considers this revelation. "What was on those pages?"

She stonily replies, "It was long ago. I hardly remember."

He realizes she will not share all of her secrets with him. "As for tonight, I wanted you far from the city and all of its distractions. Sometimes, solitude is required to discuss important matters. I need to talk to you alone," he confesses.

Nadira studies his inscrutable face. An uneasy feeling sweeps over her. Nervous about the subject of this talk, she plants a fake smile on her face and changes the subject. "I want to show you something. Come with me," she tells him.

She takes his hand and leads him topside to the observation deck, the highest point on the yacht. It offers a three-hundred-and-sixty-degree view of the horizon. They gaze out at the inky sea.

"Gregor, close your eyes."

He smiles. "What are you up to?"

"It's a surprise," she says, and he reluctantly closes his eyes. She switches off the yacht lights. The night is pitch black. "Open your eyes."

He opens his eyes. The moonlight reflects on the water like thousands of sparkling diamonds. Gregor holds his breath. "It's beautiful."

Nadira walks up behind him. Her unique perfume—a mixture of gardenia, frankincense, and spices—enfolds him. Her warm breath caresses his ear. "Sometimes, you have to look with more than your eyes," she comments.

At that moment, a school of curious dolphins surfaces around the yacht. They circle around it, leap high in the air, and swim off into the night, their fins slicing the still water.

Gregor jokes, "Did you plan that?"

"Life is often unpredictable."

"Another one of your endless supply of illuminating quotes." Gregor grins.

"I have collected them over a very long time."

He surrenders to her spell. Her alabaster skin seems to radiate in the moonlight. Her eyes smolder with an inner light. She was revered as a goddess and the inspiration for many ancient myths.

"Why are you staring at me like a hungry dog?" she asks. The expression on Gregor's face surprises her. It is the first time she has caught him off guard. Tantalized by the desire she sees in his eyes, her body instinctively responds.

"You look surreal." He is mesmerized.

A knowing smile full of mystery and promise plays on her full lips. She slides her caftan over her head, revealing a perfectly sculptured body. Gregor holds his breath.

"I feel like a swim," she mentions offhandedly.

She runs to the railing and somersaults into a perfect swan dive thirty feet into the water. Gregor walks over to the edge and waits. Nadira breaks the surface of the water. Her laughter is one of simple infectious happiness. He grins. Rarely has he seen her so relaxed and open.

"Join me." Her eyes sparkle, offering an invitation he cannot resist.

"I don't mind if I do." He strips, runs, and launches into a triple somersault. He breaks the water close to Nadira, splashing her. Gregor bobs to the surface.

"Show off," she teases.

They both laugh. He opens his mouth to speak, but she covers his lips with her fingers, turns, and swims with powerful strokes farther out to sea. She swims for a long time, distancing herself from him. But his long strokes close the gap between them. She finally pauses to catch her breath.

"I didn't think you were going to stop." He swims up to her.

Nadira looks at him, apprehensive. "I wasn't."

"I need to tell you something," he says.

"Please, don't." She starts to swim away, but he grabs her wrist.

"You can't run from me. We have to talk." He grasps her hands, pulls her to him, and clasps her in his embrace.

"I don't want to." She avoids his gaze.

"Why?" he asks.

"I am afraid of what you are going to tell me. You've read my journal," she replies.

She cringes to avoid the emotional blow. He turns her face toward him. Her eyes are bright with unshed tears. She finally looks into his eyes. Her loneliness and pain threaten to spill over in a fountain of tears, and once the dam breaks, centuries of heartache will overflow.

"Nadira, I have to go away." Gregor waits for her response.

Bewildered, her voice wavers. "When?" Her greatest fear is now reality. She allowed him inside her heart, revealed her secret, and now he is going to abandon her.

"Tonight."

Dumfounded, she whispers, "So soon? For how long?"

"I don't know," he answers and cannot relent—his decision is made.

Sadness mars her beautiful face. She asks the question that she fears the most. "Are you coming back?"

Gregor strokes her cheek. She covers his hand with hers. "I just know I have to do this."

"Gregor, don't leave me. I can change."

"Can you really? An eternity is a long time to be wrong," he tells her.

Devastated by his curt response, she is stunned to silence. She did not anticipate that his absence would hurt this much and realizes she has taken his company for granted. Jerry's words sear her conscience. *What have I done?* Tears slip down her face.

Gregor takes her face in his hands. He kisses her tears and then her soft lips. It is their first kiss, a kiss filled with sweet longing and the promise of new love. She clings to him, starved for affection. Their brief union sears her heart, but this gentle kiss is farewell. A fleeting expression of sorrow crosses his handsome face, but he remains steadfast.

"I have to do this for the both of us. Goodbye, Nadira."

He takes one last meaningful look at her. She appears very small and isolated bobbing in the vast ocean. He turns in the direction of the yacht and swims away. She watches him slice through the water with broad strokes, distancing himself from her and eventually disappearing. An aching loneliness fills the void in her heart. She yearns for love but suspects the moment has passed. Nadira treads water for a while, floating on her back, staring at the stars, and loses track of time. Time is meaningless when one faces eternity alone. She gazes up at the moon and then languidly swims back to the yacht.

CHAPTER VII

THE ASTON MARTIN hugs the hairpin turns as it creeps up the mountainous road. The view is spectacular, but who has time to admire it while traversing this twisted stretch of pavement? Gregor reaches the mountaintop and his destination. Perched among the craggy peaks of the Swiss Alps is the seat of the vampire government, the Ordinatio.

He hands the security guard his passport. Fort Knox has nothing on this place, with its formidable walls and electronic surveillance. The guard hands back his passport and wishes him "a nice day."

Gregor smiles at the expression—so very twentieth century, like a fast-food drive-through. He drives past the main gate and down a long tree-lined road to the roundabout of an extraordinary building. The drive up was spectacular, but the view from here is breathtaking. The Ordinatio is no gothic castle or fortress but looks more like a lemony sugar confection. Built in early 1620, this massive seventeenth-century baroque palace is the twin to the Rundāle Palace, both designed by the same architect. The baroque façade is lavish, with fanciful shapes and extravagant ornamentation that was in style at the time. Nestled on a mountain frosted with snow, the palace has the look of a wedding cake topper rather than vampire central. What is a better disguise for vampires than a Cinderella-style headquarters?

Amon chose Switzerland for its long history of neutrality and *laissez-faire* attitude. Here vampires have flourished politically and financially. The Ordinatio houses the government, treasury, courts, military, a bank, and all the necessities to run a small nation. It is also the main residence of their sovereign, Amon.

Amon is an enigma, even among their secretive species. Reported to be the oldest living vampire, he is possibly more than six thousand years old, but no one knows exactly. He was a high priest in ancient Egypt, has been the leader of all vampires since the thirteenth century, and is rumored to be endowed with supernatural gifts. He is Nadira's adopted father, and he alone holds the key to her secret past.

Gregor tosses the car keys to the valet and strides up the impressive double staircase into the opulent reception hall. The interior is voluminous, its grandeur meant to impress with murals, ornate moldings, coffer ceilings, and columns, all enhanced by huge crystal chandeliers. Oversized mirrors and murals grace the walls; priceless sculptures are interspersed among groups of contemporary seating. The massive space is efficient and meant to accommodate a large number of people while retaining a rich elegance. Infused with the DNA of its inhabitants, the Ordinatio is enduring and timeless.

A pretty receptionist greets him. "Do you have an appointment?"

"Yes, with Sovereign Amon. Tell him Baron Gregor Lackovic is here."

She nods and picks up the phone. "Genevieve, your visitor has arrived." She hangs up. "His assistant will be right down, Baron."

He focuses on the occupants of the hall, a variety of vampires and humans waiting for their appointments, court, or business meetings. More humans are here than he remembers seeing before. On the fringe of the hall, a group of young vampires clusters. At their center is a dark, swarthy vampire with eyes as black as coal and just as hard. He affixes Gregor with a sardonic stare, and an aura of cruelty emanates from him. The vampire reminds Gregor of the wild boar he hunted with his father—wild, unpredictable, and deadly. Gregor senses danger and a potential threat. He stares at his new adversary. The dark vampire drops his gaze first. He wonders about the motivation for the staring match with this strange vampire.

A familiar voice grabs his attention. The female vampire approaching him looks as though she stepped out of a movie— blonde, with eyes the color of the sky, a body to die for, and hotter than a habanero pepper. Her overt sex appeal conceals a sweet and sunny disposition, which is a refreshing change from the usual glum vampires. This is Nadira's adopted sister, Genevieve.

She offers the vampire greeting of trust: palms extended with wrists exposed. This is the only vulnerable part of the vampire anatomy. He grasps her hands, exposes his wrists, and then kisses her cheeks.

Genevieve grins. "Gregor, welcome back. You have been gone a long time."

"Too long, but that was not of my choosing," he reminds her.

Her face loses its happiness. "I know. But you're here now." She links her arm in his.

She is unique among vampires: assistant to Amon and liaison to the High Council. Her finger is on the pulse of government and a veritable Who's Who of vampire society.

Gregor's curiosity prompts the question, "Who is that?"

She sees who he means and a shiver runs through her. "Coatl." She spits out his name. Genevieve likes everyone but seems to despise and fear this vampire.

Gregor is surprised. "Who is he?"

"He is an ancient and was once an Aztec high priest that slaughtered thousands of humans. Now he is the head of the antihuman faction." Her speech increasingly agitated, she says, "He holds to the old ways that humans are on this planet for his amusement, to devour or torture. His blood lust is legendary." She shutters.

Gregor glances in the direction of Coatl. "Why does the sight of me provoke such animosity in him?"

"Simple—you are Nadira's companion. Coatl hates her."

"I didn't know Nadira had enemies."

Genevieve glances at Gregor. "You're kidding, right? What vampire over four thousand years old does not make an enemy or two? There is a lot you don't know about my sister."

A frown wrinkles his brow. "I am beginning to realize that."

Genevieve shakes off her uneasiness. "Please, I don't want to talk about Coatl anymore. He gives me the creeps."

Gregor takes a last glance at Coatl, who is still staring at him. A maniacal grin skulks across Coatl's face with an expression so unpleasant it shocks Gregor. Gregor shoots him an eat-shit-and-die look before refocusing his attention on Genevieve.

"Gregor, Amon wants to see you," she tells him.

"Now?"

"Yes."

"Do you know what he wants?"

Genevieve shakes her head. "I'm only his assistant. He does not always tell me his plans. Amon plays things close to the vest. He treats life like a game of chess, and we are his chess pieces."

"I don't mind being a chess piece as long as I am the king."

Genevieve giggles, emitting a high tinkling sound, like crystals on a chandelier being caressed by a breeze.

"Good, that is what I wanted to hear, your laughter." He grins.

Genevieve grins back. "I am glad you are here."

"Me too." He hugs Genevieve. "Now, take me to our leader," he says, falling into step with Genevieve.

He forgot how massive the Ordinatio is, actually larger than the Pentagon. The multistory complex is built in an enormous square grid with green space in the center. One side is devoted to the judicial branch, the second to the government, the third to supplementary departments, and the last side is residential. It's easy to get lost in the maze of hallways, but the true hub is not visible from the ground level. It consists of an underground infrastructure. Carved into the mountain itself, the Ordinatio is a veritable fortress.

They approach a set of impressive bronze doors flanked by guards. Gregor recognizes the black uniforms of the Vigiles,

the vampire equivalent of Special Forces. The guards are a formidable presence.

"This is Amon's private study. He requested you wait for
him inside. Will you meet me at the club this evening? I want
you to meet someone," she tells him.

Gregor's puzzled look prompts her to clarify. "The old ballroom," she tells him and then kisses his cheek. "Good luck!"

He watches her leave and then glances at the guards. They
open the doors to the study. He suppresses his apprehension
and enters the private domain of the most powerful vampire
in the world. The sound of the metal doors closing reverberates
through his bones as the guards seal him in the room. He isn't
sure if this was such a good idea after all.

Gregor surveys Amon's study. An expansive room with
high ceilings, it is light and airy. He snoops around for some
insight to his ruler. Many of the artifacts in the room are fas-
cinating, one-of-a-kind pieces. A lighted glass case invites a
closer inspection. He steps closer and scrutinizes its contents—
mostly ancient ceremonial objects, some Egyptian, but others
are totally unknown.

An impressive headdress occupies the place of honor. It has
two horns of gold, a sun disk with a uraeus set, embellished with
precious gems. An unusual item to find in a vampire's study;
it must carry some sentimental meaning for Amon. He has a
nagging suspicion that he has seen it before.

A large dagger captures his attention. It is unlike anything
he has ever seen. Made entirely of silver, the main shaft is a
double-edged, leaf-shaped blade featuring a triple ridge on both

sides. The entire weapon is brilliantly etched and set with blood rubies in the grip—it looks positively lethal.

Suddenly, he realizes where he has seen the headdress before. On his first trip to Egypt, Nadira showed him a secret tomb. On one of the walls was a mural of the goddess Hathor, who wore this exact headdress. He studies it closer. It cannot be the same one. *Can it?*

He hears a noise outside the doors and does not want to be caught poking around, so he moves to the window with its inspiring view of the Alps.

His thoughts drift back to his nocturnal swim with Nadira. Her reaction to his departure pierced his heart. However, he must uncover the rest of her secret. Her father is the caretaker of her secrets and must know what happened to drive her away.

His reflection comes to an abrupt halt, and his instincts alert him to potential danger. He realizes someone else is in the room and is startled to see Amon watching him. Unsure how much of his thoughts were unguarded, he quickly regains his composure. The sight of Amon is always unnerving.

Amon's physical appearance is unassuming. He is an ageless vampire of medium height whose olive skin and dark eyes betray his Egyptian heritage. He still maintains the shaven head of a priest and an intense aura that intimidates everyone.

Amon retains the disciplined tranquility of a Tibetan monk but emanates a powerful energy, seemingly without the use of any physical element. He possesses a practiced stillness that renders any meaningless movement purposeless. This is the vampire Nadira lovingly calls father and all others proclaim king.

Gregor remembers that he is in the presence of his sovereign. He drops to his knee and brings his left fist to his chest, the vampire salutation of respect. He bows his head and waits for acknowledgement.

Amon addresses him. "Baron, please stand up. All this kneeling is tiresome."

Gregor does as instructed. "My lord, I have come on a personal matter."

Amon sits and indicates he should do likewise. Amon smiles. "How is my daughter?"

Gregor is not surprised. Amon must have read his thoughts and cuts right to the heart of the matter, no pleasantries or extraneous salutations. So be it. Gregor jumps to the point of his visit. "Not well, my lord. I am very concerned."

Amon leans back in his chair, studying his daughter's companion. Gregor nervously shifts in his chair, unsure how to proceed. Amon smiles reassuringly. "Usually, the truth is best."

It is unsettling to have one's thoughts answered verbally. Gregor peers at Amon. "My lord, I am worried about your daughter. She remains secreted among humans. Other than me, she does not interact with any vampires. It is as though she is hiding something."

"Go on."

"Decade after decade, she continues in this manner. Her yearly ritual of killing criminals is the only evidence she is a vampire. I watch each year as she grows more isolated, despondent, and unhappy."

Amon's expression is unreadable. "I had not realized the extent of her self-imposed purgatory."

Gregor nods. "My lord, may I be frank?"

Amon pauses and weighs the vampire before him. "Please do."

"I love your daughter and have tried in my meager way to support her. I do not have the facts available to understand the source of her unhappiness. She allowed me to read one of her journals," he reveals.

Amon eyes narrow slightly. "Which journal?"

Stunned, Gregor wonders how many journals she has. "The one concerning Cristo," he says, and Amon's eyes darken. "The last pages are missing. I think those pages hold the key to unlocking her misery."

"Where are the missing pages?"

"Nadira said she burned them."

Amon stares out the window. "Did she tell you what was on the missing pages?"

He realizes Amon is withholding information. "She said she hardly remembers," he answers.

Amon sighs and looks at Gregor. His penetrating black eyes seem boundless. His gaze unsettles Gregor. "The pages were not destroyed. I rescued them from the flames."

Why would Amon rescue pages from Nadira's personal journal? "May I read them?" he asks.

"What do you plan to do with this information?" Amon asks.

Without guile, Gregor answers, "To better understand the woman I have loved for centuries. Help mend her shattered soul. Bring her happiness. She bleeds, I bleed. Nadira holds my heart in her hands."

A smile spreads across Amon's face, lighting up the room with his joy. "I have waited centuries to hear those words regarding my daughter." He scrutinizes Gregor. "There is something else that you do not confess." His eyes strip away Gregor's defenses. "Ah, she does not know this?"

"No, I have kept it from her, but she is beginning to suspect," he confesses.

"Why withhold your love?" Amon discerns the answer immediately.

Gregor groans. "Cristo." Emboldened, he continues, "My lord, I must know the nature of your disagreement with Nadira."

Utter silence fills the room. Amon does not answer him. Instead, he unlocks his desk drawer, pulls out a carved wooden box, and hands it to Gregor. "Here are the missing pages. After you read these, we will talk of the other."

Gregor clutches the box. "Thank you, my lord."

Amon considers Gregor. His plans for their future hinge on the cooperation of this vampire. He hopes he has chosen wisely.

Amon smiles at Gregor. "Please, call me Amon."

CHAPTER VIII

REGOR SCANS THE crowd for a familiar face. The busy club is filled with vampires and humans at the tables, at the bar, and spilling onto the dance floor. The music is loud and eclectic. He notices Coatl is front and center, surrounded by his worshipers—all dressed like Marilyn Manson wannabes. Coatl raises his glass as though toasting him. Genevieve is right: Coatl is vile but not to be underestimated.

Gregor hears his name, peers over the dancers' heads, and sees Genevieve waving her arms. She rushes over and grabs his hand.

"I have someone I want you to meet," she says.

"When did they covert the ballroom to a club?"

Genevieve shouts above the din, "We remodeled it during the height of the disco era. The perfect place to decompress, make political alliances, or just vamp-watch."

She leads him toward a table occupied by a tall Nordic vampire in a black Vigile uniform. This soldier is definitely *strac*. He sizes up Gregor in no time and stands to greet them.

"Gregor, I want you to meet my husband, Drostan."

Gregor looks from Genevieve to Drostan. "Talk about close-mouthed. You didn't say anything about getting married."

Drostan pulls out a chair. "Sit down, and let us explain."

Gregor sits. "You have my full attention."

Genevieve grins at Drostan, her face lit with love. "We got married in secret two days ago. Drostan thought it best."

Drostan explains in a calm, controlled voice, "With the current political environment, we need to keep a low profile. I am the Vigile commander and have many enemies who would take advantage of our situation."

Gregor is impressed. The Vigiles, the military strong-arm of the vampire government, are legendary. Break the law, and justice is both swift and deadly. It is an exclusive club, with very few vampires making the final cut. He had considered joining a few times but could not bear to leave Nadira. He eyes Drostan with newfound respect.

"Things are that volatile?" Gregor asks.

Genevieve ponders her response. "Yes, since Coatl's return from exile. He has been stirring the political pot. He was turned down for a seat on the council again and was not happy."

Coatl seems to be a reoccurring theme. "Why was Coatl exiled?" Gregor asks.

"Nadira didn't tell you? How strange." It is Genevieve's turn to be puzzled.

Drostan interjects the facts. "Coatl interfered in human affairs. He slaughtered an important South American government official. The official was trying to protect his family, but Coatl slew the children just for his amusement. The cover story was that the drug cartel murdered the official. Coatl was convicted and banished, but he didn't leave without a fight."

Baffled, Gregor asks, "What does Nadira have to do with any of this?"

Genevieve and Drostan glance at each other.

"It was Nadira who testified against Coatl. She had an appointment with the official and arrived at his house just after Coatl had massacred the family," Drostan reports.

Gregor slumps back in his chair. "Damn."

Drostan continues, "Coatl and his followers are fanatics. He abhors Amon's views on vampire–human relations and became the poster child for the faction clinging to the old ways. He brazenly repudiates any of Amon's laws, making himself a constant source of dissension."

Genevieve interjects, "What Drostan really means is Coatl has no regard for the law and even less for humans."

Drostan adds, "The Vigiles spend most of our time cleaning up his coven's messes. He craves only blood and power. I keep him on a short leash. Eventually, I'll have to crush him to advance our cause."

Genevieve shakes her lovely head. "Coatl, Coatl. I am tired of hearing his name." She pushes back her chair. "Enough politics. Gregor, dance with me."

Gregor is startled and looks to Drostan.

Drostan confesses, "I rarely dance and have two left feet."

Genevieve smiles seductively. "He may not be able to dance, but he makes up for it in other ways." She kisses her new husband. Her smile could melt an iceberg, including her taciturn husband. She grabs Gregor's hand, leading him to the dance floor. A pulsating techno beat vibrates the dance floor. Gregor and Genevieve join the other dancers, falling into the rhythm of the music. "I forgot what a marvelous dancer you are."

Gregor grins. "It is not a waltz, but I can hold my own. Do you remember our first dance?"

Genevieve nods. "At the Venetian Carnevale ball. My maker, Erasmo, wanted to show me off—his latest acquisition." She smiles shyly at him. "You asked me to dance. I thought you were so handsome and dashing."

"You were a vision in gold lace. Erasmo is a despicable vampire. How did you hook up with him?"

"I was eighteen, a lowly novice waiting to take my vows at the convent. Erasmo spied on me while I was about my duties as a shepherdess and then kidnapped me. My innocence was his aphrodisiac; I became his drug of choice. He turned me and imprisoned me, a bird in a gilded cage and nothing more than a plaything to be used as he wished." She smiles at Gregor. "Until the night of our waltz, then my brave knight rescued me. You introduced me to my future sister."

"I was amazed at your instant connection. Nadira said we were not leaving the ball without you. I thought I was going to have to challenge Erasmo to a duel, but Nadira cornered him. She demanded that he set you free. She must have been persuasive because you left the ball in our carriage," he remembers.

Genevieve laughs. "Have you ever sat across from Nadira at a bargaining table? She doesn't take no for an answer." They both laugh. "I was infatuated with you for a long time," Genevieve confesses.

"Really? What changed your mind?" Gregor smiles sheepishly.

"I realized your heart belonged to another."

Gregor spins her around. Genevieve's boldness takes him by surprise. He is not prepared to publicly confess his feelings about Nadira. However, he realizes that maybe this is part of the problem. For centuries, he has suppressed his love, never filling the emptiness in his heart.

"You are in love with my sister." Her emotional insight is an uncanny gift for a vampire but extremely useful in her role in politics.

"Am I that transparent?"

"To everyone except Nadira," Genevieve reassures him.

"What do you mean?"

"She loves you."

"You are mistaken," he says, but his heart soars with hope at the thought.

"Even she does not realize this truth; Nadira is so shackled by her own guilt that she does not allow herself to feel anything. She does not believe she deserves happiness so great is her need for self-castigation," she says.

"Do you know what happened to her?"

"No, even though I begged her to tell me. Her Abd, Haseem, and Jean-Louis, Drostan's—and formerly Cristo's—second-in-command, hold some pieces of the puzzle. But I believe only Amon knows the whole truth."

Gregor ponders this new revelation. "I do love your sister, more than you know. Since the first time I saw her, she has owned me body and soul."

"A difficult burden to carry century after century. What do you plan to do about it?" she asks.

Gregor is unsure how to answer. "I don't know."

"Tell her how you feel."

He ruminates on this, fearing it cannot be that easy. Nadira is a complex vampire; with her, nothing is ever simple, and altering his role as her companion will be a formidable task.

He changes the subject, asking, "Whatever became of that despot Erasmo?"

Genevieve frowns. "He arrived here last year, proclaiming his undying affection and begging me to return with him. I refused. He tried to force me. Drostan intervened on my behalf. Erasmo challenged him to combat. A very imprudent decision—it was the last time anyone ever saw Erasmo," she confesses.

As the music's volume lessens, Gregor has questions of his own. "I have always been fascinated with the Vigiles. How did Drostan become their commander?"

Genevieve's eyes light up at the mention of her husband. "Drostan was a Templar Knight. King Philip's purge wiped out his order. The surviving Templar knights fled to Switzerland, where Amon gave them refuge. Drostan was the logical choice: disciplined, loyal, and devoted to the law. He has never been defeated in battle." She beams with pride.

"Templar Knights would rather die than surrender. Their bravery at the Battle of Montgisard became legendary and the standard for every knight. You two are such opposites, how did you meet?" he asks.

"I would see him in passing, at meetings. He was always polite—professional but cold. I never considered him romantically until one day when I caught him staring at me the way males do. I asked Nadira about him," Genevieve replies.

Gregor's interest is peaked. "Nadira knows him?"

"Yes, she and Drostan were lovers before she found you. I asked Drostan about their affair. He said they were drawn together by loneliness and chemistry, but love was not part of the arrangement. You know, Cristo and all. They still respect each other and remain friends. I told you there was more to Nadira than you know."

His jealousy is aroused. The fact there was no love soothes his wounded pride, but he is loath to hear more details about Drostan and Nadira's affair. He avoids the subject. "What changed your mind about Drostan?"

"Drostan asked if I wanted to see something special. He took me to a remote mountain peak. We scaled a steep ravine and perched on this tiny ledge. The fog was so thick you couldn't see your hand in front of your face. We waited for what seemed like hours. Not my idea of a fantastic first date. I was losing patience when I heard a soft swishing sound and the vapor parted—a magnificent eagle emerged, circled us, and then disappeared back into the mist. Drostan said that eagles are raptors like vampires, lethal hunters that mate for life. He looked at me with those icy blue eyes . . . he had me at 'eagle.'" A girlish smile warms her face.

"Good date." Gregor smiles.

"Yes, it was." A wistful smile plays with her ample lips.

The tempo of the music changes as pounding rock lyrics vibrate the room. Drostan taps Gregor's shoulder. "Sorry, buddy, I saw her first."

"She is all yours," Gregor replies.

He hands Genevieve over to her husband. Drostan is right: he can't dance. He attempts some finer steps, but his two left feet trip him. Genevieve makes up for his clumsiness with grace and poise. They obviously do not notice his lack of talent and only have eyes for each other.

Gregor returns to the table to watch the parade of flesh, both vampires and humans. There seems to be an abundance of comingling among the species. He makes a mental note to ask Genevieve about it. He is oblivious to the subtle and, at times, blatant sexual invitations sent his way. *What are they compared to Nadira?* All a poor substitute. Always, his thoughts turn to her.

What a day of revelations. Genevieve and Drostan secretly married. Nadira will be choleric when she finds out. The bombshell about Drostan and Nadira leaves a bitter taste in his mouth. Nadira, always secretive about her past, never revealed any of this to him. What else doesn't he know about her? In reality, probably a great deal. It is difficult to compress a life as complicated and timeless as hers into everyday conversation.

Why would she tell him about Drostan? He has not declared his love or been celibate. His sexual encounters are limited, a physical act of release with a stranger and nothing more. Intimacy with Nadira is his dream; the climax of his love will be the union of their bodies and souls. He yearns for that day, and this endless waiting is fruitless, the price of deprivation too great for them both. Maybe her favorite proverb holds the key.

"When you love you bear a yoke."

Nadira's yoke is heavy, but his love is strong. He can shoulder her burden, whatever the price. He ponders how to change the nature of their relationship without driving her away.

His other dilemma: Amon saved the burnt journal pages. *Why would he do that? Why is he giving them to me to read?* Gregor must find out what happened to Cristo and uncover the skeleton in Nadira's closet.

He sighs, feeling very much like a fly trapped in Amon's web of intrigue, powerless to alter his destiny.

CHAPTER IX

GREGOR STUDIES THE wooden box, taking a minute to appreciate the artistry: intricately carved, inlaid with ivory, probably Moroccan, and very old. A special container, it must have held something precious. He places it on the desk and pulls up a chair. He lifts the lid, revealing fragile yellow manuscript pages with scorched edges encased in plastic to preserve their integrity. The top of the first page is torn and jagged with barely recognizable writing, the script jumbled and chaotic.

The paltry village that hosted my husband's execution. A town square embraced by stout wood buildings capped with thatch. The stone bell tower, the town's sole prominence, occupied the far side of the square. Hidden in the tower, we had a sweeping view of the scene below us.

Spectators filled the plaza. A break from the mundane, the proceedings took on a carnival atmosphere. It could have been a May Day festival; vendors hawked their wares of rancid meat pies, oily elixirs, and straw crosses. Minstrels amused their audience. A wooden pyre occupied the place of honor; serfs stacked wood onto it. Adults and children gathered to watch the novelty of a vampire burned at the stake. Those insignificant humans made a spectacle of my husband's death. I damned them all.

The crowd cheered as the processional entered the square: lay clergy preceded by priests and followed by brawny guards dragged the main attraction, my Cristo. The crowd jostled for a better view of a true rarity, a live vampire, their instinctive fear of vampires supplanted by the false courage of a mob. They ridiculed, cursed, and pelted my husband with offal. The guards bound him to the pyre's center post and secured his heavy silver chains with locks. They surrounded their prize, fearful lest the day's entertainment escape. Priests with holy water sprinkled the condemned, swung thuribles of incense, and chanted prayers. White-clad, cherub-faced altar boys sang hymns.

The crowd was restless, and the noise was deafening. These ignorant peasants did not seek salvation but rather the dark face of death. They cried for blood, the same reason my husband was to burn. The chief inquisitor presided over the proceedings. Draped in his official robes and self-important, he raised a hand for quiet. The uproar died, and silence smothered the square.

He spewed his rhetoric, "As God's anointed servant, my mission is to root out evil in all its forms. Today, we witness the destruction of Lucifer's most vile minion, the vampire. With the power vested in me by the church, Count Cristo de Mendez, I sentence you the everlasting damnation of hell." The inquisitor raised a torch, declaring, "We cleanse this demon with fire." He handed the torch to his assistant, who set fire to the pyre. The kindling ignited into a slow, painful burn.

I pleaded with Jean-Louis to do something, but he refused me. My husband made him promise to do nothing that might expose me to capture. Cristo kept my existence secret from his examiners. Jean-Louis vowed to protect me and intended to keep his word to his sovereign lord. Desperation drove me to break free and lunge toward the stairs. The knights grappled me, but I shook them off. I threatened them, baring my fangs.

Then, Jean-Louis chilled me with this declaration: "Countess, the count bid me deliver his last wish. He made me memorize it. The count beseeches you, 'Wife, do not let your husband die in vain. Do not follow me to the grave, but rather live for us both. Remember, our love is everlasting, in this life and the next.'"

The faint light of sunrise broke over the rooftops. A cheer rose from the square, buoyant on the cool dawn air. I ran to the ledge to peer down at Cristo and beckoned him with my mind. He straightened, turned his face, and gazed up at me. Our eyes met as our souls entwined. He declared his eternal devotion. Through my tears, I pledged mine. In that second, we exchanged a lifetime of love. Our happiness together had run its course.

The sun broke over the hill, filling the square with its warmth. The golden rays lit his pale skin. He struggled against the silver chains. My fingers gripped the stone ledge and painted it red with blood. I watched helpless, a spectator to my beloved's torture. His skin blistered, sizzled, and burst into flames. I closed my eyes, unable to watch. Mercifully, the flames quickly consumed him. My Cristo crumbled into a heap of ash.

The townsfolk shouted their delight. I opened my eyes, my face wet with tears. I fixated on the pyre and the humans who laughed and clapped. I shook, overcome by anguish, but something boiled to the surface. An emotion I have never felt before, all powerful, blotted out my reason. Rage—it coursed through my body, fired my blood. His execution would bring these humans no pleasure. They courted death, then I delivered its bitter taste. My powers suppressed for so long, I unleashed them on my husband's coarse murderers.

Pointing to the town, I commanded, "Exuro." The flames leapt higher and became a soaring inferno, like a blazing tree with fiery branches spreading upward. The townspeople fell silent. The priests crossed themselves. The flames danced in the air, twirled, and leapt onto all the rooftops. The whole town ignited. Sparks rained down on bystanders. Spectators screamed as their clothes and flesh were burnt. The fire consumed the guilty and innocent as their world spiraled into chaos. The surviving witnesses scrambled to douse the flames to no avail.

Overcome and my strength exhausted, I emitted a loud soul-wrenching wail, and my legs buckled as I collapsed. The knights were wide-eyed and petrified. Jean-Louis pleaded with me to flee as the flames licked the base of the bell tower. I forced a promise from him to bring me Cristo's ashes. He agreed, picked up my limp body, and raced before the inferno.

Ex Voto (Offering)

My wagon train was loaded with possessions. The servants stood on the road next to the wheat field. A group of mounted knights waited patiently. The horses tossed their heads and pawed the ground, restless for action. I stood in the middle of the field, shrouded in black mourning, the color of my future. I clutched the Moroccan box tightly to my chest. The wheat stalks swayed rhythmically with the breeze. My grasp on reality was tenuous.

I whispered, "My love, this is the field where we were to share our love. As a vampire, you never got the chance to feel the sun's warmth. I pray that in death . . . the sun will chase the cobwebs from your soul."

I opened the box just as a breeze danced across the field, embraced Cristo's ashes, which escaped upward and pirouetted over the field before disappearing.

"Adieu, my husband. Our hearts will always beat as one." I gazed up at the sun and offered my soul for my murdered husband. "Count Cristo de Mendez, I give you my oath that I would have vengeance on the humans who murdered you." Thus, I sealed my fate.

ULCISCOR (Vengeance)

The town was a charred spot on the map, leveled by the fire. I stood amidst the rubble, the stone foundation of the bell tower the solitary reminder there was a town. I reached down, scooped up a handful of ashes, spread my fingers, and allowed them to flow *back to earth. Ashes would be all that remained of the humans who murdered my Cristo. So began my quest for vengeance.*

Those that survived the fire I paid a visit. I found them about their daily tasks in the fields, at meals, or abed—it made no difference. I slaughtered them, scattered their families, and burnt their farms. Fire was now my collaborator. I deprived them of their lives, happiness, and future as they deprived me of my love. Once I was merciful, but now I was bereft of kindness. I wanted them to suffer as I suffered, to feel my pain until they felt no more.

The law held no sway with me. It forsook my husband, and now I abandoned its precepts. My hatred and lust for blood were all that remained; neither satisfied my craving for vengeance. The priests were harder to locate. The town destroyed, they relocated to other parishes. I tracked them down one by one, those wolves in sheep's clothing. The sanctuary of the church, confessional, or vespers did not hinder me. These charlatans of God all met the same gruesome fate.

I dispatched the townspeople, guards, and priests. There remained but one, the chief inquisitor, to taste my lethal kiss. His death would be the masterpiece in my requiem of death. My spies found him in fair Verona as a monsignor, his reward for executing my husband. Powerful, guarded, and surrounded by those currying favor, he was harder to eradicate.

Patience, the virtue my husband lacked, I possessed in abundance. Disguised as a nun, I easily slipped into his palace and followed his daily routine. His sins were legion—bribes, greed, harlots, and young boys—followed by his nightly flagellation as penance. The timing was perfect for my pièce de résistance. I decided to pay him a nocturnal visit. When better to hear his confession? I invaded his bedchamber, the room black like my soul, and hovered in the corner, listening to the raspy sound of his consumptive lungs. He would not die of natural causes. I had prepared an appropriate ending to his miserable life.

He tossed restlessly on his bed, the sleep of the guilty, but sensed something was amiss and sprang upright. He could not see me. I stepped into the moonlight so his weak eyes could see what specter visited him.

"Who goes there?" he asked.

"I am death," I told him.

"Art thou the Reaper?"

"As you say" was my singular reply. I felt his emerging fear, relished it, and savored its acidic taste. To sweeten the flavor, I added truth to the dish. "I am wife to Count Cristo de Mendez."

It took a minute for the name to register. A look of horror crossed his face. He begged for mercy.

"Mercy? There was no mercy for the dead. I will show you the same mercy that I showed your other conspirators," I replied.

"Lucifer's servant!" He made the sign of the cross.

"I know nothing of Lucifer. I alone hold your destiny in my hands. You murdered my husband. I condemn you to hell for all the sins you have committed in the name of your religion." Thus, I delivered my verdict.

"Spare me." He wept, slobbered like a wizen fool, and then bepissed himself. My satisfaction reached its climax. I drew him to my bosom and savagely buried my fangs into his throat. The metallic taste of his blood soared through me. I drained him to the brink of death and flung him to the floor squirming and thrashing. He wiggled like a worm as his lifeblood dyed the floor crimson.

I dragged his miserable carcass to room's center, knotted a heavy rope around his neck, tossed the end over the rafters, and hoisted him in the air. His body jerked, and his legs and arms flailed. My horrific pantomime reached its exodus. His movements subsided until one last moan escaped his lips. I staged the room and furniture to look like a suicide. The Catholic Church excommunicated suicides and deprived the deceased of a Christian burial, a fitting end to my husband's executioner.

I studied my handiwork, savoring my revenge. Vengeance was not a dish best served cold. My revenge satisfied, it was time to flee. I strode to the door, but a faint image in a polished mirror lured me closer. What loathsome creature from another realm peered outward? I moved nearer to discern its origin. A head of

> *ebony hair twisted as Medusa, a grotesque face of chalk, soulless*
> *eyes, and lips stained red with blood—horrified, I realized it was*
> *the reflection of my soul.*
>
> *I unleashed the beast within, unable to contain it. I condemned*
> *myself to darkness for eternity.*
>
> *Ita sit. (So be it)*

Gregor rereads the last paragraphs. He leans back in the chair, stares up at the ceiling, and contemplates Nadira's journal. *What now?*

He places the pages in a neat stack and slides them into the box that sheltered Cristo's ashes. At last, he fully comprehends Nadira's horrific secret. Unable to forgive herself, her guilt shackles her to this past. Fear steals her future, and regret leeches her soul. This truth is only her perception of reality. A vampire's truth is far different from a human's truth. Those were different times, violent times. Vampires hunted humans to survive, and humans slew each other over a parcel of land, religion, or simply because one was different. In fact, humans are crueler to each other than any vampire is.

He understands better than most the seductive power of the dark side. Once embraced, it is hard to forgo, but Nadira taught him how. Now it is his turn to rescue her; he holds the key to her salvation. His love will unlock her prison door and set her free.

CHAPTER X

"**D**O YOU TRUST him?" Amon stares into Genevieve's eyes. She is uncomfortable with his line of questioning and nervously squirms under the scrutiny. "Let me rephrase the question. Would you trust him with your life?" he asks.

Like usual, Amon's face is unreadable. This is another one of his character tests, and Genevieve cautiously contemplates her response.

"Nadira respects and trusts Gregor. She has for centuries. He loves her almost to the point of obsession. Someone told me that with love, you can move mountains." She smiles at Drostan, who blushes. "The answer to your question is yes. I would trust him with my life."

Amon smiles, satisfied with her answer, and focuses on Drostan. "I know you have just met Gregor, but I would value your opinion. Do you agree with your wife?"

Honored by Amon's compliment, Drostan understands flattery is a flimsy platform to stand on. He is responsible for internal security and the military, an overwhelming task at times. Background checks are a routine part of the job, and of course, the companion of the king's daughter was thoroughly investigated. He bases his answer on the facts gleaned from Gregor's security dossier.

"My lord, I provided you with his dossier, which I assume you read," Drostan says, and Amon smiles. "He has no infractions with the law, no disputes with vampires, and prudent investments have made him financially independent. It appears the overall the focus of his life is your daughter."

Amon switches the question around. "So, Drostan, would you trust Gregor with you wife's life?"

Drostan is accustomed to Amon's chess strategy, so he plays the game. "As you trust him with your daughter's life."

Amon laughs. "Checkmate, Drostan." He glances at Genevieve. "Cancel my appointments for the rest of the afternoon. Let us not keep Gregor waiting. Send him in."

Gregor walks up to Amon's desk and slides the Moroccan box across it. Amon considers the vampire across from him and then leans back in his chair.

"So, now you know it all." Amon studies Gregor for any insight to his feelings.

"Yes, now I know," Gregor answers, giving no indication of his thoughts.

"Did you find what you were searching for?" Amon decides to play cat and mouse until he is positive of Gregor's intentions.

"Yes and no."

Amon weighs Gregor's answer for a moment and decides to fill in some of the gaps in Nadira's story. "When Nadira came to me in China, she was on the brink of madness." He remembers his heartbreak upon seeing his daughter shattered almost beyond repair. "It took many years of patience to bring her to reality then stability." He stares out the window for a few moments, lost in thought. "You know, it was finding you that proved the pivotal point in her recovery."

Gregor is puzzled. "Me?"

"Rescuing you gave Nadira purpose and direction. You provided companionship and lessened her loneliness, filling the vacuum Cristo's death left in her life. I am indebted to you for saving my daughter's life," Amon tells him.

"She saved me from certain death," Gregor confesses. A new vampire with no mentor, his thirst was unquenchable—a savage predator killing indiscriminately. She dragged him from the darkness back into the light. Amon considers these truths. "I did not realize how powerful Nadira is," Gregor adds.

Amon didn't wish to confide this potentially dangerous information just yet. Nevertheless, Gregor needs to understand the ramifications of a relationship with his daughter. It is time to trust him with the whole truth.

"No one knows the extent of her powers, least of all Nadira herself. I kept it a closely guarded secret. In Egypt, I glimpsed a fraction of those powers. I made her my acolyte to hone her skills. More powerful than any other vampire, including me, she may have limitless powers," Amon says.

Rocked by this new information, Gregor contemplates the repercussions. "The information in these papers is dangerous." Gregor indicates the box on the desk.

"Yes, I was waiting for you," Amon reveals.

Gregor's hunch was right: Amon *did* want him to read the journal. Amon picks up the box and walks over to the fireplace; its blazing fire roars behind the grate. He opens the lid, one by one tosses the pages into the flames, and watches them burn.

"They have served their purpose," he says.

Fascinated, Gregor stares at the fire as the plastic shrinks and the pages curl, blacken, and then disappear. In this one act, he erases Nadira's past. Amon tiredly sits down and fixes Gregor with a riveting stare.

Uneasy, Gregor returns his gaze. "Where do we go from here?"

"As your lord, I demand a pledge of silence about the matters we are to discuss." Amon leverages his power as sovereign to force Gregor's complicacy. If Gregor wants the truth, he must swear an oath.

"I don't know what we are about to discuss," Gregor says, afraid of committing to an unknown oath.

"You must do this without foreknowledge based on your faith, loyalty, and trust. Do you so pledge, Baron Lackovic?" Amon demands.

The formal title disturbs Gregor. Amon has trapped him again. If he hopes to be with Nadira, he must promise. He is either all in or all out. Gregor's heart skips a beat, and his palms sweat. He kneels on the floor, fist to chest, and swears to Amon, "I so pledge on my life, my lord."

In this one action, Gregor commits to their shared destiny. Amon's face changes expression, a look Gregor is unfamiliar with but one his opponents across his chessboard see routinely: triumph.

"You asked what Nadira and I disagreed about more than seventy years ago," Amon says.

"Yes." Gregor's mouth goes dry. He waits for Amon to drop the other shoe.

"I asked her to succeed me on the throne," Amon answers.

Gregor imagined a disagreement on politics, family matters, or something else, but he never guessed Nadira would be next in line to the throne. "Nadira?"

"Yes, my daughter. Nadira is the logical choice. She is one of the oldest living vampires, her opinions on human–vampire relations match mine, and she garners a great deal of respect and support from other vampires," Amon says.

"Not Coatl," Gregor counters.

Amon frowns. "So, you have met Coatl. He clings to the ancient ways, viewing humans as a source of food only. Killing humans is archaic. My daughter's pharmaceutical blood bank radically changed our reliance on humans. I spoke to Dr. Graetz; he's invented a synthetic blood."

"Nadira never told me any of this," Gregor confesses.

"She wouldn't. I asked to her to keep it a secret."

"How long until it's available?" Gregor asks.

"We do not have a launch date, but maybe a year." Amon allows Gregor to assimilate this latest tidbit. "The new millennium brings a shift in our relationship with humans. We need to rethink the nature of our connection. Vampires evolved from humans, becoming a new branch of *Homo sapiens*. We sacrificed reproductivity for immortality. Humans achieve immorality through children, and vampires reproduce by adoption. We are both adaptable species." Amon pauses, lost in thought. He knows Gregor's cooperation is paramount to the success of his plan. Therefore, he must guide Gregor toward the successful conclusion of his vision. Gregor clears his throat, which jolts Amon from his musings. "In the future, vampires will live openly in society." Amon voices his full vision, thus committing it to action.

Gregor, amazed by the far-reaching implications, says, "A new world. No more living a lie and hiding in the shadows."

"Change always has a price. Many humans and vampires will resist this move. A war among our factions is inevitable. We will need a strong ruler who can make the hard decisions, a vampire who acts as liaison between humans, and a pathfinder to claim our rightful place in the world. I believe Nadira is that vampire and asked her to be my successor."

"What happened?" Gregor asks.

Amon glances at him. "I think you know. She refused, objecting to certain conditions of the ceremony. She ran away, hiding among humans, and has remained hidden for almost a century. I think the time has come to try again."

Gregor is doubtful. "Do you really believe she is capable of this arduous task? She is too fragile. It would destroy her."

"True, she is not physically strong, but she is in a unique position. She never joined a coven, preferring to live with humans, which gives her a different perspective." Amon pauses. "If we can bring her here, I can help her. My daughter possesses an inner strength and resiliency she fails to acknowledge. Her past adversities would have destroyed a weaker vampire."

Gregor walks to the fireplace and stares at the fire. Nothing remains of Nadira's journal pages. It is a finished chapter in the story of her life. Now Amon plans to write a new chapter.

Amon studies Gregor. "The only thing Nadira lacks is a strong partner by her side." He waits quietly for Gregor's answer.

Amon offers him the brass ring, Nadira, if only he has the courage to grasp it. It is one thing to have a dream, but it takes strength to make a dream reality. Gregor studies his inscrutable sovereign. He must decide to stand beside Nadira or give her up. Life without her is nothing. Her destiny is his destiny. "What do you want me to do?" Gregor asks.

Amon smiles his enigmatic smile. "I have a plan."

CHAPTER XI

NADIRA STARES AT the desk calendar. The full moon has waxed and waned since Gregor's exodus. His departure left a void in her life, at times threatening to consume her with loneliness. Food has lost its flavor—necessary for survival only. Her memories of Gregor make poor bedfellows, and rest eludes her. Always at her side, she took him for granted—the sound of his voice, his smile, and a thousand other little things he did to fill her day. His infectious smile was a salve for her unhappiness.

She replays their last conversation repeatedly until exhausted. Self-critique is her forte, a skill she honed with centuries of practice. Her indifference drove him away. She still tastes their kiss, so sweet and full of promise. His absence has brought the truth into sharp focus. She loves him.

Strange, he is very different from her great love. Cristo was bold, earthy, and lusty, an impulsive man with a big persona.

Gregor is a subtle and disciplined intellectual with a depth to him that Cristo never possessed. Passion sparked her love for Cristo, but her connection with Gregor is deeper. They are similar to the point of sharing the same thoughts. Each day, she wonders if he will return to her and concocts schemes to win him back.

She glances at the meaningless papers stacked on her desk. At one time, work brought her satisfaction, but now it is just an empty routine. Frustrated, she rifles through the documents on her desk.

"I told you, I can't find the contract," she complains to Jerry, who has just appeared in the doorway.

Jerry walks around the desk, scans the documents, pulls out the contract, and hands it to Nadira. "Sign it where I've indicated," he tells her.

She jerks the paper out of his hands. Her reaction is a radical departure from her usual behavior. Prior to Gregor's disappearance, Nadira was kind, polite, and controlled, but her increasingly agitated state has the whole office walking on egg shells. "I know where to sign it." She scribbles her signature. "Are you happy?" she snaps.

Jerry studies Nadira. She is haggard, with dark circles under her eyes. She's pale, even for a vampire. He has never seen her so distraught. "Obviously you aren't," Jerry remarks.

His offhanded comment incenses her. Nadira glares at him, her irritation growing expediently. "Not what?"

"Happy." He walks around the other side of the desk and plops down in the chair. "Is it Gregor?" He offers her a shoulder to cry on, but she rebuffs him.

"Nothing is wrong. It is none of your business."

Softly, Jerry says, "Boss, we're all concerned about you. Everyone in the office is worried. We all care about you."

His words strike a chord that resonates in her aching heart. Her eyes tear up. The sound of the phone ringing startles them. Jerry answers it.

"She's right here." His expression is grave as he hands the phone to her.

"Genevieve? What's wrong? It can't be!" She pauses as her face goes white. "I'll come right away." She hangs up. Her whole body begins to shake, and her eyes well up as she peers at Jerry. "My father is dying . . ." she stutters but cannot finish the sentence. She clutches her chest as though in pain.

Jerry rushes to her side. "Please don't cry." He embraces her while she sobs into his shoulder. "Those damn bloody tears will tip everyone off that you're not human."

The office doors swing open. The staff knows the unwritten rule: when the doors are closed, do not interrupt. Startled, they both stare at the intruder.

Gregor stands in the doorway. Nadira catches her breath. Her relief at his reappearance leaves her speechless. Now she understands why women flock to him. It is as though she has been blind. His beauty leaves her breathless and makes her heart skip a beat.

"Gone for a little while and you jump into the arms of the first man you see," Gregor teases. A devilish smile scurries across his face, and then he winks.

"Gregor," Nadira whispers. Her voice cracks and relief washes over her. She can face anything with Gregor by her side. She tries to regain her composure but can't contain her joy. She runs to him, practically leaps on him, grabs his face, and kisses him passionately. Gregor's arms swing around her, enfolding her.

Jerry watches the two locked in an embrace. He quietly leaves the room, closing the door behind him.

"I missed you," she says

"I can tell. Maybe I need to go away more often." His eyes sparkle with delight.

"Don't joke about leaving me. I would die."

Gregor studies her. She looks as fragile as opaque glass: translucent and easily broken. Her haggard appearance alarms him.

"Forgive me?" she asks.

"For what?"

"I will never ever take you for granted again," she tells him in a rush of words, hardly stopping to take a breath.

"Slow down. What are you trying to say?"

"I won't wait another moment to say what's in my heart. You've waited patiently all these centuries while I've played the fool," she tells him.

Gregor cradles her face in his hands. "You're misguided but no fool. I would rather wait patiently beside you than live without you."

Nadira can't contain her tears as they slide down her cheeks.

"Don't leave it unsaid," he whispers and kisses her salty tears.

The words she hasn't spoken in centuries slip easily from her lips. "I love you."

Gregor stares at her. "What about Cristo?"

"All my life, I hungered for love. My first love was my father, who betrayed me. What followed was a vast emptiness. Eventually, Amon loved me as a father should. I never experienced that all-consuming passion of true love until Cristo. He was my husband and lover. Ours was a fervent love. I believed my capacity to love died with him, but I learned that life without love is only existence." She peers into his eyes, his soul, and sees only his love for her. "But my love for you is different. We are two sides of the same coin."

Gregor's love suppressed for centuries overflows. His voice is husky and choked with emotion. "I have loved you since first I beheld you, an angelic vision gazing down from your black charger, beseeching me, 'Come with me if you wish to live.'" He pauses. "Since then, you've owned me body and soul. You are my obsession. I love you more than blood, more than life itself. I shall never leave your side so long as I have breath in my body."

They kiss again, basking in the happiness of shared love, locked in an embrace, seemingly oblivious to the outside world.

Gregor strokes her hair. "Love, I could remain as thus . . ." He tightens his embrace. "But I have some urgent news. It is bad news." He feels her shudder.

She pulls away and the intimate moment is lost. "I know. Genevieve rang," she tells him, overwhelmed with conflicting emotions of newfound love and fear for her father. She does not know which way to turn. "I must go to Father," she says.

"The minute I heard, I came to get you. Hans is waiting downstairs. I have the plane on standby. Thought you would not be up to vampire aeronautics. You must be strong; we are surrounded by humans and mustn't expose our true identities," he reassures her and takes her hand, kissing it. "I am here, beloved. Let me share your sorrow."

Beloved. She has not heard that term of endearment since Cristo. It dawns on her that Gregor will always be there for her. She will never face life alone. The thought bolsters her courage. Nadira pulls herself together. "I am ready."

Hand in hand, they step outside of her office. Gregor stops and speaks to Jerry, who nods and shakes Gregor's hand. She glances around the office space at the humans peering over the cubicles, their eyes staring at her. She feels their overwhelming support, which comforts her. Gregor returns to Nadira's side.

"What did you tell him?" she asks.

"That your father is very ill, you are leaving for Switzerland, and to schedule a teleconference with the board of directors in two days. He and Haseem are to join us in Switzerland in a week. I told him that we don't how long we will be gone."

Obviously, Gregor has everything under control, releasing Nadira from the pressures of decision-making. Her concern for Amon blocks all reason. She cannot imagine life without him, a fixture in her life since she became a vampire, and berates herself for avoiding him all these years. He honored her with the offer to be his heir, and she ran away like a spoilt child. *Will I never learn?*

Gregor hurries Nadira into the Limo. "Hans, the airport. How are you holding up?" he asks her.

"I have broken my father's heart, and he has given up on life. I can't lose Amon again." Her voice is brittle.

"Let's hope that does not happen. You know how melodramatic vampires can be. Let's wait and see."

"Gregor, I was terrible to Amon the last time we were together. We argued. I was wrong, just being stubborn," she confesses.

Gregor is amused. "You? Wrong . . . stubborn? I can't imagine."

"How can he forgive me? I have avoided him for over seventy years. I owe him my fidelity, my love, and my life." She is so contrite that he tries to assure her.

"He is your father. Forgiveness is a forgone conclusion."

Gregor wraps her in his arms. Nadira peers up at him with such profound grief that he pities her.

"It will be all right. I promise you," he soothes her.

Nadira breaks free of Gregor's embrace. Panicked, she cries, "I have to go my apartment."

"Nadira, the plane is the opposite direction. We will be late. Haseem will bring anything you need."

"You don't understand. I forgot something," she cries. Her tears creep down her cheeks. Gregor realizes she is on the verge of hysteria. He tries to comfort her, but she collapses in his arms, sobbing uncontrollably. Gregor strokes her hair, cradling her like a child.

"Hans, swing by my lady's apartment. We have something to retrieve," Gregor directs him.

"Yes, sir." Hans gazes into the rear view mirror.

Nadira whispers between sobs, "Thank you. Amon gave them to me."

"We have plenty of time. It's your plane—it won't leave without you." He smiles, taps her on the chin, and then kisses her nose.

She settles in his arms, pulling strength from him. It's a unique experience for her to have someone she can trust and rely on. She lays her head on his chest and listens to the steady rhythmic beat of his vampire heart. Unlike a human heart that varies in intensity and rhythm, vampire hearts beat like the rising and setting of the sun—predictable and eternal.

She feels the car slow and come to a stop. Gregor cups her face with his hands. He looks deeply into her eyes.

"Are you ready?" Gregor asks.

Hans opens the sunroof. They lock hands, fly upward, and land on her balcony. Nadira releases his hand, runs to her library, and heads to the hidden safe. She opens it and pulls out the earring box. Gregor is bewildered but waits for her to enlighten him.

Nadira glances at him. "Amon gave me these before our disagreement."

She removes the earrings, displaying them for him. The earrings refract the light and illuminate the room as though the blood of their nation is in each stone. The earrings are part of the *La Linea de Sangre*, the Bloodline set, passed down to each vampire ruler since the beginning of time. The implications that she has the earrings are staggering. Only the next ruler would possess the earrings. The reigning sovereign presents the set to the heir in a secret ceremony. This is the stuff of vampire legend.

Her eyes reflect her conflicting emotions: a mixture of awe, fear, and sorrow. "I must accept his proposal. I have wasted centuries because of fear. I will waste no more," she says.

Gregor's eyes never leave her face.

She stares quietly at the painting and then turns toward Gregor. "My love, I kept you at arm's length. Every time I felt something more for you, I pushed you away," she admits.

"I know." Gregor is very still, realizing Nadira is on the brink of an epiphany.

"My pitiful excuse was Cristo's memory. But one can only deceive oneself for so long. I chained myself to a cage of my own creation, a prison forged with bars of shame, regret, and guilt. I focused on punishing myself and passed up happiness to wallow in my misery. Regret lasts forever, but I can cast off my shackles of shame and guilt. I am a vampire and will live as such from this day forth. No more hiding from my past." She manages a weak smile.

He smiles at her. "We have a plane to catch."

Gregor sweeps Nadira in his arms, planting a gentle kiss on her lips. Nadira grants him a grateful smile that speaks volumes.

CHAPTER XII

THE GULFSTREAM 550 rests on the apron of the Innamorati corporate hanger, its engines powering up for takeoff. Vampires do not usually travel via plane, but business trips with humans require a company jet. The crew waits for the limo to release its passengers.

The pilot addresses them. "We are ready for takeoff. Estimated flight time is six hours to Switzerland."

Gregor nods. "We leave immediately."

Gregor bundles Nadira onto the plane. The male steward seats his two passengers and then secures the outside door. The plane taxis down the runway, picks up speed, gains altitude, and then banks out over open water. Nadira blankly stares out the window. Gregor covers her with a blanket and sits down across from her. He watches his charge, so vulnerable and fragile, arousing his protective instinct.

"Nadira."

Lost in her private reverie, she does not hear him at first. Nadira's penchant for brooding prompts him to repeat himself. He must divert her agile mind from thoughts of Amon's impending doom. She glances at him. He smiles reassuringly.

"Will you tell me about how you became a vampire?" he asks.

She looks at him as though he has lost his mind. "Now? Are you sure you want to hear this?"

The memories associated with the beginning of her life are so heart-wrenching that it is easier to forget them than repeat them. Only Amon and Cristo knew the story of her life.

"It is a long flight. We have time," he says.

He hopes to gain more insight into this multifaceted woman who has captured his heart. "It would be a great honor to hear the story of your first encounter with our ruler," he says expectantly.

Nadira looks out the window, a mixture of pain and sadness etched on her pale features. She faces the first challenge of their blossoming relationship: sharing the story of her life and trusting him without reservation. Soft classic music fills the cabin, lulling the occupants and setting the mood for her heartbreaking saga.

"I guess I should start at the beginning so you will understand how meeting Amon changed my life," she says, and Gregor closes his eyes, settling back in his seat. "This is the fairy tale of a Persian princess." Her voice is laced with irony. "It was the year of a rare lunar and solar eclipse. I was the sixth child and first daughter of an Akkadian king. He prayed for a daughter. I was his favorite, showered with love and affection and denied nothing. My life was idyllic."

Her voice transports him to her childhood. In his mind's eye, he can see her: a delightful child, spoiled, lavished with attention, and cherished by a doting father.

She sighs and continues, "But all fairy tales have a tragic twist of fate. Mine is no different. I grew into a great beauty that delighted others but enraged my father. He became overly protective and hid me from public view." She stops, and sadness mars her lovely face. "My father rejected all offers for my hand in marriage. He would not give me up until a rival king offered to make me his queen in a political alliance. My future husband was handsome, a benevolent ruler, and a decent man. He would have given me a crown, children, and a mortal life. My father was furious with his proposal and, against his vizier's advice, spurred the offer. First, my mother and then I begged him to bless the union. I pleaded for an opportunity for love and happiness. My father would have no rival for my love and vowed that no man would have me."

Her story churns up a wave of bitterness that floats on the surface of her consciousness like sea foam. She stares at Gregor with her eyes shimmering.

"After four thousand years, the sorrow remains. How fickle the heart. My father's ultimate betrayal: he locked me in my quarters, forcing me to bribe my escape, only to have my plot exposed. Captured and bound in chains, I returned to the palace and was forced to watch my coconspirators be beheaded. He offered me to the goddess Lilitu of the blood sect as his present, gift-wrapped in virginal white and given to the high priests in an archaic ceremony. My father's prophesy that no man would have me was fulfilled. The priests were not human. They ravaged me one by one until I was near death. Finally, the high priest took my life in an orgy of blood."

Her father's treachery is the reason trust is so elusive for her. She closes her eyes, wishing these memories gone, the pain erased, but they are woven in the fabric of her mind, forever with her until the day she ceases to exist. Nadira's face hardens, but she puts the pain away.

"The priests were vampires?" Gregor asks.

She gazes at him with empty eyes and an unfathomable expression. "Yes. They took my virtue and my life. Now it is hard to decide which is more important. I became a high priestess and would have remained so until a chance encounter altered my destiny."

She pauses and stares out the window. The pieces to the puzzle of her life begin to fit together for him. Her story, hidden from him for centuries, becomes his gateway to understanding her.

"Caravans from the East whispered tales of a powerful and seemingly immortal Egyptian priest, a God. We suspected the priest was a vampire. I volunteered to go to Egypt and uncover the truth. Our caravan journeyed at night, arriving during the festival of Thoth."

Visions of exotic caravans, the grandeur of ancient Egypt, and mystical rituals fire Gregor's imagination, a magic carpet ride out of the *Tales from the Arabian Nights*.

"You must remember, I was a king's daughter, accustomed to luxury, but nothing prepared me for the grandeur of Egypt. Temple walls that touched the sky, gossamer tunics of the finest linen embroidered with gold, the air fragrant with expensive perfume, and everything inlaid with Kush gold and precious gems."

Gregor smiles encouragingly, eager for this next chapter in her story.

"Arrayed in my finery, I was taken to the grand temple and presented to their order. They summoned the high priest. Terrified, I knelt on the incense-laced altar, unsure of what awaited me. The room vibrated with the rhythmic chanting of the priests. It made my blood burn, my head swim, until it reached a crescendo. Then, a hush fell over us. Fear gripped me and paralysis seized my body. A mysterious priest clad as the god Anubis entered the sacred room. He glared down at my pitiful form quivering in the dust. I prostrated myself before him. If I could have disappeared into the limestone floor, I would have."

Gregor shares her feelings of awe, apprehension, and terror. He notices a look of serenity cross her face.

"But the gods had another destiny planned for me. The priest's next action shocked me. He blessed me with ancient verse, touched me with his staff of power, and bade me stand beside him as his equal. Our connection was immediate. The jackal-headed priest was Amon."

Her obvious love for Amon radiates from her very core, touching Gregor's heart. No wonder she worships him; he saved her from brutality and a loveless life.

"Our destinies were intertwined. He became my mentor and I his acolyte. He loved me as a father and gave me guidance and purpose. Egypt, obsessed with life after death, was the quintessential haven for a vampire. Amon and I became powerful and worshipped as gods. It is a tempting thing to be a god. It remained so for thousands of years. Eventually, the pharaoh's lineage weakened. A new pharaoh felt threatened by our power and wished to dispose of us. Amon felt it was time to return providence to humankind. We simply vanished from the pages of history, never to return. But that is a story for another day."

Nadira finishes, exhausted, leans back, and closes her eyes. Gregor is speechless, unable to find words to describe his conflicting feelings. Her saga spans a tumultuous period that altered human history. Genevieve was right: there's more to Nadira than anyone knows.

"Quite a story," he whispers.

Nadira opens her eyes, but they are different, black and endless, like the night sky bereft of stars. He has seen this look before. Amon's eyes have that same expression, as though the knowledge of the world lives there. There is something else harder to articulate—a sensation of raw energy pulsating just below the surface of their physical bodies.

"Maybe I will write a novel someday. But who would believe it? Truth is stranger than fiction."

A knowing smile plays across her face; she read his mind, as Amon did in the study. He never noticed the similarity between the two, but now it is striking. He must be careful to guard his thoughts until she sees Amon.

In an attempt to distract her, he chimes in, "A book about vampires would do well, and humans are crazy for us. We are quite the rage. Look at the vampires in movies, television, and even commercials that sell everything from candy bars to car headlights. The truth about us is even more fantastic and less horrific than humans can imagine."

"Reversing the propaganda spewed by the church has been difficult, but our PR department has made great strides in the digital age. Public opinion has shifted dramatically in our favor, advancing our assimilation into human society. Vampires are the next evolutionary phase of humans, but unlike Neanderthals, it makes sense that we coexist with our siblings. The two species working together can change the world for the better."

Her ideas of human and vampire interrelations intrigue Gregor. They mirror Amon's vision for the future.

"Amon is the key to this transformation. He must not perish," she says.

"He is quite the visionary." *More than you will ever know,* he thinks.

She looks out the window until her eyes flutter shut and she falls into an exhausted stupor. Gregor studies his sleeping beauty and ponders all that she said. She is right about everything but one fact. Amon may be the catalyst for transformation, but she will be the instrument of that change. Her yoke will be heavy indeed.

CHAPTER XIII

THE ROOM COULD be the cheap set of some gothic horror movie. Red flocking smothers the walls and a velvet-draped four-poster bed dominates it. The long hair of the woman kissing his stomach festoons Coatl's muscular chest. Her lacy lingerie barely covers the bruises and bite marks marring her bronzed skin. He lifts her slender wrist to his lips, kisses it, and bites down. A soft moan escapes her lips; she closes her eyes in ecstasy. A perverse smile tugs at his face. He flips her onto her back and imprisons her wrists. Amused, he watches her struggle to free herself, but she is no match for him. He pins her down with his knees and nips her breasts. She moans, writhing underneath him. Her eyelids flutter open.

"Bite me," she begs.

He is more than happy to comply, biting her shoulder. Blood washes over her slender shoulder and down her breasts. She grasps his face, holds his gaze, extends her tongue, and slowly licks the blood from his lips. His passion-charged smile exposes his canines.

"More," she growls.

His mouth travels down her hard body toward her inner thigh. She grabs a handful of his hair.

"Yes," she whispers.

He plunges his fangs into her femoral artery, causing her body to stiffen and arch up. She cries out; the delicious thrill of bloodletting is more than she can bear. Her passion fuels his lust. He jerks her head back, exposing her neck, his fangs poised over her carotid artery pulsating tantalizingly close to his lips.

Breathless, she insists, "Do it."

His mouth descends on her unprotected skin. A loud knock at the door startles them. Midbite, he pauses, grits his teeth, and waits.

There is more furious knocking at the bedroom door.

"Lord Coatl, I am sorry to interrupt, but I must speak to you on an urgent matter."

He rolls off the woman and perches on the side of the bed, gathering his self-control. "Damn," he curses.

"You're not leaving?" his partner complains. Her disappointment fervent, she grabs his arm, her smile intoxicating, but he hesitates.

"Duty calls," he laments.

She provocatively reaches behind her back, unhooks her bra, drops it to the floor, and arches her back, rubbing her breasts against him. His arms imprison her. She responds with a rough kiss, savagely bites his lip, and draws blood. Her eyes glisten with desire. "Just a reminder of what you're missing, lover," she taunts.

He wipes the blood from his lip, stares at her a moment, and then backhands her across the face. She falls backward, laughing a taunting laugh meant to provoke him to greater violence. He could snap her silly neck at any time, but he won't. She is the only woman who can arouse him. The more blood and pain, the more she likes it. Better yet, she brutalizes him. She is a true sadist and not afraid of him. He thought about turning her a few times, but there is something stimulating about a human with the same appetite as his.

"Beydaan, you're as twisted as I am." He smiles, pleased with his mistress.

"That's what you pay me for, isn't it?" Her smile is wicked and enticing.

He found her in a Somalian brothel. He ordered something special that night and was thrilled when she glided into the room. She is a delicious exotic beauty with skin the color of wild honey, amber eyes, and long legs. He thought she would be the night's entertainment—then, dessert. He was sadly mistaken. His violent foreplay did not faze her until it escalated out of control. She fought like a tiger, but he easily overpowered her until she produced a switchblade and skewered him. He found her refreshing, a human with pluck and not afraid to fight back. He laughed, extracted the blade from his chest, and introduced himself as the vampire Coatl. Nonchalantly, she demanded more money. Her warped sexual appetite compliments his primal need to debase humans. He purchased her contract on the spot—that was three years ago.

He laughs, wraps himself in a robe, and leaves the room. His chief adviser, Aleksei, is pacing the living room floor. Aleksei is a worrywart, meticulous, and lacking any scruples, which makes him a valuable ally.

Aleksei focuses his attention on Coatl. "I am sorry to interrupt, but I intercepted news of a pressing nature."

Aleksei's nervousness infuriates him. His advisor has more tics than a dog. Between his handwringing, pacing, and jerking eyebrow, it's enough to drive him to slaughter this feckless human. He strolls over to the sleek glass bar and rummages around the liquor bottles. The meaningless activity cools his passion. He pours himself a drink and then studies Aleksei, who wilts under his scrutiny.

"What is so urgent that you interrupt my pleasure?" Coatl asks.

Aleksei swallows hard to calm his nerves. Lord Coatl hates to have his leisure time disrupted, and more than one lackey has lost his life doing so. Aleksei pastes an insincere grin on his face.

"My lord, I have received a choice piece of information. Nadira returns to the Ordinatio."

"The pigeon returns to the roost." A vicious smile affixes to Coatl's face.

Coatl tosses back his drink. He strides over to Aleksei, slapping him on the back. Aleksei flinches and clumsily covers his fear. Coatl smiles, basking in the fear he elicits. He rules his subjects with force and terror.

"We have much planning to do. Amon is ill and vulnerable; this is the time to strike. Their defenses are down. If we move cautiously, we can kill two birds with one stone." He laughs at his own joke.

"My lord, our army is not of sufficient size to deal with the Vigiles," Aleksei counters.

Coatl scowls at him. "Trivialities, my friend. Just step up recruitment. There are plenty of young humans out there who would give anything to be immortal. Stupid children think being a vampire is like the movies." He laughs, but it's not a laugh at all, more like a low-key growl. "Remember, you are the flunky. Your job is to fret and work out the details. I am the visionary." Coatl jabs his finger in Aleksei's chest. "Increase our ranks."

Aleksei shivers. "What about Nadira? She is powerful," Aleksei whines.

"She *was* powerful. Living with humans has made her weak. She is easily disposed of." Coatl's eyes narrow.

Aleksei is not convinced. "Her companion, Gregor?"

Coatl ponders this potential problem. "He concerns me. Gregor is intelligent, powerful, and devoted to her. He is not easily dismissed."

Aleksei drones on about potential problems, anxiously wringing his hands and pacing. Coatl tunes him out and reclines on the couch, lost in his own thoughts. An outsider among his species, his ideas and methods have been deemed extreme, so his resentment toward his own kind and humans has festered over the centuries.

His fondest memories are of the Aztec, a savage and superstitious people. His powers dazzled them. Believing him a god, they worshipped him. It was not the first time humans thought him a god, but it was the last. As a deity, he did as he pleased without consequence, indulging his appetites without restraint. His voracious appetites for blood and power consumed many of the indigenous tribes of the region. His blood rituals altered the Aztec culture. Bestowed with the title "The Serpent," he bears the same moniker to this day. Pity it only lasted a brief interlude.

His species could not ignore him forever, and during the Great Persecution, the High Council sought him out. His extreme violence was unavoidable to combat the vampire slayers. He hunted them down one by one, and each met with a particularly horrific demise. Celebrated as a hero, he sat on the High Council until his excessive appetites became an embarrassment. Shunned by his own kind, he was discarded after he served his purpose, and his resentment festered into hatred. It was easier in the old days when most vampires shared his beliefs.

But the times have changed. The politically correct view is coexistence with humans. Humans are disgusting creatures who think they know everything about vampires, creating television shows and movies with werewolves. *Werewolves, a secretive species, would hardly communicate with us, let alone be seen in our company. The myths about mirrors, garlic, and stakes in the heart are all rubbish. Humans know nothing about us and are not our equals. Just as the zebra and the lion are not equal—one is the prey and the other the predator. Amon's visions of a brave new world with comingling of the species will result in our extinction; vampires will go the way of the dinosaur.*

In this new era, vampires are reverting backward to their human origins. Most vampires feed on packaged blood, bottled like beer or soda. They have forgotten how to be predators, the thrill of the hunt, the sensual draw of blood, or the taking of life—all vanishing.

As for humans, there will be no coexistence. Mankind's own history provided him with the answer. His stint with the Gestapo solidified his ideas. He was an officer assigned to implement the master plan and was appalled by Hitler's final solution, not for moral reasons but for a more practical motive. The extermination of humans over an asinine prejudice was shortsighted and a waste of valuable resources. He understands that one does not eradicate humans, but rather you dominate them. His plan is a simple one: subjugate the human population and divide them into two categories, slaves and food.

Vampires are the master race; it is our time to reign. Once in power, he will abolish all the idiotic laws that favor humans. Vampires will take their rightful place in the world. No more skulking in the shadows. *We will rewrite history.*

He must bring his plan to fruition, crush Nadira, and steal the crown. His revenge will be slow and painful. First, annihilate Nadira's family. Then, kill her. He will save Genevieve for his pleasure. His twisted soul craves her sweet and gentle nature. The opportunity to corrupt and torment her thrills him. Beydaan satisfies, but she is human. He must restrain himself and not kill her with punishment. The amount of abuse Genevieve can withstand is limitless.

The sound of his name creeps into his subconscious, interrupting his grandiose daydreams. Aleksei is staring at him. He tries to remember the topic of conversation, and then it comes to him.

"I do not have a plan regarding Gregor. Together we will devise a strategy to sway him to our side or remove him. Let us focus on the bigger challenge: building our army," Coatl says.

Aleksei bows. "Yes, my lord."

"You are dismissed."

Coatl waves him away like a buzzing fly. Aleksei scurries out of the room. Coatl saunters to the bar and pours another drink. He is close enough to his dream that he can taste its sweet success. The Council will pay for denying his rightful council seat. After he defeats the Vigiles, he will rule and all will pay homage to him, a satisfying thought. He sips his drink and rolls the stringent liquor in his mouth.

"A fine Kentucky bourbon," he purrs. His voice echoes in the vacant room. He contemplates the empty Waterford tumbler. It is beautiful and fragile, like his enemy. He squeezes until it shatters. The simple gesture satisfies his desire to destroy. "I will break Nadira like this pretty crystal." His hand is cut and seeping blood from the laceration. Turning it over, he laps up the blood and savors its life-sustaining properties. The intoxication of blood ignites his body, each a slave to the other.

His lust inflamed, he strides to the bedroom and kicks open the door. Beydaan lounges on the bed. He tosses off his robe.

"We have unfinished business."

"It's about time." She smiles seductively and extends her hand as an invitation.

CHAPTER XIV

T HE MEDIATION ROOM, with its white walls, tatami-mat floors, and muted lighting, is the perfect environment for reflection. A philosopher at heart, Amon is bent over, reading an ancient papyrus. One of the many that he rescued from the Royal Library in Alexandria, it is a complex philosophic essay by Socrates. He misses his debates with Socrates, whose agile mind challenged all his concepts about life and death. Amon adopted the Socrates method of questioning and answering that encourages critical thinking. A source of annoyance to the weaker minded, it makes for stimulating conversation with those possessing greater cerebral capacity. Facing his greatest challenge, he would welcome advice from the Greek philosopher. It will require all of his mental powers to untie this twisted knot.

He finishes reading the manuscript, rolls up the papyrus, and places it in the Tibetan cabinet filled with scrolls and ancient volumes. He prepares to meditate, closing his eyes, taking his usual lotus position, and clearing his mind.

His daughter is coming home. Her rapid departure seventy years ago left a void in his life that remains to this day. In truth, he is glad she disobeyed him. She sacrificed great power for love, and it was with love that he released her, bestowing upon her the gift of freedom and time. During her absence, her understanding of humans has evolved. He demanded too much from her; she was not ready, but now she is poised to fulfill her destiny.

He knew she was special. Her humility impressed him from the beginning. A quick study, she became his student, picking up the bizarre rituals and archaic languages with ease. Each vampire possesses a unique talent or gift. Her training took on a new dimension when he discovered an untapped reservoir of raw energy and a talent for manipulating it. Her ability to control the weather was astounding. Many of Egypt's ancient climatic disasters were by her hand.

She is singular: the rare vampire with a conscience who enjoys the company of humans, a unique combination perfect for their vision of the future. He never fathered any children, so she became his daughter. She filled the vast emptiness of his heart with love. Her love is without reservation, at times consuming her, a trait that almost cost her her life. The loss of Cristo broke her, releasing her darker nature and scarring her permanently.

Now he prepares for her arrival. It will herald the start of the game that, once begun, must reach his intended conclusion. His tentative first move was met with success. She snapped up his bait, Gregor. He can't guess at her reaction to the truth about his illness. The labyrinth of possibilities is endless. His mind overflows with options and strategies until his thoughts are a tangled web.

He organizes his thoughts by thinking in terms of his favorite game, chess. *Once Nadira arrives, my major players will be on the field. She is my queen, the most powerful opponent in chess. She is weak at present, at her most vulnerable, and requires protection, lest even a pawn take her. After training, she will run the game, because only she knows the strategies necessary to win it. Her movements are both calculated and unpredictable.*

Gregor is her king. I am a solitary ruler, but my queen cannot rule alone. The king is my pivotal player. He is strong, shrewd, and loyal to the queen. Although new to the game, he is quick to learn, as evidenced by the success of his present task. He will protect the queen until she is ready to lead, always guarding her flank. Once the queen is prepared, they will move as one, indestructible. If the king is lost, we lose the game.

My knight, loyal Drostan, obedient to a fault. He is absolutely lethal and unstoppable, his movements ordered and limited to a defined direction. He is the knife that I wield to remove corruption. He will weaken the rook by toppling his defenses. My knight treasures the law and maintains stability in the regime.

Genevieve is my gentle pawn. Her movements are gracefully simple. Directed and influenced by the other pieces, she will support the queen, sacrificing herself for the knight. Loyal to the ones she loves, she is the bait. Therein lies her value: the rook covets her.

Coatl is the dark rook. His motivation is power, and he seeks the crown. His tools are violence, force, and intimidation, but his Achilles's heel is his perverse appetite. The rook's strategic movements are linear, never three-dimensional, except for an occasional unpredictable play. He will clash with my queen and her king. Coatl must be emasculated or the game will be lost and the world thrown into chaos.

The last chess piece is the bishop. Myself. As the game master, I set the game in motion. I must move carefully, decisively, or the game will be lost. The stakes are high. The future of vampires and humans is uncertain. Time is running out. I do not know if I will survive the game, but I must win it.

CHAPTER XV

NADIRA AND GREGOR wait in a car outside the Ordinatio. Gregor glances over at Nadira. She is dressed in a tailored black pantsuit, her hair captured in a tight chignon. Her appearance is formidable, a carefully staged façade, masking her inner turmoil. Her apprehension is infectious.

"How do I look?" she asks.

"Like the prodigal daughter."

He offers a halfhearted smile and watches her reaction. She produces the whisper of a smile, but her eyes dart nervously about. He cups her chin, looks deeply into her eyes, and sees fear but also something else—determination. He gives her an encouraging look, offers his support, and wonders what is next. She turns his hand over and kisses it.

"Are you ready?" he asks.

She nods, adjusts the visor mirror, and slips the Bloodline earrings into her earlobes. She studies her reflection and wipes the trepidation off her face. Gregor inhales sharply. The earrings proclaim to all that she is heir to the throne. Her eyes glitter, and her lips form a tight line. This is the Nadira that he knows—strong, powerful, and brilliant.

"To every new thing there is a beginning," she whispers.

Gregor finishes the thought, "So let us begin."

They get out of the car, and she comes to his side, takes his hand, and gently kisses him. He wraps her in his embrace, pausing to gather strength. Holding hands, they ascend the double staircase and stride confidently into the Ordinatio reception hall. Nadira and Gregor hesitate in the entrance, the morning sun casting a soft glow around them. A hush falls over the occupants as everyone stares at the couple, captivated by their appearance. With a regal bearing, Nadira moves toward the reception desk. The crowd parts to allow them passage. Some vampires bow, and others curtsy or nod. All these acts of fealty are spontaneous and unrehearsed. Nadira acknowledges each person with either a nod or a smile.

Coatl spies his nemesis from the corner of the room. He stares at her with unveiled hatred. She senses his malevolent presence and meets his gaze without fear, safe with Gregor at her side. She smiles at him. Infuriated, he can stand no more and storms out of the hall, trailed by his supporters.

Gregor whispers, "No one said this was going to be easy."

She tightens her grip on his hand. They reach the desk. The receptionist is flustered, awkwardly curtsies, and clears her throat.

"Princess, the Sovereign awaits."

She attempts to bow, loses her balance, and falls onto Nadira, who puts out her hand and steadies the clumsy girl. The receptionist turns crimson with embarrassment.

The reception hall is as quiet as a church, the audience waits on pins and needles for the next event on this extraordinary day. Princess Nadira returns after almost a century wearing the Bloodline earrings that mark her claim to the throne. Remarkably, some vampires already pay her homage. The seasoned vampires noticed Lord Coatl's abrupt exit. Humans mill about, clueless to the subtle nuances of vampire politics. Anticipation fills the room as the heir apparent writes the next chapter in vampire history. A wave of whispers sweeps the hall, and speculation on today's outcome runs high.

Drostan and Genevieve, surrounded by a small detachment of Vigiles, march toward Nadira and Gregor. Nadira smiles as her sister rushes forward to greet her, skipping all pretense of formality by hugging and kissing her on both cheeks.

"Sister, I have missed you. I see you wear the Bloodline," Genevieve says.

Genevieve welcomes Gregor with the formal vampire greeting and then kisses his cheek. Her eyes widen. Her gift of perception is razor sharp.

"Things have changed since I last saw you." She glances at Nadira and winks. "We have a lot to talk about," she says, and Nadira gives her a puzzled look.

The crowds' patience is rewarded when Drostan steps forward, kneels, places his fist to his chest, and bows his head. "Princess, I pledge the allegiance of the Vigiles from this day forward," he proclaims.

With military precision, all the Vigiles kneel, salute her, and shout, "We so swear by our blood!"

The overwhelming support from Drostan surprises Nadira and Gregor. The military's backing is crucial to her success. She recognizes a familiar face among the kneeling soldiers.

"Jean-Louis, my old friend. It is good to see you," she says.

Jean-Louis glances up. "*Oui*, it has been a long time, Countess. I mean, *Princess*."

Nadira scans the crowd and speaks to the Vigiles. "Please, rise. I accept your pledge this somber day of my return. I vow to prove worthy of your loyalty and trust." She walks to Drostan. "Thank you, Drostan."

"Princess, your status demands additional security. I wish to appoint a detachment of royal guards to protect you," he tells her.

Nadira studies Drostan. She would like to skip the guards, but she must be prudent and reward his public demonstration of allegiance.

"I agree on one condition. Jean-Louis will be the captain of these guards, if he agrees," she offers.

Drostan smiles broadly and clears his throat. "Princess, Jean-Louis has already agreed."

Nadira makes a stern face. "Am I that predictable?"

Drostan answers, "In some things like loyalty you are. Other times, not at all."

Gregor and Genevieve both chuckle. Nadira rolls her eyes.

"Jean-Louis saved my life more than once. His counsel is wise and his discretion immeasurable. He is the logical choice," she offers in her defense.

Gregor takes her hand and kisses it. He grins mischievously. "Of course, Princess."

Nadira tries to maintain her decorum, but the joke is on her. Gregor disarms her with his mocking smile. She suppresses the urge to kiss his twitching lips. Drostan's next action surprises her. He greets Gregor with the informal vampire greeting. She is intrigued.

"You two have met before?" she asks.

Her curiosity is aroused, but before she can ask another question, Genevieve interrupts them.

"Amon is waiting for you," Genevieve announces.

So much has happened this morning that she was able to forget about Amon's illness. Now she must face her greatest fear. He has always been a powerful father figure and mentor. How will she deal with a diminished or feeble Amon?

Her plan is simple: she will protect him and offer him her strength and love. She will become his project, a reason to live. Amon will once again be her mentor, and this should motivate him. She feels better now having worked out the details.

She looks at the crowd pressing around her, both vampires and humans. They wait patiently for her next decision, hanging on her every word or expression. A wave of apprehension sweeps over her, but a potent idea takes hold. Ruling is like running her corporation: she is the CEO, and each person has their special job. *If we all do our job to the best of our ability, we will succeed.*

She glances at Gregor, who is staring at her with those extraordinary eyes, and thinks, *Your job will be to love me.* Her heart swells with pride and love. She is ready.

"I want to see my father," she commands.

Amon stands on the terrace of his study, deep in thought. The view of the Alps is an inspiring background for self-reflection. He turns toward the French doors. "Enter," he says.

Nadira, Gregor, Genevieve, and Drostan enter the study. The guards shut the doors behind them. Amon's eyes light with pleasure at the sight of his daughter, her love for her father clearly etched on her features. She cannot curb her enthusiasm but runs onto the terrace, embraces him, and lays her head on his chest. He wraps her in his comforting embrace, strokes her hair, and kisses the top of her head. He gazes at the others.

"Leave us," he commands.

They bow, back out of the room, and close the doors behind them. Nadira raises her head, looks him dead in the eye, and frowns. "You are not ill!" She is too astute to be deceived and frees herself from his embrace, waiting for his answer.

Amon chuckles. He forgot how keen she is. "No, I am not." A self-satisfied grin tickles his face. "That is why I dismissed the others. I knew the minute you touched me you would know the truth. I could not take a chance the others would discover my deception."

Nadira ponders this revelation. "Who else knows?"

Amon smiles knowingly. "Only Gregor. I sent him to retrieve you." Amon carefully scrutinizes Nadira.

She starts to protest but thinks twice about it. "Why the ruse?"

Amon is glad to see she is controlling her emotions, which is a very good first step. "First, I wanted to see my daughter. We have been separated too long." He fixes her with a stern look.

Nadira has the good grace to accept his gentle reprimand. "Forgive me, Father. I am a disappointment to you." She bows her head.

Amon shakes his head. "You are never a disappointment. I am proud of you. It took courage to refuse me. Answer me this: there are many means of escape, so why did you choose to live as a human?"

"I sought salvation among humans, but it came to naught. The shame lingers," she admits.

"My child, redemption comes from within. It germinates from the light that resides in all of us. You glimpsed darkness for a split second. It caged your heart, keeping you bound with regret. No one on this earth can forgive your sins but yourself. Free your heart, embrace the light, and liberate yourself." He is surprised that she does not understand this concept yet. "Gregor came to me very concerned for your well-being."

"That is why he left me? To see you?" she asks.

Amon nods. Her face softens at the thought of Gregor pleading with her father for help. This information fills her with joy and boosts her confidence.

"Yes, he loves you very much. I am pleased with your choice, my child," he says.

My child—she missed those two beloved words and slowly raises her eyes, meeting his gaze. They communicate silently with their minds, catching up on information lost during decades of separation. Amon's attention shifts to the earrings.

"I see you have accepted my gift."

Nadira swallows hard and nods.

"Are you prepared to fulfill all aspects of the ceremony?" His eyes narrow.

Nadira's face hardens. "I cannot complete the final ritual."

"My child, you must. It has been done this way for centuries. It cannot be undone."

"I will not." Nadira is adamant.

Love softens his face. "We will not think on this at present. Your training will begin immediately. We have time to resolve the other issue. Time answers many questions." He smiles.

"Father, I understand you missed me, but something troubles me," she says.

She is quick, he thinks and verbalizes her own question. "Why the drama of my impending death? It was necessary to tie up some unresolved issues, proclaim you heir, determine alliances, and root out my enemies. My illness will achieve all of this. Don't you think?"

"It would indeed, my lord." The complexity of Amon's plan impresses her.

"We must keep this secret for now. I have secured our nation's safety, and we have prospered, but it is not enough. I realize the future of vampires hinges on coexistence with humans. Your destiny is to unite our two species. This became clear when you fell in love with a human and then chose to dwell among them. You retained your humanity, a blending of both worlds. Most vampires live for blood, but you do not. You thrive on love and your future is limitless with Gregor by your side."

"Gregor said you were quite the visionary," she adds.

Amon smiles. "An intelligent vampire."

She steps back into his embrace and lays her head on his chest. He enfolds her in his nurturing cocoon. Eventually, she will emerge a new creature of his making. He strokes her hair as they gaze at the Alps.

"Are you ready to play the game?" he asks.

Secure in Amon's presence and bolstered by Gregor's love, she asks, "What do you propose?"

Amon smiles.

CHAPTER XVI

J EAN-LOUIS LEADS NADIRA and Gregor down the corridor to the private residences. They turn down a private wing banked on both sides with impressive views of the Alps. At the end of the hall are two extraordinarily carved wood doors flanked by uniformed guards who come to attention at the sight of them. Jean-Louis releases the doors.

He addresses Nadira. "Your apartment, Princess."

The apartment exudes a sense of luxury, a richness layered over time. A massive stone fireplace flanked by long sectionals fills the great room. A wrought iron chandelier anchors the ceiling. The bedrooms, office, and conference room radiate off this main living area like spokes on a wheel.

Nadira walks out on the terrace and Gregor joins her.

"Nice digs," Gregor jokes.

"Guards will be posted outside your doors 24/7. If there is anything you need, just ring." Jean-Louis bows and leaves, closing the doors behind him.

Nadira looks out at the snowcapped mountains. Gregor slides up behind her and wraps his arms around her waist. She leans back against him. They stay like this for some time, drinking in the silence, lost in thought. Nadira turns around, facing Gregor, and gazes into his eyes. Her invitation is unmistakable, and he responds to it with a kiss. She slides her lips over his, lighting the flame of passion.

"I have waited all day to get you alone," she says.

"Have you now?"

He runs his hands up her back and around her shoulders and nips her neck. She unbuttons the top of his shirt, running her hand across his chest. A shiver runs through him, and she responds with a provocative smile. He grabs her hand.

"Stop," he insists.

Taken aback, she asks, "Don't you want me?"

Gregor smiles. "Look at me. What do you think?"

His face is flushed, his breathing rapid, and his erection evident. However, his eyes are the most compelling, lit with an inner fire like the magma of a volcano succumbing to eruption.

Nadira is mesmerized. "I think you want to ravish me." Her voice is husky, but she is puzzled. "Why stop? It has been so long. Let us consummate our love."

Gregor keeps her at arm's length, wrestling for control. "Beloved, I have waited centuries. Can we not wait a short time more?"

"Wait for what?" she asks.

She tries to make sense of Gregor's request. Her lust, once inflamed, is hard to extinguish. Gregor reaches in his pocket, takes out an antique box, and kneels down.

Formally, he asks her, "Princess Nadira, will you have me as your husband?" He opens the box, and cradled inside is a medieval gold band encrusted with large vivid green emeralds.

Nadira is stunned. She looks from Gregor, to the box, and then to the ring. The events of today are almost overwhelming. His proposal is more than her frayed nerves can handle. Tears escape her control, slipping down her cheeks.

"I know it has been an eventful day. Maybe my proposal is ill timed." He smiles sheepishly.

She wipes her face. "Perfect timing. We begin this new phase of our life together. I accept you as my beloved husband."

He slips the ring on her right ring finger and jumps to his feet. He sweeps her up, plops down on the couch, and cradles her in his lap. "I ask that we wait to consummate our union until after our joining ceremony," he says.

"I want Amon to perform the ceremony," she requests.

"Of course." He runs his hand through her hair. She rests quietly in his lap. Memories flood her of another time, another man who held her this way. She lays her head on Gregor's chest, listening to his heartbeat. Her gratitude is immeasurable—to be loved by two different but great men. She draws comfort from his masculinity, and a sense of peace soothes her soul.

"Nadira, why didn't you agree to become heir when Amon first asked you?" he asks.

Her coveted peace evaporates. She knew his curiosity would prompt the question that she has evaded all these decades. "I refused to perform the final ritual of the ascension ceremony."

He continues to stroke her hair and kisses the top of her head. She snuggles closer to him, hoping he will ask no more.

"What final ritual, love?" he asks.

She debates telling him the particulars of the secret ritual, but he must know the truth. She takes a deep breath. "The final ritual when I plunge the Qayin dagger into my father's heart. The price of the throne is Amon's life."

A shudder racks her. They sit in silence, each loathe to discuss the horrific act that would force her to commit patricide. No wonder she ran away. Gregor's apprehension grows now that Nadira wears the earrings and Drostan swore his allegiance to her. Nadira bolts upright and stares at Gregor, astonished.

"I would never ever agree to kill my father. I would give my life for him. How can you think that?" she exclaims.

Her ability to read minds has him at a disadvantage, but he is relieved that she clarified her position. His apprehension dissipates.

"I am sorry, love. How will you succeed if you will not complete the ritual?" He pulls her closer.

She settles down and snuggles comfortably in his arms. "Amon says time and inertia are companions and that any obstacles will eventually resolve themselves." She allows her exhausted body to melt into his. "Please, let us discuss happier topics."

"I forgot something," he says.

Suddenly, Gregor lifts her off his lap, gets up, and walks over to a console table. Nadira is perplexed. *What is so important that he would interrupt this intimate moment?* He returns with the Moroccan chest and hands it to her.

"An early wedding present," he tells her.

She takes his gift. Her hands shake, and her eyes well up. "I lost this a long time ago," she whispers.

"Amon rescued it. I asked for the box after I learned about Cristo. I thought you might want it," he adds.

She runs her hand across the carved wood, her emotions tumultuous, rendering her speechless. His thoughtfulness touches her heart. He sits down, and his arms instinctively enfold her. It has been centuries since she felt so cherished and loved, and she revels in the feeling.

"Do you like the ring?" he asks.

"Very much."

She holds up her hand, admiring her ring. Gregor captures her hand in his, intertwines his fingers with hers, and then kisses the ring.

"It is beautiful, Gregor. Where did you get it?"

Gregor smiles at the memory. "I purchased the ring from a Turkish jeweler commissioned by the king of Spain to make it for his queen. The queen went mad. The king wanted no part of a ring that reminded him of his lost love. The jeweler was stuck with it. The staggering cost of the emeralds almost bankrupted him. I purchased it knowing someday I would ask you to marry me."

"What a sad story. A mad queen—I hope this not an omen of my future." She grins at him.

"Let's hope not." He kisses her nose.

Nadira sits up, staring at him. "Gregor, I want to thank you." She is so serious that he decides not to tease her.

"For what?"

"For everything: the wedding present, loving me despite my flaws, waiting for me all those years, for being you." Her eyes shine with love, and the expression on her face astounds him.

"Anything worth having is worth waiting for." He grins.

"One of my quotes. You remembered."

"I remember everything you tell me." His pupils darken as the tone of his voice deepens.

Her body responds with a skipping heart and throbbing loins. She smiles seductively. "It will be hard to keep this vow of celibacy," she teases.

"I know."

They laugh and fall backward on the sectional. Several sweet minutes pass of kissing, fondling, and discovering each other before Gregor frees himself from her ardent embrace. He catches his breath.

"You delicious vixen, using your womanly wiles to weaken my resolve," he teases.

She smiles up at him. "How am I doing?"

"Very good."

She reaches for him, but he shakes his head.

"Nadira, it is important to me that we wait until the night of our joining."

His plead is so genuine that she takes it to heart. She sits up, smooths her tousled hair, and grins at him. "No sex. I do not understand. But I will try," she concedes. She jumps up and grabs his hand. "I have something to show you."

"Where are we going?" he asks.

"Trust me."

With Gregor in tow, she marches out of the room, flings open the outer doors, and strides down the hall. The startled guards trip over themselves to keep up. She turns toward the guards and points to the youngest. "You come with us. The rest return to your post," she orders.

The guards do as told. Nadira navigates the labyrinth of hallways and doors until Gregor is hopelessly lost. The young guard runs to keep up with her. She opens a door with *EMPLOYEES ONLY* stenciled on it.

"Wait here," she tells the guard.

She looks inside to make sure the area is vacant and pulls Gregor through the door.

"What are we doing?" Gregor asks.

"Sssh!"

She puts her finger to his lips, leads him down a service corridor to an innocuous door, unlocks it, and pushes Gregor in. Closing the door behind her, she joins him in an empty supply room. She flips on the lights. The room is nothing special, a typical supply closet stocked with mops, brooms, and cleaning supplies.

"Are you planning to do some cleaning?" he questions.

"Watch." She walks to a clock on the wall, opens the glass face, and turns the hands. The floor shutters, and the whole room moves upward. "It's a secret elevator shaft that travels from the roof down to the underground infrastructure."

"Who else knows?" he asks.

"Amon and myself. Privacy and freedom are the sacrifices monarchs make for their people. But discretion is sometimes necessary. This elevator, a series of secret passages, and stairs allow us to move about unnoticed with some semblance of freedom."

The elevator comes to a stop, and the back wall opens to a deserted rooftop. They step outside into the dark space. The muted glow of curtained windows and stars casts a hazy iridescence. The view is spectacular; you can almost reach out and touch the mountaintops.

"I used to hide here when I was troubled or needed to be alone. I wanted you to know where to find me or come here when you need solitude." She stares up at the inky sky. "There's the North Star, my talisman." She points to the star and glances at him. Her eyes sparkle, filled with the light of so many stars.

"It's beautiful." He caresses her cheek. "You're cold."

She is shivering. "A little."

He enfolds her in his arms and rubs her hands until she stops shivering.

"Gregor."

"Yes?"

"I am afraid," she whispers.

"Me too. But we are together, and together we can face anything."

Together—she likes the sound of that.

# CHAPTER XVII

THE ORDINATIO CONTAINS a large fitness and entertainment complex. It has a sparring facility for martial arts, boxing, fencing, and other contact sports. Nadira and Gregor join Drostan near the boxing ring. Nadira and Drostan are clad in sweats.

"Are you ready for the first phase of your training?" Drostan asks, and she nods. "I am in charge of the physical portion of your schedule. We will meet here daily to begin strengthening your muscles and increasing your speed and agility. Once we meet the physical goals, you will graduate to weapons. Agreed?" He looks from Nadira to Gregor.

"I am just here for moral support." Gregor throws up his hands.

"Good, she will need it," Drostan says.

Nadira glances around. "I don't see any weights."

Drostan frowns. "No weights. We will use another technique. I have chosen our best sparring partner for you. His name is Kashta. He is Nubian. The Vigiles nicknamed him 'The Colossus.'"

"That doesn't bode well for me," Nadira mumbles.

Another vampire enters the sparring area. He is a giant roughly hewn of solid ebony, with muscles as dense and solid as the wood itself. The floor vibrates with each of his steps.

Gregor whistles. "Shit. That is the biggest man—vampire or human—I have ever seen."

Nadira shakes her head. "Am I supposed to fight him or climb him?"

Gregor is nervous; this vampire is four times Nadira's size and weight. His protective instinct kicks in. "Drostan, I don't think this is a good idea. Maybe start with someone who is more her size," Gregor requests.

"Amon commands it. If Nadira cannot protect herself from her enemies, her reign will be short."

"She has guards, and I will protect her," Gregor insists.

"What if the guards are killed or you are not with her? I must prepare her to defeat any assailant," Drostan says.

Nadira raises her hand. "Drostan is right. A ruler who cannot protect herself cannot hope to lead others. I trust my father and Drostan's judgment." She takes Gregor's hand. "Beloved, your concern for me warms my heart. Did not Sun Tzu say that a leader leads by example, not by force? So I ask, would you have me weak or strong?"

Gregor looks over at Kashta. "I would rather have you alive."

Nadira kisses him on the cheek. She whispers, "He is not as big as he looks." She walks into the center of the sparring area to Kashta. He *is* as big as he looks. She swallows hard and looks up at him. Now she knows how David felt when he met Goliath, only this will not turn out as well for her. Up close, she notices Kashta's skin is latticed with scars. Instinctively, she reaches out and gently touches a tortuous mark on his forearm. She peers into his eyes, the portals of his soul, and sees the shadows hiding there. Amazed, he stares at her. She comforts him with a soft smile.

Drostan shouts, "Kashta has been instructed to treat you as any other sparring partner."

Kashta bows awkwardly and addresses her in a deep, booming voice. "Princess, do you want padding?"

"No. Thank you, Kashta." She grits her teeth.

They bow to each other, and the match begins. Nadira moves cautiously, reasoning his size equates to slowness. *If I can stay out of his reach, this might not be too bad.* She bobs and weaves around this unmovable mountain. Kashta stands rock still, studying his opponent. The match continues this way for a few minutes until he moves in a flash, catching her off guard. She realizes that he has vanished and whips her head around, trying to locate him. Nadira spots him too late.

She sails through the air, slams into the wall, and slides face down onto the wood floor. Catching her breath, she sits up and tries to focus. It feels as though a freight train ran her over. Blood floods into her mouth from her split lip.

Gregor runs toward Nadira. His anger up, he barely contains himself.

Drostan grabs him and pins his arms. "Your liege has ordered this. You will stand down."

Drostan's tone catches Gregor's attention. He fixes on Drostan's face, realizing the Vigile commander won't tolerate any disobedience.

Nadira stands up, her balance unsteady as she wobbles over to Kashta. She wipes the blood from her mouth, plants her feet, and puts her hands on her hips, a dazed arrogant smile nailed to her face. "Have you had enough?" she asks.

Kashta scrutinizes her. His deep rumpling laughter fills the air.

"Let us continue," she tells him.

She moves slowly and carefully around her opponent, occasionally landing a blow or kick, all as ineffective as a fly biting an elephant. Kashta repeatedly tosses Nadira in the air or plants her face in the mat. Each time, Nadira gets back up, staggers to Kashta, and says, "Continue."

The match is painful to watch. Gregor is powerless; frustration overwhelms him at his inability to protect her, a difficult lesson to learn. Drostan understands it will take more than sheer physical strength to defeat Kashta. He did not reveal to either of them that Kashta has never been defeated in a match. Even he was unable to best him. The sparring, if you can call it that, continues for over an hour.

Amon surveys the match from the back of the venue. Drostan and Gregor do not notice him so intent they are on Nadira's beating. Kashta sends Nadira spinning across the wood floor on her ass. She ricochets off the wall and comes to a dead stop against the boxing ring. Stunned, it takes a minute to regain her equilibrium. She weakly pulls herself upright, wipes the blood oozing from a cut over her right eye, and uses the ropes to hoist up. She wavers against the side of the ring, musters what little strength she has left, and hobbles toward her opponent.

"Hold!" Amon orders.

Startled, the occupants of the room look in the direction of the command. Amon advances toward them. In an instant, Gregor sprints to Nadira, catching her before she collapses. One eye is swollen shut and the other bruised. Her skin is marred with cuts and bruises. Gregor scoops her up in his arms just as her legs buckle and cradles her broken body.

She concentrates on his handsome face. Softly, she asks, "Did you see?"

He nods.

She adds ironically, "I was about to make my move. I could see the fear on his face." She manages a lopsided grin.

Gregor's voice cracks with emotion. "I saw you. I think he was about to surrender."

She smiles, satisfied that he understands.

Kashta approaches Gregor and peers down at his sparring partner. He has never seen a vampire—male or female—endure such abuse. "Princess, you fought well. Do you know how I defeated you?" he asks.

Nadira studies his marred dark face and shakes her head.

"A warrior must use all his weapons." He points to his head. "Intelligence." He points to his massive biceps. "Strength." Lastly, he points to his chest. "Heart. The most important is heart. When the other two fail, the heart will bring victory. You fought with heart today, never surrendering. We will work on the other two. Eventually, you will prevail against me."

She smiles. "Thank you. Tomorrow?" Kashta nods and bows. Amon studies his battered daughter and touches her cheek. Nadira whispers through cracked lips, "Father."

"I am proud, my child. You did well," Amon praises her.

Nadira winces as she smiles and peers at the most important men in her life. Her grip on consciousness slipping, she says in a small voice, "My love, I shall pass out now."

Gregor studies her shattered face. His heart aches for her, but this burden he cannot share. "Beloved, I will keep you safe until you awaken." Her head lolls backward as she blacks out, and he seethes with anger and glares at Amon. "Amon, this is too much."

Amon does not answer but stares at Gregor a long time. Gregor shifts Nadira in his arms, and she moans in pain. Uncomfortable, he tries to avert his gaze, but Amon will not release his hold. Gregor's anger cools and then disappears under Amon's intense scrutiny.

"Are you ready to listen?" Amon asks, and Gregor nods, now contrite like a scolded child. Amon continues, "It tore my heart to watch my daughter abused, but I want her to persevere. I will do anything to achieve this goal. What father withholds skills from his child necessary to survive in this world? Our future rests on her shoulders. You are her partner and must help her succeed. Smothering Nadira will make her weak; she will resent you."

Drostan looks from Nadira to Gregor. He sees the pain etched on Gregor's face. "She is stronger than she appears and will rejuvenate by the morrow."

Amon urges Gregor, "Take her to your apartment. She needs sleep."

Gregor gazes down at her and brushes the limp hair from her face. She is far from beautiful now, battered and broken. Her beauty never mattered to him; it was her spirit that captivated him. Today, her spirit triumphed when her body failed. He cradles her close to his heart and leaves the sparring arena.

Drostan glances at Amon. "I have never seen a man so obsessed with a woman." They watch him go.

Amon regards Drostan. "His possessiveness will only bring him pain. He waited so long for her that he is fearful she will disappear. In time, he will learn to release the falcon's jesses. Only then can she truly soar."

"A good pun. Nadira will allow no man to dominate her. How well I know." Drostan's off-handed comment grabs Amon's attention.

"Really?" Amon watches Drostan's expression.

Drostan stares back blankly. "Do not try your mind tricks with me, Amon. I do not covet Nadira. I had my chance. I am thankful for Genevieve, the most gentle and loving wife a vampire could have."

Amon continues to scrutinize Drostan, forcing him to drop his gaze.

"Damn you, Amon," Drostan concedes.

Amon smiles, satisfied he made his point. Drostan scans the practice area. The mats are scattered and the equipment twisted. There are pools of blood staining the floor.

"None of my men lasted more the fifteen minutes with Kashta. My match was finished in thirty minutes. She continued for over an hour," Drostan reveals.

Amon thought the sparring session would be over in thirty minutes. After forty minutes, he received no report on its progress, prompting a trip to the gym to assess the situation. Watching her continually stagger to her feet to meet her adversary, he realized that he had underestimated her courage and tenacity. This match confirmed his suspicion that his daughter possesses the necessary grit to rule their nation. "I know," Amon says.

"Is that why you requested Kashta as her sparring partner?" Drostan asks.

Amon stares at the floor painted with his daughter's blood before answering. "Yes."

CHAPTER XVIII

NADIRA, GREGOR, GENEVIEVE, and Drostan lounge in the reception hall. They casually watch the parade of vampires and humans. The vampires maintain an air of decorum developed from years of practice and politely go about their business. The humans are not as disciplined, barely containing their curiosity about the future leader and openly gawking at the foursome.

Bored, Genevieve asks, "Will they be here soon?"

Nadira makes a face at her. "I sent the car for them—they'll be here soon. Keep your panties on."

Genevieve absentmindedly twiddles her fingers. Drostan grabs her hand and kisses it.

Gregor glances at them and smiles. "I enjoy this twenty-first-century slang. 'Keep your panties on.'" He looks at Nadira meaningfully. "Now that is one piece of lingerie I would like to take off." A sensual smile plays across his lips, and she playfully slaps his arm. "If we were not in public, I would kiss more than your hand," Gregor jokes.

Nadira blushes. "Reprobate," she teases, but she enjoys the sexual banter as much as he does.

Drostan chuckles. "Nadira, I know you have a propensity for quotes, but what's the source of this urban slang?"

"My human assistant, Jerry, is very current. He tells me I sound like I have been in mothballs for centuries. I guess I have."

Genevieve giggles at the thought.

Drostan just grunts disapprovingly. "He sounds irreverent to me. A human should show more respect for his employer."

Nadira laughs. "Irreverent. Now there is an understatement. Jerry doesn't believe in social stratification. Humility is not his strong point. Why should he be? He is by far my best employee. He is truthful, has an outrageous sense of humor, and is overall a nice piece of eye candy who happens to be my friend."

"Eye candy?" Genevieve cocks her head.

"He is very handsome." Nadira grins mischievously.

Drostan glances at Gregor. "Should we be worried?" Drostan asks.

Gregor shakes his head. "No, he is a good sort of chap. He is human, after all."

"I have my own piece of eye candy. I married it." Genevieve pats Drostan's cheek.

"Thanks for tossing this old dog a bone," Drostan concedes.

They all chuckle.

Intrigued by Nadira's concept of a human friend, Drostan asks, "A human friend? Isn't that a contradiction in terms? How does a human go from a meal to friend?"

They all look at her for an explanation.

"Cease thinking of them as food. We were all human once. Vampires have more in common with humans than differences," she elaborates.

Gregor says, "That reminds me. Genevieve, I have noticed an increased number of humans at the Ordinatio."

"They're employees of the Ordinatio, familiars, or partners of vampires. Since the new Vampire Act, there are more humans working and living here," Genevieve explains.

"New Vampire Act?" Gregor is puzzled.

Drostan rolls his eyes. "Now you've gone and done it. Genevieve's favorite topic!"

Despite Genevieve's saucy pout, her enthusiasm is unmistakable. "It should be. I helped draft bill 985.A, which states that vampires cannot arbitrarily create a new vampire without the consent of the human involved. Furthermore, the vampire mentor assigned instructs them on vampire laws, powers, and responsibilities. It is a pivotal role in the transformation from human to vampire. The result has been less new vampires but a higher success rate after transition," she says, finishing her speech.

Drostan nods in agreement. "We lost a lot of new vampires during the first year. Fifty percent of the Vigiles' time was spent chasing them. Now we rarely deal with new vampire infractions."

Gregor looks at Nadira. "I can attest to the importance of a good mentor to a young vampire."

She flashes him a brilliant smile of thanks.

The whispered conversations of the crowd fall silent. The foursome looks in the direction of the entrance. Jerry and Haseem stand on the landing. Jerry scans the massive area and lets out a low whistle.

Nadira's assistant caught the crowd's attention not for his behavior but for what he is wearing. He is dressed head to toe in black and sporting matching Oakley sunglasses, a caricature of what a real vampire would look like. Genevieve snickers.

Drostan sneers, "Humans."

Nadira strides over to greet them.

"My lady." Haseem bows.

Nadira takes his hands. "I am glad you are here. Where is Adrian?" Nadira asks.

His partner's name always brings a smile to Haseem's face. "He is wrapping up his film. He will close the apartment and then join me in a month." Haseem wears a dubious expression and rolls his eyes toward Jerry. "I brought your human." They glance at Jerry.

"I see." She adds.

Gregor, Genevieve, and Drostan join them.

Jerry takes off his sunglasses. "Nice crib."

Nadira says, "Jerry, what the hell are you wearing?"

He looks down at himself and smiles. "I wanted to blend in." He notices that no one else is dressed like him, but he shrugs it off as one of life's awkward moments. "There are no handbooks on what to wear to your first vampire gig."

Amused, Gregor suppresses a grin.

"You have been watching too many movies." Nadira is clearly annoyed.

Drostan adds, "You might as well wear a sign that says 'bite me.'"

Jerry looks startled and swallows down his fear. They all laugh except Jerry, who looks uncomfortable.

Genevieve breaks the ice. "I am Genevieve, Nadira's sister, and this ogre teasing you is my husband, Drostan."

Jerry approaches her and starts twisting his wrists around. They stare at him, dumbfounded. He notices the four vampires' reaction to his greeting and turns bright red with embarrassment. "I thought there was some secret handshake."

Drostan's mouth twitches. "There is if you're a vampire."

Jerry is mortified by his series of social blunders, two of them in as many minutes.

"I can't believe it. Jerry is speechless." Nadira smiles and they all laugh, breaking the tension.

"My bad. I wanted to make a good impression, but I screwed up." Jerry shakes off his awkwardness and then turns on the charm. His smile dazzling. "I am glad to be here, boss."

Genevieve admires Nadira's human assistant. "I see what you mean." She winks at Nadira, who grins back.

Gregor slaps Jerry on the back, causing him to jump. "I, for one, am glad to see you. You can help Nadira plan our joining ceremony." Gregor hugs Nadira.

"You are secretive. Show me the ring!" Genevieve squeals when Nadira sticks her hand out.

"Look who's talking about being closemouthed! Who got married and didn't tell anybody? But I forgive you. Will you be my lady in waiting?" Nadira asks.

"Try and stop me." Genevieve and Nadira embrace.

Gregor approaches Drostan. "Would you do me the honor of being my groomsman?"

Drostan glances at Gregor and then Nadira. He does not answer but peers at his wife, who winks at him. Jerry does not miss the interplay between Drostan and Nadira. He catches the look of longing on Drostan's face. With Nadira and Gregor, he discovered that vampires have a tendency to underestimate human intuition, often dropping their emotional guard around him. He can't blame Drostan—they all fall in love with Nadira.

"I would be honored." Drostan shakes Gregor's hand. "We will be brothers."

Gregor smiles. "I would like that."

Jerry charges over to them and shouts, "Group hug!"

He tries to span his arms around all four vampires, who look at him as though he has lost his mind. He smiles impishly. "I got carried away. Congrats, boss." Out of the corner of his eye, he sees a beautiful Asian vampire staring at them and points her out. "Who is that?"

Genevieve smiles. "Ayame. She is lovely, isn't she?"

He translates her name. "Iris flower." Captivated, he glances at Ayame, who smiles back.

Drostan winks at Gregor and prods Jerry. "You speak Japanese?"

"Fluent. I'm an Air Force brat. I grew up in Asia. I speak Japanese, Mandarin, Cantonese, Korean, and Vietnamese."

Nadira has never seen Jerry so taken by a woman. Jerry has dated an endless parade of beautiful females, none lasting more than a month, each just another pretty face to turn his head. When asked about his turnstile approach to women, Jerry has always just shrugged and mumbled something about empty heads and gold diggers.

He whispers to Nadira, "She won't bite me, will she?"

"No, it is against our laws, unless you want her to." Nadira suppresses a smile and wonders what her assistant thinks vampires do.

"Want her to?" He looks naively at his boss, mystified.

Gregor approaches him. "Once you have been with a vampire, you never go back to a human."

Jerry eyes Gregor, trying to decide if he is pulling his leg. He glances at Drostan, who winks at him. In that second, they share a male bond—whether human or vampire, the lure of the opposite sex is both mysterious and powerful.

"Boss, if you don't need me right now, I'll go check out the local action," Jerry announces.

Gregor teases Jerry. "You sure you can handle her, sport?"

Jerry grins, his bravado returning in full force. He smiles at them. "Can she handle me?" He makes a beeline to Ayame. They watch as Nadira's human introduces himself to Ayame, and within a minute, she is laughing and smiling.

Nadira is fascinated with this unexpected turn of events.

"Damn! What did he say to her?" Gregor asks.

Drostan answers, "'I taste good.'"

The others laugh, but Nadira is not amused. She pokes Drostan in the chest. "When I lived with humans, there was one thing I did not miss. Do you know what that was?"

"Pray tell me," Drostan answers.

"The vampire's morose sense of humor." She makes a scornful face.

Startled by her defensiveness, he tries to lighten the mood and smiles charmingly. "You have to admit, he is a cocky son of a bitch."

Genevieve adds her two cents, "I like him. A lot. He would make a great vampire."

"Hey, don't try to turn my assistant." Nadira shakes her finger at her sister.

They watch as Jerry and Ayame disappear into the crowd.

Gregor observes, "I don't think it's us that you have to worry about."

His comment prompts a round of laughter. Nadira wonders if Gregor is right, but thoughts of Jerry vanish when groups of well-wishers swarm the foursome, congratulating Nadira and Gregor on their coming union.

CHAPTER XIX

NADIRA AND GENEVIEVE rush down a seemingly endless tunnel, Genevieve buried under a stack of papers and files. Their frantic pace is halted by Nadira's curiosity about their surroundings.

"Is this the subterranean service network?" she asks.

Now we're going to be late for the meeting, Genevieve thinks. She forgot how many questions her sister could ask in a day. Her head aches with the insistent quizzing.

Swallowing her frustration, she answers, "The mountain is honeycombed with maintenance conduits, storehouses, you name it. Trust me, this underground universe is immense. The tunnels are a shortcut to the council chambers or courtrooms. I have gotten lost more than once."

The underground labyrinth houses everything necessary for the survival of a small nation, including a communication center and a military arsenal with Humvees, garages, a commissary, and even a medical clinic for the employees. Nadira, fascinated by the vastness of this one tunnel, inspects it closely. The upper levels were excavated with modern moles, leaving a smooth-finished tunnel, but lower levels are older, cut with manual labor, resulting in roughhewn passageways.

"Have you gone all the way to the end?" Nadira asks.

Genevieve shakes her head. "No. For all I know, a whole coven could live down here and none of us would see them for years."

Nadira makes a mental note to research the schematics for this area and be better acquainted with this underground universe. She decides to speak to Drostan about scheduling security patrols down here.

Genevieve switches topics in the hopes of getting Nadira back on track. "Are you auditing court today or council meetings?"

Nadira thinks a minute. "Council meetings. I'll catch trial proceedings later. Amon wants me immersed in administrative duties. He even gave me homework."

Genevieve giggles. "Little old for school, aren't you?"

"At least it's a break from my daily punishment with Kashta." She makes a face.

"How's that going?" Genevieve asks.

"It brings a new meaning to the word 'pulverized,'" she says, and they both laugh. "I am improving. I don't get my nose broken anymore."

Genevieve grimaces. "Good thing our bodies repair rapidly. I know I couldn't do it."

"One unexpected benefit: I am able to keep my vow of celibacy. I am too exhausted to even try to be sexy," Nadira admits.

"I respect your willpower. I can't keep my hands off Drostan." They pass a restricted section with a metallic sign that reads *BIO LABORATORIES*.

Nadira stops and peers in the window. "What's this?" She glances at Genevieve.

"The new lab for your Dr. Graetz," Genevieve answers.

"Is he here? I want to go in and catch up," Nadira says. Before Genevieve can stop her, Nadira pushes through the double doors.

Genevieve shakes her head. "We are going to be to be late, not like anybody cares or anything," she mumbles to herself. She saunters further down the corridor, occasionally glancing back for Nadira. Finally, she stops and waits, tapping her foot impatiently. Uneasiness grips her like something or someone is watching her, something unseen and foreboding. She tries to shake it off, does not see anything untoward, and wonders if her mind is playing tricks on her. However, she trusts her intuition, which is uncanny. Other vampires have more dramatic abilities, but hers is a subtle talent of empathy, whether vampire or human. She notices the figure stepping out of the darkness but can't distinguish who it is until he speaks. The voice is unmistakable—it is Coatl.

"Good morning, Genevieve. You look especially lovely today," Coatl says.

Coatl leers at her like a starving man. She steps back and clutches her files, trying to create an invisible barrier between her and the vampire she loathes. Even the way he says her name makes her skin crawl, and he always looks like he wants to eat her. She nervously glances in the direction of Nadira. A lurid expression slithers across his face, and his lips curl up over his fangs. He steps toward Genevieve, and she instinctively backs up.

"I said good morning." His eyes are hooded, but his lust is unmistakable. She catches her breath.

"What do you want, Coatl? I am late for a council meeting." She musters her courage, looks him straight in the eye, turns on her heel, and walks away. He grabs her arm, and feels the shiver run through it.

"No need to be rude. I just want to talk about my petition to the council. That is all. Have you submitted yet?" he asks.

"We've had this discussion before. Yes, I submitted it with the other petitions. It is up to the council to decide if they vote on your proposal." She jerks her arm away.

He addresses her in an oily sweet voice. "You know, if you would support my candidacy, I am sure they would agree to vote on it. The council respects your opinion."

"Coatl, you overstate my influence. I cannot show any favoritism."

Coatl slithers up to her, close enough for her to feel his hot breath on her neck. He whispers in her ear, his voice a rough caress, "I respect your opinion more than you know. I can make it worth your while if you help me." Her silence encourages him, and his lust overcomes his discretion. "I will give you anything. I can show you things and make you feel incredible."

At first, Genevieve thinks he is joking, but then she realizes he is not. She has seen this look before. Her maker stared at her the same way. He stole her and made her a slave, a trophy, until Nadira rescued her from that lascivious life. She will never go back and decides to jolt Coatl back to reality. "What about my husband?" Genevieve asks.

"He doesn't have to know. It can be our secret." His expression darkens, and he leers at her hungrily. Puzzled she has not answered, he adds, "Or I can kill him, if you want."

Shocked that he suggested murdering Drostan, she realizes he is mad and pushes past him. He jerks her backward, imprisoning her in his arms. Her files tumble to the ground. Terrified, she stares into the oblivion of his eyes.

"I will have you one way or another," he snarls.

Trapped, she feels his arms tighten around her, and she opens her mouth to scream.

"Coatl!" The sound of someone saying his name shatters his delusion.

Nadira is standing, hands on hips, staring at them. Coatl releases Genevieve, who stumbles to the ground. The desire drains from his face and is quickly replaced another emotion: hatred. He sneers at Nadira.

"Why, if it isn't the queen bee herself. Welcome back, Nadira." He marches up to her, but she doesn't move. "Tired of playing with humans, so you return to your own kind. Lucky us," he adds sarcastically and walks around Nadira, sizing her up. He stares at the earrings; the evidence of her succession inflames his animosity. "Nice earrings. It does not look like Kashta has killed you yet."

"What do you want, Coatl?" Nadira says flatly, unable to avoid a confrontation with this foul creature.

"I thought it was obvious what I want." His maniacal laugh echoes down the corridor.

Nadira shakes her head, never losing eye contact with him. "Not to me."

"Surely you can read my mind," he sneers.

She peers at him, and her eyes widen in disgust.

He smiles. "Now you understand."

His voice drips venom. She assesses her opponent and steels herself for a confrontation. He hesitates for a moment, uneasiness washes over him, and his instincts scream caution, but loathing clouds his reason. She should fear him as most vampires do, but she never has, and the thought infuriates him. He is the stronger vampire and must strike while she is weak. His anger grows red hot, demanding release. He slips the leash on his control. His expression changes, and this tips her off to his intent.

His hand slices through air, missing his target, which has vanished. He swings his head around, searching for his opponent. Surprisingly, he finds her on the opposite side of the tunnel waiting for him. Her movements were so fast she was almost invisible. A blinding rage overpowers him, and he attacks, hurtling a series of offensive jabs at her.

She parries some of the blows while others hit their target. She is faster than him but not as strong. His assault escalates as she visibly weakens under the barrage of abuse. He focuses all his attention on killing her, forgetting a vital tactic in any skirmish: protect your flank.

Genevieve creeps up behind him and delivers a flurry of crippling kicks to his back. Unfazed, he whips around and backhands her, sending her spinning to the ground. Nadira takes advantage of the distraction to mount an offensive strike. However, Coatl, an experienced and lethal killer, anticipates her move and pins her to the wall. They lock eyes, his fetid breath fouling her cheek, and their noses touching. She turns her face away.

"I have you right where I want you," he croaks.

"I will not give you what you want." She stares at him defiantly.

"We'll see, Princess," he taunts. Still, he senses no fear. He wants her to beg for mercy, cry out in pain, and suffer. He gazes into her eyes, two unreadable black pools that reflect his ineptitude.

Genevieve pleads, "Don't do it, Coatl."

He looks at her and then at Nadira. The slight change in Nadira's eyes tells him all he needs to know. She is not the only one who can read minds. Hurting her sister is the ticket to Nadira's pain. His face twists sardonically. "No, Princess. I will not hurt you. You will watch while I torture your sister."

Nadira's eyes widen with alarm, and she struggles against his grip. His malevolent laughter rings in her ears. Suddenly, his hands are gone from her neck, and without the extra support, she falls to the ground. She sees Coatl dazed and struggling to his feet across the tunnel from her. *What just happened?*

Gregor's strong hands lift her up and pull her into his arms. "Are you all right?" he asks.

"He was going to kill us," Genevieve says, shaking.

A controlled fury takes hold of Gregor; he strides over to Coatl, grabs a fistful of his hair, and drags him back to Nadira and Genevieve. Coatl struggles, hisses, and bares his fangs but is powerless against Gregor.

"Is this true?" Gregor asks.

Coatl is frustrated and confused as to how this younger vampire is able to manhandle him. Furious, the last of Coatl's restraint vanishes. He spews out his wretched plan. "Yes. I will torture her sister. Then, I will rape Nadira and drain her life." His lips stretch over his fangs, his eyes lit with perverse pleasure.

"I've heard enough!" Gregor roars.

His self-control snaps, and he pounds Coatl's face, rocking his head backward and then proceeding to pummel him unmercifully. It is a lopsided struggle; Coatl never lands a blow, astonished that a less-experienced vampire has overpowered him. Gregor's fury, once unleashed, is ruthless. Genevieve and Nadira watch Gregor vent his wrath on the now unconscious vampire. Gregor wrenches Coatl by the throat, preparing to bite him. Biting another vampire without his or her consent is the ultimate humiliation.

"I hope he kills him," Genevieve confesses.

Genevieve's comment triggers her father's warning about Coatl. *Do not kill him or taste of his blood.* Nadira glances from Genevieve to Coatl. She forcefully grabs Gregor's shoulder.

The momentum spins him around, almost knocking off balance. His mind clears, but he screams, "Let me finish the enemy!"

"Stop!" she commands.

His fist freezes in midair. He stares at the woman he loves, and her eyes plead with him. He releases his grip on Coatl, who drops to the ground in a heap. "He would have you dead," Gregor quizzes.

"Yes, my love. But my father commands he live," Nadira explains.

"Why?" Gregor is bewildered.

She studies her fiancé. *Why indeed?* Coatl is a centuries-old burden best removed before he can do more damage. She and Amon have disagreed on the subject many times. But Amon is unmovable regarding Coatl, demanding no harm come to him and no one taste his blood.

"I do not know. Amon says Coatl is a necessary evil. No matter the reason, Amon is our liege lord and must be obeyed." She caresses his face. "I do not want his tainted blood in you, Husband."

His control is loath to return. A favorite quote from Sun Tzu's *The Art of War* comes to mind. "Opportunities multiply as they are seized." Success in battle is based on taking advantage of an enemy's vulnerabilities. His enemy lies vulnerable at his feet, a viper that needs to be crushed under the heel of his boot. *What better opportunity?*

He glances down at Coatl's inert body and kicks him a few more times, eliciting a moan from the battered vampire. His discipline returns, fueled by love for Nadira. "So be it. Come, let us leave this sack of shit," Gregor utters.

Nadira helps Genevieve pick up her papers and files. Genevieve peers over at Coatl crumbled in the dust. She marches to him, kicks him in the face, and spits on his inert form. "I curse you, Beelzebub," Genevieve swears.

Surprised, Gregor glances toward Nadira for verification.

"One of his many names," Nadira confirms.

Genevieve rejoins Nadira and Gregor. Nadira wraps her arm around her sister. They walk away, leaving Coatl marinating in a pool of blood.

CHAPTER XX

AMON SITS PATIENTLY, filtering through the barrage of accusations regarding Coatl. Genevieve is overwrought, hovering in the background and wringing her hands. Her husband furiously paces back and forth like a caged lion, occasionally stopping in front of him and shouting.

"I will kill him," Drostan swears.

Surprisingly, Nadira and Gregor appear unruffled, sitting quietly and holding hands.

"The vile and disgusting things he said to my wife. He threatened your daughter . . . made an attempt on her life. He must be eliminated," Drostan demands and continues to stomp around the room.

Amon eyes his loyal knight and asks, "Nadira, where were your guards?"

Nadira and Gregor glance at each other. She blushes and clears her throat. "I dismissed them. I did not require them in the council meeting."

Amon chastises her with a look. "You won't make that mistake again, will you?"

Nadira shakes her head, embarrassed that she put herself in such a vulnerable position. "No, my lord," Nadira concedes.

"We all owe Gregor a debt of thanks for rescuing you and Genevieve." Amon glances at the occupants of the room.

Drostan stops pacing and offers Gregor his thanks. "I owe you a debt for saving my wife that I can never repay." Drostan grasps his hand.

Gregor shrugs his shoulders and nonchalantly addresses his hero status. "That is what families are for. We take care of each other—you owe me nothing."

Amon studies the three of them. "Gregor, how did you happen to be down there?"

Gregor glances at Nadira sheepishly. "I know how stubborn your daughter can be. When I heard she dismissed the guards, I sought her out."

"For once, I am glad you were over protective," she says.

Amon smiles, very pleased with Gregor. Coatl's attempted assassination of Nadira came sooner than expected. He is glad Gregor's plan to protect her was successful. Still, it was a narrow escape.

"What are we going to do with Coatl?" Drostan folds his arms across his chest and glares at Amon.

Gregor nods. "I agree with Drostan. We must do something about him. He grows more daring. To attack Nadira and Genevieve in the Ordinatio? He is too bold. It undermines your authority."

"What say you, Daughter?" Amon glances at Nadira.

Nadira contemplates his simple request. She realizes this is another test, one of many to come. Glancing at Drostan and Gregor, she notices they are a united in their hatred of Coatl. Good, they will need this bond in the future. Why would Coatl be so reckless as to attempt to murder her now? A piece of this complex puzzle is missing. Finally, she answers the question. "Something is amiss for Coatl to act rashly. I believe to execute him now is imprudent. He has a large following, and his death would divide our nation. I say play for time to uncover his plot."

Amon shoots Nadira a look of approval. "I agree. To cut the head off the snake and not destroy the body only releases the rage but does nothing to resolve the problem. How did Coatl get past the Vigile defenses? Where are the holes in our security? What was he doing down in the service tunnels? We must address these questions first and formulate a strategy to deal with him."

Drostan is loath to let Coatl get off so easy and protests.

Amon raises his hand. "You will not harm Coatl. Have our spies gather information on him and his covens. The thrashing Gregor gave him will make him think twice about attacking my daughter. He is treacherous and must be taught a lesson. You will have your opportunity when the necessary due diligence is done and the timing is right."

Amon approaches Drostan. "I know it is hard for a warrior not to act. Let us reason with our head and not our heart, that is our advantage over Coatl. The rewards of patience are sweeter than revenge, my friend." Amon rests his hand on Drostan's arm. "We must act as though nothing untoward happened. We cannot tip our hand." He addresses everyone. "Appreciate how close you came to losing someone precious to you. You deserve a break. Go out tonight and celebrate."

Frustrated, Drostan glares at Amon, but he obeys his king, salutes, and leaves with Genevieve in tow.

Amon addresses Gregor. "Thank you for saving my daughter. Why didn't you kill Coatl?"

"My lord, I wanted to destroy him. Nadira asked me to stop, so I did."

Gregor peers at Nadira, whose face is expressionless. Amon contemplates his daughter. He knows she is holding back something. "Did you bite him?" Amon asks.

Gregor shakes his head and does not notice Amon's tense expression, but Nadira does.

"You stopped because Nadira asked you? Your control does you justice. It is not time to eliminate Coatl, even though he is a thorn in our side. He still has his uses," Amon says.

Amon and Nadira study each other. Gregor realizes they are communicating silently; he is the odd man out. He gets up to leave.

"My lord, if you will excuse me, I think you would like to speak to your daughter in private." He bends down and kisses Nadira on the cheek. "I will wait for you in our apartment." He bows and leaves.

Amon watches him leave the room. "He is learning rapidly and will make an excellent consort for a queen," he says, and Nadira waits for his next query. "Why did you answer my question the way you did?"

Nadira answers deliberately, "That is what you wanted me to say for the others. Coatl is not stupid. For him to make his play this soon is either a sign of desperation or a major flaw in character."

"Which do you think?" Amon asks.

Nadira peers at the fireplace, staring into the fire, lost in thought. It is hard to sort out her emotions regarding Coatl, and formulating an unbiased opinion about him is difficult. Coatl is an ancient vampire, a contemporary of Amon, powerful and respected among his likeminded peers. Nevertheless, he disgusts her and represents everything dark and ugly about her species. Any positive action on his part has an ulterior motive.

She thinks for a moment and then answers, "A character flaw. He lacks impulse control. He must feed his appetite—that is his Achilles's heel."

"Gregor is not the only one who learns fast." Amon's expression does not change, but his eyes register his admiration. "I planned to wait until you finished your physical training to hone your gift. But Coatl has moved up our timetable. We will start our sessions tomorrow. I do not want you caught unprepared again."

"Will it be like Egypt?" she asks.

"No. We manipulated the climate and performed magical tricks meant to impress humans but very little else. Now we will work on the tangible transformation of energy."

Nadira's puzzled look prompts him to clarify.

"Let me explain. Energy exists in all forms of matter, and the quantity of energy is based on the particles in an object. It is a simple physics principle. You will learn to harness this energy and then transform it into another form," Amon explains.

"It sounds similar to what I have done before."

Amon shakes his head. "Not quite. Your previous experiences will seem like parlor tricks compared to what I will teach you. The ability to control this energy is of paramount importance since matter cannot be destroyed." He pauses, allowing Nadira to assimilate this new information. "You glimpsed a small portion of this in France."

Nadira shudders. "Yes. I could barely control myself. Father, I am afraid to unleash that force again. It took me a long time to learn to suppress this gift." To unleash her inner monster is her worse nightmare.

He reaches over, takes her hand in his, and reassures her. "Do not be afraid, Daughter. I will be at your side every step of the way. Together we will conquer your fears and develop your powers."

"Father, what would I do without you?" she asks. Nadira slides out her chair, sits at his feet, and lays her head on his lap.

Amon strokes her hair and ponders her question. *What will I do without my beautiful daughter? What will we all do if I fail?* The challenges facing them are staggering, and her decisions will alter the future for all vampires. She alone will implement these changes by sheer force of will. Her success or failure is based on his ability to build her confidence and transform her into a powerful ruler. A tall order for anyone, but he knows that she is resilient and possesses a strength and energy that, once disciplined, will be unlimited.

The task seems overwhelming for both of them. He closes his eyes, focuses on the positives, discards the negatives as trivialities, and allows a grand design to form.

Nadira senses Amon's mind is far away, plotting and planning. She feels safe and closes her eyes, awash in this comforting feeling. Time passes as she luxuriates in the peace and tranquility of this moment, knowing it is a fleeting gift.

The sound of his voice startles her. "Daughter, I will always be with you. I have not revealed that there is a secret ceremony between the sovereign and the heir, an ancient ritual performed since the beginning of time. The sovereign shares his blood and, thus, his memories and knowledge with the next ruler. It is called the Enlightenment."

She asks tentatively, "Will we perform the ceremony soon?"

"No, first we will work on focusing your gift with meditation. When you are proficient with directing energy transformation, we consummate the Enlightenment," he tells her.

"Good." Nadira is relieved it will be later. Amon's vast knowledge as well as the previous regents' to be assimilated by her—the very thought is daunting. *How will I accomplish this?*

He reads her thoughts and answers, "Together, as we always have." He smiles reassuringly.

She answers his smile with an expression of relief, pleased that with Amon, words are meaningless.

CHAPTER XXI

The club is crowded. The lighting sets a dark mood with a sporadic flash of color from the laser show. The music is loud, pulsing, and sensual, with dancers moving rhythmically to the beat. Vampires and humans grind together in an orgy of dance. The entrance of the next regent and her entourage goes unnoticed. Gregor finds them a table close to the dance floor. The bar overflows with customers, definitely the right place to have fun.

The foursome sits back and watches the action. One of Coatl's young covens occupies a table on the far side of the dance floor. They nervously glance in the direction of Nadira's table, and once noticed, the jumpy vampires shoot worried looks at each other.

Drostan leans toward his companions. "I see Coatl's groupies but no sign of the man himself."

Nadira comments, "They know what happened."

Drostan makes a hand gesture that he has eyes on them and indicates the black-clad Vigiles scattered about the room.

The groupies whisper among themselves, nervously get up, and leave. Nadira watches them abandon their prized table, which is quickly snatched up.

"So much for living in harmony," Nadira adds.

She scans the dance floor and sees Jerry dancing with Ayame. They are engrossed in each other. She wonders how serious the relationship is and points them out.

"Damn!" Gregor comments.

"They look good together. He can move well for a human," Genevieve says, taking Drostan's hand.

He chuckles. "You don't have to stroke my ego. Everyone at this table knows I can't dance. It doesn't stop me from trying."

Jerry sees them from the dance floor, whispers in Ayame's ear, takes her hand, and leads her through the gauntlet of dancers toward Nadira's table. "What's up, boss?" he asks, and Nadira smiles indulgently.

Ayame is shocked by his casual reference to the princess. Genevieve, Drostan, and Gregor glance at each other.

"Ah, the source of Nadira's urban slang." Drostan uses his best Bela Lugosi accent to say, "You must teach me this slang, human." He smiles and bares his fangs. His look is so sinister, almost threatening. Jerry turns pale, Ayame frowns at Drostan, and Nadira studies him, not sure if he is joking.

Gregor breaks the tension. "Jerry, can you teach me some phrases? I will teach you our customs and etiquette. First lesson: do not greet the heir apparent with 'What's up?' It is a sign of great disrespect."

Jerry is mortified by his mistake. He is a stranger in a strange land and cannot treat vampires like humans. It's easy to forgot how lethal they are. Ayame filled in many of the blanks about vampires, both in bed and out. He smiles at the thought and catches Nadira watching him.

"If you would like to attend, there are classes for our human employees. The classes cover vampire culture, history, and the skills necessary to successfully work and live with vampires," Genevieve adds.

Jerry nods. "I would like that very much."

Genevieve replies, "Good, I will sign you up. One starts tomorrow, but I must warn you that it includes a confidentiality agreement. The penalty for any breach of contract is final."

Jerry laughs. "Do I have to stand in the corner if I blab?"

The look on Genevieve's face silences him. "No, the penalty is death," she adds.

Jerry swallows hard. His voice wavers. "You're not kidding, are you?"

"I am never flippant about the end of a life. Do you want to sign up?" Genevieve asks.

All the vampires are watching him expectantly, guessing he will chicken out. Jerry looks at Ayame, who smiles at him. He nods. The others do not miss the interaction.

Nadira smiles at Ayame. "Please sit." She indicates the chair next to her, and Ayame bows and nervously sits down. Nadira pointedly looks at Gregor and Genevieve, who catch the hint.

Genevieve approaches Jerry. "Will you dance with me?" She turns on a brilliant smile.

Jerry's nervousness slips away. Confident in his ability to dance well, he replies, "Yes, I would like that."

She takes his hand and leads him onto the dance floor. Drostan watches his wife leave with the human, and his face darkens with jealousy. He missed some subtle interplay, but he is at a loss to understand what.

Gregor smiles. "Come, brother, let's get a drink. I will explain it to you. The women want to talk," he says, and Drostan follows him to the bar.

Left alone with the next queen, Ayame's trepidation grows. She closes her eyes and concentrates on suppressing her anxiety.

"May I call you Ayame?" Nadira asks, and Ayame nods. "I am concerned about your relationship with my assistant. Humans can be very exciting for us. Their fragility and exuberance for life, the way they think, and even their smell draws us to them. They've been our prey for so long that we are naturally attracted to them."

Ayame's composed face has a strange expression, but Nadira chooses to ignore it. "Vampire–human relationships are unique, even stimulating at first. They possess something precious that we have lost: hope. Eventually, we grow tired of the human who is not our equal. Similar to how the cat playing with the mouse grows bored and then eats it."

Nadira notes a subtle change in Ayame and concentrates on her thoughts, which are astonishing. Ayame is insulted and desperately trying to hide it.

Nadira pushes on. "Jerry is not only my assistant but also my friend. If you hope to gain some favor with me through him, you are mistaken. I do not want to see him hurt, physically or emotionally. I consider him part of my family. He is special . . ."

Ayame cuts off Nadira's speech and responds passionately. "He is special. A person like him comes along only once in a lifetime. The saying 'he is comfortable in his own skin' applies to Jerry." She pauses and like her namesake, the iris, unfurls her petals as she opens up her feelings about Jerry.

Nadira allows her to continue just to watch the marvelous transformation in this lovely vampire.

"I was the harbinger of death, a killing machine, the denizen of Yomi. Life became a distant memory . . . until a beautiful human asked me in my native tongue to dance. Your assistant is the very essence of life, squeezing the last drop of vitality out of every day. He is generous, sharing his experiences with me, teaching me to see them anew. He schooled me in our precious gift of eternal life."

Nadira is stunned to see Ayame's eyes filled with tears.

"I forgot how to laugh, but he taught me how. I lost my joy, and he found it for me. Your assistant has captured my heart." Ayame peers down at her hands and struggles to bridle her emotions. She rarely allows her self-control to slip. Hers is a life of strict discipline, devotion to her vocation, and ritual. Jerry freed her from these constraints.

Nadira sits quietly, giving her time to sort out her feelings.

"What am I going to do? He is human, and I am vampire. I love him," Ayame confesses.

"Have you told him your profession?" Nadira asks, and Ayame shakes her head. Nadira does not answer at first but instead contemplates Ayame and Jerry's dilemma. She faced a similar quandary with Cristo. She repeats what Amon told her,

"My father says the truth is always best. As far as the difference in the species, time has a way of sorting out all problems."

Nadira glances at the dance floor where Jerry and Genevieve are making their way back to the table, Gregor and Drostan close behind them. "It appears everyone is returning. Dry your tears—your secret is safe with me." She pats Ayame's hand, and Ayame manages a lackluster smile. "How was the dance?" Nadira asks her companions.

Jerry addresses Drostan. "Your wife is an excellent dancer. You are a lucky man."

Drostan is taken aback. Maybe this human can be civilized. He smiles at Genevieve, who grins back. Drostan replies, "I know."

Jerry notices Ayame is upset. He sits next to her, wrapping his arm around her in an attempt to comfort her. She snuggles closer, offering him a grateful smile. She addresses the group. "We have to be leaving." Jerry and Ayame stand, and she bows. "Thank you, Princess."

Jerry takes her hand, and together they blaze a path through the dancers. The foursome watches until they disappear from sight.

Drostan exclaims, "In a thousand years, I would never had guessed your human, and of all vampires, Ayame!"

Genevieve comments, "He is smitten with her, kept talking about Ayame this and Ayame that. Doesn't he know another woman, even a vampire, gets jealous?"

Nadira peers at her sister and smiles at the remark. Genevieve always wants to be the belle of the ball.

"They left in a hurry. What did you say to her?" Gregor asks.

"Nothing, I just repeated something Amon shared with me." Nadira grins at Gregor, who eyes her suspiciously.

The tempo of the music changes with a decidedly Middle Eastern flair. Nadira looks in the direction of the dj.

Gregor gets up and formally bows to Nadira. "Madam, this is our song."

"'Hal,' my favorite."

"I know." His eyes sparkle with delight.

Nadira smiles at her fiancé, her heart leaping with anticipation. She sinuously slides from her chair. He takes her hand, leads her to the dance floor, and pulls her to him, body to body. They stare into each other's eyes.

The music starts slowly. Nadira's body moves to the familiar rhythms of her native Persia. Her fluid hand movements and undulating hips blend into an elegant sensuality. Gregor matches her movements perfectly. The tempo increases, and the two circle each other, synchronizing their dance to the rhythm. Their bodies are only inches apart. His hands glide over her, and hers caress his torso, their movements erotic and beautiful. The sensual lure of the music and their physical closeness creates a palpable sexual tension hard to ignore. For Gregor and Nadira, lost in the song and each other, the surrounding dancers fade into the background.

The audience watches, spellbound at their exquisite dance of love and passion. The dancers' graceful gestures are physical extensions of their feelings, a rare glimpse at something so intimate between two people. The crowd parts to give them room and then encircles the couple.

The music reaches its climax. Gregor clasps her tiny waist, and she gracefully arches backward, her hair brushing the floor. Her hands keep gently moving to the fading strands of the santur. The music fades to silence. She remains poised in this dramatic posture until Gregor snaps her upright. They stare at each other, breathless.

Nadira brushes a few damp strands of hair off her face. "Thank you for the ballad. It reminds me of my home," Nadira whispers. With breasts heaving and eyes lit with passion, she gives him a radiant smile.

"I thought you might like it, my love." His eyes smolder with a look that inflames her desire.

She catches her breath, and her knees tremble.

He smiles provocatively, reading her need.

"I forgot what a good dancer you are." She imagines what else he excels at—Gregor does not do anything half way.

"I thought it was time to remind you of my many talents," he says and flashes an inviting smile.

Flustered, she says, "I thought you wanted to wait."

Gregor studies his fiancée. He feels her heart pounding like a jackhammer against the palm of his hand. "I may have to rethink this vow." He kisses her hand like a cavalier.

"You know, men don't kiss ladies' hands anymore," she purrs. Her lips form a saucy pout.

"Don't you miss having men slobber all over you?" He winks.

"Yes," she whispers. She stares into his eyes and sees her desire reflected in them.

Their eyes caress one another, oblivious to their surroundings. He draws her closer, her breasts imprisoned against his hard chest, their loins entwined in a snug embrace. Cradled in the safety of his arms, she feels lightheaded and her legs shake. His heated mouth pushes open her yielding lips.

Genevieve's shout breaks their amorous spell. "That was hot! I thought the two of you were going to do the nasty right on the dance floor. Gregor, you really *can* move."

"Many thanks, fair lady." Gregor disengages himself from Nadira and bows awkwardly.

Nadira fights to regain her composure. Amused, Gregor watches her sequester her passion.

Drostan slaps him on the back and drains the last of his desire. "You'll have to show me some of those movements," he tells Gregor, who gazes directly at Nadira.

"I would gladly show you what I can do," Gregor admits.

Drostan glances back and forth between the two. "Nadira, I don't think he is talking to me."

His comment strikes them as funny, eliciting a flurry of laughter. A piercing chirp breaks the reverie. Drostan's cell phone vibrates with a text. "Got to go to work, some vampires being bad," Drostan says. He pulls Genevieve to him and kisses her soundly. "Keep my side of the bed warm until I get back." He tells Nadira and Gregor, "Meet me at the helipad in an hour." He signals the other Vigiles in the club, who silently disappear.

The Ordinatio helipad is a hot bed of activity. Two Black Hawk helicopters stand prepared on the helipad. Ground crews run back and forth, making the helicopters mission-ready. A squad of

Vigiles carrying heavy-duty firepower run toward the choppers. The sound of the rotors is deafening.

Genevieve, Nadira, and Gregor huddle together, waiting. Drostan strides over to them. In action, he is a very different vampire: all business and no nonsense.

"We have Intel on one of Coatl's more troublesome covens. Amon gave us the green light to bring them to heel." He looks at Gregor. "Brother, watch over my wife while I am gone."

Gregor promises, "You already know that I will guard her with my life."

Genevieve hugs Drostan. Blood-tinged tears escape her control, sliding down her cheeks.

Drostan brushes one away with his finger. "I'll be back," he tells her.

"I know."

He strokes her face, gives her one last smile, steps back, and signals the soldiers. "Let's roll," Drostan says.

The Vigiles scramble into the Black Hawks. Drostan jumps aboard and signals lift off. The choppers angle off into the night. Drostan stares down from the helicopter doorway at his wife. His image shrinks as the helicopter gains altitude. Genevieve, Nadira, and Gregor watch as the helicopters disappear, the sound of the rotors growing fainter.

Genevieve continues to stare up at the empty sky.

CHAPTER XXII

Drostan and his second-in-command, Red 2, cop a squat on the chopper floor, studying a large map. "Operation Red Intel has the targets located on the 2nd floor of this building. We will enter here and here." Drostan indicates the highlighted areas on the map. "The objective: secure as many live targets as possible. A simple snatch and grab of the prime targets."

Red 2 queries, "Are the targets armed?"

"Heavily," Drostan responds.

He imagines the combatants are probably a couple of new vampires playing G. I. Joe, but it is better to be vigilant. Any vampire can be deadly. He glances at his squad, seasoned veterans that he trusts with his life. After a long hiatus from violence, the soldiers banter back and forth, all eager to do their job. They prepare for the landing, tightening straps and checking weapons and ammunition.

Amon finally gave Drostan the green light to take down one of Coatl's covens, an insignificant one, but it sends the right message to Coatl. Retribution for breaking the law is swift and decisive. He personally owes Coatl some payback for Genevieve and Nadira.

The chopper pilot shouts back, "Two minutes to LZ!"

Drostan scans the terrain and assesses the landing zone, an abandoned industrial complex, a wasteland of empty buildings and derelict equipment. It offers cover for them but a slight tactical advantage for the enemy.

Drostan barks, "Saddle up!"

The interior light switches to red. Drostan assumes his command position, presses his headset, and orders, "This is Red 1." He hand signals Red 2, counting down his fingers—three, two, one—and then silence.

The Black Hawks touch and go; the soldiers disembark and secure the landing zone. The choppers take off and remain on station two clicks away. The soldiers stealthily advance single file, stacking on the target building's outer wall. They disperse rapid time with weapons drawn and adopt a basic wedge offensive formation.

The building is an empty administrative building, five stories high, and missing half its windows. The structure, outside doors, and fire escapes are intact, offering multiple exits for the soldiers. They slip up to the surrounding buildings and stack foundations, waiting for the signal to advance on the target.

Code name Newbies, two coven sentries armed with automatic weapons are visible at the building's entrance. Red 2 signals his men, who take the Newbies out with tranquilizer darts. They drop unconscious to the ground. The squad advances onto the first floor, fans out, checks corners, and sweeps the lower level. They position themselves at the main staircase. Red 2 signals the advance, and they ascend the staircase. Drostan indicates hard stop at the second floor landing. Outside the main conference room doors, they tranquilize two more Newbies. The soldiers rush the doors and affix explosive charges to them.

Behind the doors, a massive table dominates the conference room. A gang of young vampires packs around it. It could be a goth Halloween party—everyone is wearing heavy makeup, black leather, metal studs, and chains.

The coven leader, Daniel, is a high-strung teen with unruly mop of hair that he nervously pulls. He hardly seems threatening, but appearances are deceiving. His irresponsible and unpredictable behavior makes him a dangerous vampire. He parades on top of the table, waving an AK-47 around and shouting, "What are you pussies whinnying about? You are vampires, invincible, powerful, and immortal. No one can kill or stop us." He discharges his weapon overhead in a show of bravado meant to impress his followers, who whoop and make a conciliatory display of support.

Except one scrawny vampire, Jay, who pushes through the group toward Daniel. "Daniel, maybe it wasn't a good idea to kill Claude," Jay says.

Daniel glares at Jay. "Claude disobeyed me. I am the coven leader. You must obey me without question."

The other vampires look at each other, unconvinced.

Daniel notices their lackluster response to his comment. He threatens them with his weapon. "Any questions?" he asks.

Jay waves his hands. "No. But we're not supposed to kill another vampire, that's all."

Daniel doesn't like Jay's tone and aims the gun at him. "So what if I did? Who is going to stop me? You? That'll be the day! All you do is snivel and piss your pants when there's trouble."

Jay backs off. "I've heard about these Vigiles. They sound like mean sons of bitches."

"They are just some urban legend, a scary story to frighten chickenshit vampires like you." Daniel snickers. "As I was saying—"

A loud explosion accompanies the conference doors ricocheting across the room. The blast knocks some young vampires off their feet. Vigiles rush the room, tranquilizing their targets with military precision. It is more like a turkey shoot—Newbies drop like flies, definitely no match for the experienced soldiers. A few vampires fire their weapons haphazardly, missing the soldiers and hitting the ceiling or each other.

Drostan presses his headset. "Go loud!"

The soldiers return live fire using ultraviolet rounds made specifically for new vampires. The bullets hit their targets, disintegrating them instantly. Bodies start to pile up or disappear altogether. In a matter of minutes, Daniel sees his entire coven in chaos or vanishing before his eyes. Outgunned, he makes a mad dash for the door.

Red 2 starts to pursue him, but Drostan shakes his head.

"Red 2, secure the room. Call for RVAC of these idiots. I'll get the little bastard."

Drostan is in hot pursuit of the prime target. They play hide-and-seek in this shell of concrete and rebar. Drostan stalks his objective with military efficiency, checking corners, doorways, and blind spots. Driven by panic, Daniel's flight is erratic, desperate, pulling over shelves in an effort to slow down his shadow. He climbs down fire escapes, runs across the roofs, and shimmies down elevator shafts. Constantly, he glances backward for signs of his pursuer. He realizes too late that he underestimated the tenacity of the older vampire.

Drostan is minutes behind Daniel, using the mechanical conduits above to mirror his moves. When Daniel turns down a blind hallway, Drostan sees his opportunity, jumps off the roof, slides down the elevator cable, and swings over to the open elevator doors. In one fluid motion, he vaults through a shattered window onto the fourth floor, cutting off Daniel's escape route. He turns a sharp corner, honing in on his prize. Suddenly, his weapon flies out of his hands. Daniel steps around the corner, surprising Drostan. The slippery teen tricked him.

"Got you."

"So you have. Now what, kid?"

"Now you surrender." Daniel shoots him a cocky grin.

"Never!" Drostan's eyes narrow.

"Listen, old man, just surrender and save me the trouble of killing you."

"No, you little bastard," Drostan answers.

"Then die!" Daniel bellows.

Drostan is surprised the cheeky bastard caught him unawares, but he only has a second to consider his options. Daniel raises his weapon and, at point-blank range, unloads his clip into Drostan. Bullet casings litter the floor. The impact jerks Drostan like a puppet on a string. He collapses onto all fours, bleeding from a myriad of wounds.

Daniel slides closer to inspect his handiwork and decides that wasn't too hard. He crouches down for a better look. His victory is short lived when his victim reaches up, grabs his throat, and growls at him.

"Dumb shit. You should respect your elders. We're hard to kill," Drostan tells him. He staggers to his feet, drilled with more holes than a gun range target, and flexes his rippling muscles, freeing his wounds of the bullets that drop to the floor.

"What the hell?" Daniel barks.

Drostan straightens up, cracks his neck, and says, "You're under arrest!" He hoists Daniel in the air.

The kid futilely struggles to free himself. "I'd rather die," he hisses at Drostan.

"So, be it." Drostan reaches backward into a hidden scabbard in his uniform and draws out a silver retractable broadsword that springs open at his touch. The long sword glistens menacingly in the feeble light. "I keep this for close encounters of the vampire kind." Drostan offers him, "Last chance."

The two study each other. Daniel laughs. "Are you senile? You're gonna fight me with a sword?"

"No, I'm going to kill you with a sword," Drostan answers.

"A sword can't kill me, stupid." Daniel spits in his face.

In the blink of the eye, Drostan impales Daniel through the chest with the broadsword. A look of utter disbelief registers on Daniel's face. He staggers backward and stares at the sword sticking out of his chest.

"You stabbed me?" Daniel cries incredulously.

He slides to his knees, his bravo ebbing away with his life. No longer the arrogant coven leader, he looks like a frightened child. Drostan kneels next to him, holding him upright.

"Did you think this was a video game, kid?" Drostan asks.

"The vampire who made me said we were immortal. I thought it was like the movies: strength like a superhero, incredible sex, and shapeshifting stuff. My maker told us that we were his army and would rule the world. Nine months ago, my biggest worry was going to the prom and if my dad would lend me the car." At the mention of his father, Daniel's eyes shine with unshed tears and the light fades in them. "I convinced some of my friends to join me. Now they are dead. We're just kids."

Drostan pities the naive vampire. "Young vampires are extremely vulnerable."

Daniel's breathing is raspy, and his chest makes a sickening sucking sound with each breath. He looks beseechingly at Drostan, managing a wan smile. He gasps for air and then clings to Drostan's hand. "Promise me you'll kill the lying son of a bitch!"

"Daniel, what is your maker's name? I give you my oath you will be avenged," Drostan promises.

Daniel tries to focus on Drostan. "His name is Coatl." Daniel coughs, and blood bubbles between his lips and slips down his chin. He peers into Drostan's eyes. "I'm afraid." Daniel's voice is barely a whisper.

"I know," Drostan reassures him. Drostan brushes Daniel's hair out of his eyes and offers a gentle smile.

The bass tone of helicopter rotors captures their attention. They glance out the shattered windows at the Black Hawk hovering outside the building. Daniel's eyes glaze over, his last breath escapes his lips, and his head drops backward. His body crumbles to dust and slips between Drostan's fingers. All that remains of Daniel is scattered by the turbulence inflicted by the chopper.

Drostan broods on the young vampire's short life robbed of any future by Coatl's madness. Coatl will pay for his crimes no matter what Amon orders. He promised the kid. Drostan always keeps his promises.

He retrieves his sword, presses his headset, and reports, "Red 2, prime target is KIA."

CHAPTER XXIII

Nadira and Genevieve join Drostan in the martial arts arena. Fashioned after a Japanese dojo, it is a large Spartan room with wooden beams and shoji screen doors. Two competitors arrayed in black Kendo *bogu*, protective armor, kneel across from each other on the wooden floor. Kendo is a modern Japanese martial art evolved from ancient swordsmanship practices, or *kenjutsu*. Humans practice Kendo using bamboo swords, *shinai*, but vampires pass on the bamboo, preferring real katana swords.

The match begins with the traditional bow and elaborate drawing of the swords. A stylized form of ritual posturing is next, displaying the opponents' skill and discipline. Once the match begins in earnest, it is loud affair, with the combatants shouting and fiercely attacking each other. The blade movement is rapid, a visual blur punctuated by a swish of air and the solid thud of the metal connecting with armor.

The audience crowds the arena to get a better look.

Nadira asks, "Who is that?"

"Shen Feng," Drostan answers.

"Amon's chancellor."

Drostan nods. "Yes. He is a master of martial arts. The katana is his weapon of choice."

Nadira notices the size of the audience. "It's too large a crowd to watch a simple sparing match."

Genevieve asks, "Who is the other vampire?"

Drostan answers, "I don't know."

Shen and his opponent fight viciously, charging and bullying each other. The swords sail gracefully through the air. Both vampires are obviously experts of this martial art. Shen's challenger dominates the conflict, employing short intense attacks and then a *Katsugi-waza*, a surprise attack with his weapon. Shen counters with *Nuki-waza*, but his timing is slow, and the unknown opponent finishes with the *Debana-waza* technique, winning the match.

The combatants bow to each other. They remove their headpieces, or *men*, revealing the second vampire is Amon. The crowd goes wild, cheering and chanting. Amon formally bows to his subjects.

Nadira comments, "The old chess player. The cat is out of the bag now." The others don't understand the full meaning of her comment and give her the once-over.

Drostan off-handily remarks, "I guess he wasn't dying after all."

Amon catches Nadira's eye, winks, and then nods to Shen. Nadira wonders what Amon is planning. In an instant, Shen vaults through the air, lands in front of her, and swings his sword in wide arch, stopping a fraction of an inch from her throat.

The crowd gasps. A low murmur ripples through it as they speculate on a motive for the attack and guess her reaction. Nadira exhales slowly. Amon did not tell her this was part of the plan. She thinks it is an overly dramatic display but typical of her father. She prefers a more subtle touch.

Shen demands, "I challenge you to combat."

Nadira scans the crowd, who watches her every move, waiting in anticipation. She knows what he expects of her. She squints at Shen. "Are you sure?"

He nods.

Nadira glances over at Amon, whose eyes twinkle mischievously. So, this is his answer. She addresses Shen and then bows. "I accept your challenge." Drostan tosses her a blade. She deftly catches it, swings it gracefully around her body, and finishes in a crouched stance. She grins. "Let's play."

Shen and Nadira rush forward, vaulting over each other and locking weapons. They abandon the formal Kendo style, opting for a more eclectic style of swordplay. Nadira alternates offensive thrusts and stylized leaps in the air. The only sound in the arena is the whistling of the weapons and the metallic clink when the blades clash. Shen counters with aerial flips and twists, giving the match the appearance of a Chinese circus act rather than a sword fight. The conflict takes a deadly turn when Shen makes a bold move, somersaulting in the air and landing to her left side. He twists his body while simultaneously slashing outward toward his antagonist. The razor sharp blade slices through the soft flesh of her triceps. She steps backward, blood gushing down her arm, which hangs useless at her side. She gingerly touches the gash in disbelief and gazes at the blood dripping from her fingers.

She notices the crowd waiting and watching. Worst of all, she sees her father, accompanied by Kashta, staring expectantly. Their presence reminds her that failure is not an option; this is more than a match. If she wants the crown, she must bleed for it.

Gregor enters the arena and sees Nadira injured and hemorrhaging. He bolts forward, but Drostan restrains him.

Drostan shakes his head. "Stand down, brother. Only she can do this."

Gregor shakes off Drostan's hand and backs off. He watches helplessly while the woman he loves battles a master swordsman. His eyes find hers and send a silent message of encouragement.

She is grateful for his presence, and his love bolsters her resolve. She focuses on Shen, hisses, and bares her fangs. Her counterattack is so furious that he can barely defend himself. Her aggression takes him by surprise. Relentlessly, she drives him into a defensive position where he's unable move. Slowly, he loses ground until she pulls one last trick out of her hat. She flips backward over him, lands behind him, and rakes her weapon across his legs. Shen crashes to the ground. Nadira uses her blade to pin his shoulder to the floor. Skewered like a kabob, he wilts under her ferocious glaze.

She stares down at her opponent, demanding, "Do you concede?"

Shen breathlessly nods.

Nadira tosses her sword across the floor, catches her breath, and then extends her hand to him. "Shen, I would rather work with you than fight you." She pulls him up and asks, "Why the challenge?"

Shen answers truthfully, "Amon has a great deal of respect for you. I was testing you to see if you deserve his respect."

"Did I pass?"

"A+," he answers. They bow, acknowledging the other's skill.

Gregor runs to her side. "I was worried. Let me look at your arm." He pulls back her sleeve and finds the flesh intact and the bleeding stanched. The only evidence of her injury is her bloodstained clothing.

"I told you I can take care of myself," Nadira says.

"What was that about?" Gregor asks.

"Amon's special brand of theatrics. He enjoys a bold statement. The match with Shen was just that. His unofficial announcement that he is not dying. In one quick move, he curbs his enemies' intrigues."

"Was Shen's attack a surprise?" Gregor asks.

"Yes. Amon didn't forewarn me. It was imperative that I best Shen. Everyone knows he is a master swordsman. My victory dispels the rumors that I am vulnerable. After the incident in the tunnel, Coatl's covens have been busy spewing lies regarding my ability to rule. Today, Amon and I quelled those rumors. A good day's work, if I do say so myself," Nadira says.

She is very pleased with Amon's plan and grateful he did not divulge any of it so her reactions were genuine and not rehearsed. Gregory is studying her, his pride clearly etched on his face. She kisses his cheek and wishes they were alone, which rarely seems to happen. Immediately, they are engulfed by well-wishers congratulating Nadira on her win.

Nadira scans the audience for Amon and locates him standing apart. They study each other until a tender smile relaxes his face. He bows his head, places his fist to his chest, and salutes her. She bows her head and looks up, but he is gone.

She smiles to herself. *How like my father—the whole match planned, executed, and delivered with a theatrical flourish. Vampires will remember this day and talk about it for years. The day the heir bested the master swordsman, Shen.* Suddenly, Nadira has an epiphany: Amon made a statement without uttering a single word and birthed a legend.

Her legend.

CHAPTER XXIV

T HE MEDITATION ROOM is devoid of jarring distractions, almost sterile with its lack of embellishment. Amon and Nadira are seated in the lotus position opposite each other and clad in white, seamlessly blending into the white walls. A serene ambiance infuses the room.

Amon senses Nadira's apprehension and smiles reassuringly. "You have mastered the art of meditation. Today, we will perform a small exercise."

Nadira's perplexed expression tugs her beautiful face into a frown.

"In Egypt, I held back. You learned so rapidly and your gift was so powerful that I was afraid. The events in France confirmed my fears. Your power, once unleashed, is hard to contain," Amon tells her.

Nadira studies Amon. "And now?"

"Now it is necessary. Drostan exposed Coatl's plot to seize the throne and rule the world. You stand in his way, and he will stop at nothing to remove you."

Nadira interjects, "So do you."

Amon is pleased with her concern for him but is undaunted. He assures her, "I can take care of myself, but the recent attack on you has changed our plans. Kashta is satisfied with your physical progress. I believe you are ready for the next step. It involves a source of great power. Voltaire said, 'With great power comes great responsibility.'"

Nadira is not convinced that she is ready for great power.

Amon continues, "Your gifts are useless without the ability to channel this energy. Energy exists in everything. It's interconnected and part of the infinite whole. We become conduits for this energy, bending and molding it to our will"

"What is the source of this energy?" Nadira asks.

"What do you think?"

Nadira knows Amon answers every question with another question, prompting his pupils to critically reason out their own answer. She contemplates her response carefully. "Humans would say from God. I do not know God. In Egypt, we were gods."

"Are we gods?" Amon queries her.

"No, we have no more control over the future or our destiny than humans. Humans, unable to explain our powers, labeled us gods, wizards, or shamans. The church damned us as demons and witches for centuries. I know we are not human, demon, or God but something in between, neither good nor bad but a mixture of both. We are vampire."

Amon nods in agreement. "What is God?"

She considers his question. "I have long pondered the idea of a divine being who is all-knowing and powerful. When Jesus lived, I felt his teachings brought me closer to my answer. His philosophy was to love your neighbor as yourself. My neighbors were humans and, thus, my source of substance. I could not reconcile my slaughter of humans with his doctrine. A philosophical quandary as my alternatives were limited to animals or starvation; instead, I chose life. Thus, I ceased tormenting myself with the question of God." Nadira waits for his response.

An enigmatic smile animates his face. "The answer has haunted us since the beginning of time." He ponders his answer. *Is she ready for the truth?* "Science explains many things, but some are beyond its grasp. For example, physical objects are organized of atoms and subatomic particles—where do these originate? If there is no divine power, how do we account for their existence? Science has various theories, including the Big Bang—all ambiguous at best. The most interesting questions aren't answered by science or supported by fact."

Nadira asks, "Such as?"

"A myriad of questions. Why are we here?" He indicates their surroundings. "Is everything a coincidence? Or is there a higher plan at work? What are vampires? Humans say we are dead, but do the dead laugh, love, or exist for an eternity? How do we explain the transformation from human to vampire? Blindly, we grope about, seeking an answer so simple yet so elusive."

Nadira follows his line of reasoning and hazards a guess. "An infinite power?" She looks to Amon for affirmation, but his expression is indecipherable.

When he finally replies, his response is unexpected. "'And the earth was without form, and void: and darkness was upon the face of the deep.'"

She finishes his verse, "'And God said, Let there be light: and there was light.' The book of Genesis."

Amon smiles. "Use whatever name you chose. Something greater than ourselves."

Nadira's mind reels with a barrage of abstract thoughts. Over the centuries, she puzzled over the secrets of the universe but never came close to a satisfactory answer, only more questions. Lost in thought, she fails to notice Amon watching her, reading her.

He reaches out and touches her arm, startling her. "Maybe the truth is a fusion of both. Do not be troubled with this revelation. The next concept will further tangle your intellect." He pauses for effect. "Where do vampires go once they cease to exist? Humans believe when they die that their souls travel to heaven, paradise, or are reincarnated, no matter the word. But the question remains: is this a tangible place or just a repository for the individual's energy?" Nadira's quizzical expression prompts him to add, "We shall harness this same energy today. Energy is never created or destroyed, just transformed."

Amon sits back and watches Nadira's eyes widen in wonder. He smiles at her. "As for me, I aspire to transcend to this alternate plane of existence. We are minuscule, and the universe is infinite. The possibilities are limitless."

"You crave death?" She scrutinizes her father.

"Death of the flesh is the liberation of the soul," Amon answers. "As long as I remain trapped in this physical body, I am unable to merge with the universal stream of consciousness. To remain stagnant, ceasing to evolve, is nonexistence and the death of potential."

Befuddled, she doesn't understand her father's meaning. However, she knows this talk of death distresses her and wonders what he means by merging with the universe. It does not seem a valid excuse to leave the ones you love. She ponders his comment but fails to come to any conclusion.

Amon senses her impasse. "I have given you a lot to think about. We need to clear our minds for today's exercise. Put away these baffling thoughts for a later day. Empty your conscience."

They resume their lotus positions opposite each other and close their eyes. A silence settles. Nadira struggles to suppress her uneasiness. Amon waits patiently until his apprentice is ready to proceed.

"The energy we harness ebbs and surges like the tide. You must not fight this synergy but allow it to flow freely. Your mind must be buoyant. Release your hold on the tangible and grasp the infinite. Belief in your abilities will result in a successful lesson. Can you do this?"

She takes a deep breath and nods.

"During the rest of the session, our communication will be telepathic. The chatter of speech is distracting."

He mentally instructs her to focus on a point to her left. She concentrates on the area. *Now picture a star twinkling in the sky,* he tells her. A mental picture forms in her mind, and a tiny spot of white light appears to her left and twinkles. He bids her to center all her attention on the light. She stares at the spot until it grows larger and brighter and pulsates.

Amon stares at the empty space to his right and generates another spot of light, but his does not flicker and is much larger. The two lights flutter to the left and right of Amon and Nadira. He coaches her to focus all her energy on her light, which changes color to brilliant neon blue. Simultaneously, Amon rivets his attention on his dancing light and flips it to neon blue.

Amon instructs Nadira to move her light directly in front of her. It skips into place and then hovers before her. He telepathically slides his light in front of him. He prompts her touch his hands. Nadira extends her palms forward until she feels Amon's hands touching hers in the same position. Their minds converge. The lights merge, pulsate faster, and increase in size and brightness.

He encourages her to feel the energy around her and to allow it to flow through them. Brows knit together, she devotes her full attention to the task. The pulsating light changes to a brilliant white, expanding as if it were the sun, beams spiraling off like a pinwheel. The brightness envelopes them, blinding in its intensity, until a kaleidoscope of color infuses the room. Bouncing off the walls and ceiling, the energy reaches the boundaries of the structure. Wave after wave of it rocks the small room, unable to contain the raw power until a small explosion releases it. The blast hurtles Amon and Nadira across the floor.

Stunned, they lie motionless. Amon props himself on one elbow, peering at Nadira. Their faces and clothing are begrimed with soot. She struggles to sit upright. The ceiling is black, the walls are charred, and the tatami mats look like shredded wheat. A thin veil of smoke hangs in the air. It takes a minute for both of them to comprehend what just happened.

Amon produces a lopsided grin. "A successful lesson."

"You think!" she replies, overwhelmed by the experience. Their strained laughter fills the smoky room and extinguishes the tension.

"We'll have to work on your control," he says, and she stares at him. "I believe it is time to show them."

"Show who?" she asks.

"The council," he answers.

The High Council of Elders are the most powerful vampires in the realm. This is the official announcement of her candidacy for the throne and her plea for their support. She worries—another hurdle to overcome with an uncertain outcome. Amon watches her nervously fidget and senses her anxiety. She peers at him with an apologetic expression, hair askew, soot-stained face, and wide-eyed, reminding him more of a frustrated chimney sweep than the next heir.

Nadira asks in a small voice, "When?"

He smiles. "Very soon."

CHAPTER XXV

GREGOR AND NADIRA are free climbing the North Ridge of Piz Badile Mountain. The North Ridge is a soaring summit of granite and buttresses rated a fifth class terrain among climbers. They move easily up the ridge without equipment or fear.

Gregor jokes, "Hey, slow poke. If you don't hurry up, we are going to miss it."

Nadira peers up at Gregor's retreating butt. The sheer face of the mountain is latticed with fissures, but good handholds are scarce. She spots an arête, grits her teeth, and bumps up. Both climb faster, springing like mountain goats from handhold to handhold. Gregor reaches the summit first, waits for Nadira, and pulls her up.

Nadira teases, "Are you happy now, Mr. Impatient?"

They both turn to watch the sunrise. A flash of crimson and then orange fires the sky and skips across the mountain peaks.

In the bracing cold, they can almost hear the heartbeat of the world shrouded below the clouds. Nadira leans against Gregor, who wraps his arms around her. Secure in his embrace, she nestles against him, basking in the seclusion.

"I never get tired of watching the sun greet the day. Do you remember your first sunrise?" she asks.

"How could I forget? You took me to the top of the great pyramid at Giza to watch it. I waited fifty years for that first golden welcome to a new day. Do you remember that trip?"

"It was like going home. Amon and I lived there for a very long time," she answers.

"What was Egypt like?"

Nadira expounds, "Magnificent. A richness of culture unequaled in history. No other empire reached the heights that Egypt did. It was an exhilarating experience, but it seems like a distant dream."

"Your life is punctuated by human civilizations. All gone in the blink of the eye," Gregor says.

"Poor humans. Their lives are encapsulated in eighty or so years. Our lives span centuries, eras pass, civilizations rise and fall, but we remain. I have tasted them all in one form or another. I have seen humanity at its best and worst. I have been privy to the secrets of the pyramids, the seven wonders of the ancient world, and debates on the floor of the Roman Senate. I witnessed firsthand what horrors humans will inflict on each other, smelled the blood of slaughtered Christians, stacked Muslim corpses during the crusades, and walked the fence line at Auschwitz. I have tutored under Plato, watched Michelangelo paint the Sistine Chapel, heard Mozart's first performance of *The Magic Flute*, and saw a human walk on the moon. Immortality is a two-edged sword, both a curse and a gift. Mankind builds empires, and we watch them crumble to dust."

"The building of an empire was how I felt about war. It wasn't about the taking of life, it was more about the military strategies used to seize a nation, the eventual conquest, and the sheer thrill of victory," he confesses.

"Not many empires to conquer now. Business is the virgin territory; we create companies from nothing or strategically take them over. Like a game of chess but more thrilling with higher stakes."

"I am not much of a chess player, but I am learning," Gregor adds.

"You're a quick study. I can teach you," she offers.

Gregor tightens his grip. "I bet there is a lot you can teach me."

She smiles up to her cheekbones at the innuendo. They stare at the sunrise, appreciating the quiet radiance.

"I forgot how much I enjoy your sister's company. Genevieve is a paradox: both sassy and sweet," he remarks.

"Much to her own determent. Remember, we had to kidnap her from her maker."

"Do you rescue all of the down and out vampires or just Genevieve and me?" he says.

"I guess I only save the best. Someone rescued me not once but twice. My father's betrayal broke my heart. The temple priests used me as their whore and broke my soul. After Cristo's death, I clung to a shadow of life. Both times, Amon saved me from oblivion. What would it say about me if I did not repay the kindness?" She stares into his eyes. "You were a rough black opal—once polished, your beautiful colors shine. Helping you was the key to my wholeness. Together, we are complete."

Grateful she chose him, he kisses her, a long, slow, lingering kiss.

"I brought you up here for a reason. I need to be alone with you," she tells him.

Gregor grins. "This sounds interesting."

She stutters, "Do not distract me. We need to talk."

Gregor playfully grabs her and grins mischievously. "Okay, talk."

Her playfulness evaporates. "Amon plans to formally announce me as his heir during the next council session," she blurts out.

Gregor pauses, rolls his eyes, and lets loose a long whistle. "That will stir the hornet's nest," he says.

"Precisely. That is Amon's plan. He wants the elders to officially declare their loyalties." She continues, "Things will be dangerous."

"That's an understatement. Coatl will flip out. I am worried about your safety." He wears a concerned expression.

"I have to show you something. Wait here. It might dangerous to be next to me." She flies to a large outcrop on the side of the mountain.

Intrigued, Gregor raises his eyebrows. *What does she want to show me on the top of a mountain?*

A copper sun chases fluffy white clouds across the azure sky. Nadira scans the horizon and concentrates on the sky. She raises her arms and commands, *"Tempestas!"*

The sky darkens, dirty gray clouds eclipse the sun, and thunder rumbles in the distance. A snowflake smacks Gregor's nose. He glances up at the plump white flurries spiraling downward. Thick snow starts to fall, gently surrounding them like a snow globe. The sound of thunder grows louder. Called thundersnow, it's both dramatic and beautiful.

Spellbound by this unexpected climatic change, Gregor is both frightened and amazed by the extent of her powers. He often thinks of her as divine. She could very well be the Sumerian goddess An commanding this storm.

Nadira points toward the horizon. *"Fulgur."* She directs the elements as a conductor would an orchestra. Lightning strikes the mountaintop, illuminating the craggy peaks and jarring the boulders. The force of the blasts makes it hard to stand upright. Nadira transforms herself into a lightning rod, attracting the storm's energy.

He is terrified when it strikes her repeatedly. He shields his eyes from the brilliant light and feels the tremor in his bones. But she appears impervious to its effects, turns toward him, and extends her hand, beckoning him. Mesmerized and drawn to her like a magnet, he leaps onto the ledge beside her. He notices her eyes are a solid milky white, eerily beautiful. She touches his face, discharging static electricity into him. He feels its power rushing through his body, causing his skin to tingle. Instinctively, his arms encircle her, his mouth clinging to hers.

Their kiss triggers a prism of lightning to encircle them. They dissolve into each other as though welded together. Their souls converge, intertwine, and fuse. Theirs is a union of infinite power, no longer two individuals but one entity, two bodies with one soul and conscience.

Dazed by the experience, their kiss ends and the electricity dissipates. He notices her eyes revert back to their burnished ebony hue. His love radiates a warmth, and she basks in it.

She whispers, *"Sol,"* her breath caressing his face.

The lightning ceases, and the gray clouds evaporate. The sky lightens, replaced by a cerulean wash populated with cotton candy clouds. They peer at the magnificent rainbow spanning the mountaintop. The couple quietly watches the clouds roll overhead. The iridescent sky paints the mountain with a surreal glow. Love binds them together as time disappears.

"Words cannot express." He gazes at the horizon.

"Do not use them, my love." Nadira puts her finger on his lips and reads his thoughts. She takes his face in her hands and kisses him ardently until both are breathless.

Gregor vows, "Beloved."

"I told you I could protect myself." Nadira smiles coyly, melting his heart.

"I see."

Nadira is a chameleon, reflecting the ever-changing hues of her surroundings, camouflaging herself in splendor. He wonders if he will ever discover all the infinite layers that make up this amazing woman. He certainly hopes not.

Nadira rests her head on his chest. He inspects the sky; there is no evidence of the dramatic climatic display. All that remains is a grandeur and tranquility sheltering them, the perfect setting for their love.

Nadira raises her head and smiles at him. Impishly, she challenges, "I'll race you down."

He sees joy dancing in her eyes combined with a freedom she rarely experiences. "You're on," he counters.

They both run to the edge of the ridge and jump.

CHAPTER XXVI

THE COURTROOM, THE site of heated debates and verbal sparring, is quiet today and empty except for a handful of vampires. The agenda on the calendar is a closed meeting of the High Council.

Seated behind a long courtroom table, Nadira, somberly clad in black, awaits the verdict of the High Council. Genevieve, the official recorder, is to her left, and on her right side, Shen acts as legal counsel. They face an impressive dais of twelve imposing vampires: the High Council, the oldest and most seasoned vampires, are unanimously voted to this influential position. Legal and governmental issues not resolved in the lower branches are brought before the High Council. Their decision is final, with no appeals. Amon sits at the pinnacle of this system as its sovereign lord. His word is absolute.

The council members are clad in their formal judicial robes as befits this important hearing. The vampire government is divided into three branches—legislative, judicial, and executive—or the *trias politicia*, based on centuries of gleaning the best policies from human institutions. The result is a hybrid form of government, marrying a constitutional republic to a monarchy. The belief in a good king is embedded in the vampire consciousness along with an innate independence, hence the successful blending of two opposite political principles. This marriage has been effective for millennia. Seven vampires, including Amon, have been sovereign, each selected by the prior ruler.

Amon's coronation took place in AD 1221, and his regimen has weathered many storms; the worst was the Great Persecution. Prior to this time, the killing of vampires was a random occurrence, but over the centuries, the systematic slaughter of vampires took on epic proportions. The carnage escalated out of control, resulting in the execution of all young vampires. Amon saved their species, unleashing Coatl and the Vigiles on the slayers. A blood bath ended the genocide. In the aftermath, vampires became displaced persons who would never be safe until they had a homeland and formed a cohesive republic. Amon chose Switzerland for their headquarters. Over the next centuries, the Ordinatio was constructed and a national identity embedded. In this environment, vampires have flourished.

Apprehension about the outcome of today's meeting plagues Nadira. Her future hinges on the goodwill of these twelve vampires. Although it is not necessary for the council to approve her status as Amon's heir, without their support it would be hard to govern.

Amon rises from his seat, walks to the podium, and formally addresses the council. "I have called this meeting of the council to make an announcement. I have chosen my successor."

A murmur runs through the council members. Amon waits for the speculation to run its course. He continues in the ancient vampire language, choosing his words carefully.

"I, Amon, the Hidden One, Sovereign of the Ancient Gods, King of the vampires, chose Princess Nadira Naram-Sin as my heir." He delivers his declaration in a strong commanding voice.

The council members look at each other. The statement sparks a flurry of conversation, and the room reverberates with controversy.

"Your choice was not presented to the council for a vote," a dignified African council member says. The other members nod and shower him with approving looks.

Amon replies firmly, "Councilman Menas is correct, but he forgets history. Our rulers are never elected. The selection is solely at the discretion of the reigning sovereign. It is my prerogative to choose my successor without input from the council. I tell you now as a courtesy and sign of respect."

The council members whisper among themselves.

A Chinese representative named Da Xia speaks up. "Our esteemed spokesperson meant to say that the council has questions regarding your choice."

"Of course. That is the reason for this meeting, to address any questions or concerns," Amon answers.

It is not the only objective of the meeting. Amon plans to bolster support for his candidate and catch any traitors in his net of intrigue.

Menas speaks up. "Thank you, sire. My first question is why did you choose the princess?"

"Nadira is an ancient, older than most of you on the council." He waits for them to acknowledge this fact. "I have been her mentor since our time in Egypt and have personally trained her. She has sat on the council in the past." He stops and waits for the expected questions.

"Yes, she did so admirably. However, she resigned abruptly seventy years ago. She left our society to live among humans. What is to prevent her from abandoning her duties again?" Da Xia asks.

Amon smiles with admiration. Vampires do not pussyfoot around. They cut right to the heart of the matter. He glances at Nadira, indicating she should answer the question.

"Esteemed council members, I resigned after a disagreement with my father," Nadira answers, and the council digests this information.

The flaxen-haired female council member Gudrun has her own question. "You've lived among humans for many years. You must have a unique perspective on them. Would you please share your insights?"

Nadira thinks, *Good, the questioning is proceeding as we envisioned.* She answers, "My father and I are in accord with our ideas on humanity. We must coexist for the betterment of both species. I believe as he does that we must live openly in human society."

A loud banging from the dais disrupts the cross-examination. The Italian council member, Quintus Flavius, is rapping his gavel on the table. Nadira knows very little about him except that he was a Roman senator. His interruption is unforeseen. Nadira studies the offender. His features are a carbon copy of the Greek gods, but his tribulations as a vampire have hardened his countenance into a guarded wariness, an arresting face but no longer handsome.

Shen leans toward Nadira and whispers, "Watch out. He is a fierce proponent for the old status quo of no comingling between species. He prefers we remain in the shadows, feeding on humans. Not a forward thinker, he clings to the old ways and believes that vampires have survived for centuries this way. Why change?"

Indignant, he cross examines Nadira. "Princess, do you really believe this is possible given the way humans have viewed us for centuries? Have you forgotten the Great Persecution that took the lives of thousands of vampires, including your husband?"

Nadira understands Quintus is opening the door for debate, but fortunately, she is prepared. "Yes, I do believe we can coexist. I did it for centuries. The humans who persecuted us are long dead, and the days of vampire hunters over. Who can blame humans for their fear? We have hunted them for food since the beginning."

"My point. They still are a major food source. How has that changed?" Councilman Quintus rebuts her statement and then leans back, satisfied with his argument.

Nadira glances at Amon, who nods. She drops her bombshell. "My pharmaceutical company has developed a synthetic blood that will sustain us and negate our reliance on humans for food."

Her last statement generates buzz among the council members. Quintus is stunned but conceals his reaction. Amon smiles at Nadira. Her answer is the prefect counter to Quintus's move.

Councilwoman Gudrun asks, "When will this product be available?"

"Our target date for market is one year." Her answer generates more mumbling among the occupants of the room.

"We have not had a female sovereign in over two thousand years. I, for one, think it's time we had another," Councilwoman Gudrun says, declaring her support, and nods at Nadira.

Quintus is not finished with Nadira. He makes an innocent-sounding statement. "Living among humans and suppressing your gifts must be difficult. You must have great control."

Nadira does not answer at first. She waits to see where his line of questioning is going.

He adds, "I have heard rumors of an altercation between you and another vampire. You and the sovereign's secretary could barely defend yourselves. If it had not been for your paramour, you would have been killed. How can you rule if you cannot defend your own person?" He leans back and smiles.

This new information stuns the council. They argue among themselves. Nadira and Amon glance at each other. Their traitor is exposed; no one knew about the incident in the tunnel except the five of them. The only other vampire was Coatl. Therefore, Quintus must have connections with Coatl. Amon's eyes narrow slightly as he answers Quintus.

"The princess has been training since she returned home. We will gladly provide a demonstration of her abilities if you wish," Amon offers.

Da Xia answers, "We would be very grateful, sire." He bows to Amon and Nadira.

Quintus is not finished. "What sort of disagreement did you have with your father?"

Nadira knows he is fishing for information. She must answer carefully. "He asked me to succeed him."

There is a collective gasp from the council members.

Quintus's eyes narrow. He can smell a secret. She is concealing something, and he will root it out. "You did not wish to succeed him?"

Amon's eyes caution her, and she answers flatly. "I am honored to succeed him. The nature of our disagreement was regarding the ceremony."

Quintus contemplates Nadira and strikes at the heart of the secret. "The ceremony. Was there a part of the ceremony you found difficult?"

Nadira weighs her answers and decides on the truth. "Yes, I will not consent to perform the final ritual."

Pandemonium breaks out, and the council members argue among themselves, each of them speaking over the other. Amon focuses on Nadira, who stares back, telepathically reassuring him she knows what she is doing. He acknowledges her decision. Genevieve and Shen are puzzled. They are not privy to the details of the secret ceremony.

Shen leans backward in his chair and asks Genevieve, "Do you know what ritual they mean?"

Genevieve shakes her head. "Not a clue."

They look at Nadira for clarification, but she remains poker-faced.

Amon raises a hand for quiet, but the council continues to squabble until he raps his gavel for silence. "Continue, Councilman Quintus," he orders.

Quintus enjoys the turmoil his question elicited and basks in the limelight. He opposes Amon and Nadira's views regarding humans and would like to derail Nadira's candidacy for the throne. He hones in on her answer like a dog on the scent of a bone. "Are you prepared to perform the ritual now?" he asks.

Nadira gazes at the occupants in the courtroom. She stares at Amon and replies, "No."

The courtroom explodes. Amon gazes at his daughter with love clearly written on his face. She deviated from his plan to lie about the final ritual. He studies the occupants of the courtroom. The council members haggle with each other. Quintus wears a self-satisfied grin. Genevieve and Shen look to anyone for an explanation. Only Nadira sits impassive amidst the turmoil.

"Silence!" Amon shouts. The room is instantly as silent as a tomb. He continues, "I have a question for my daughter. When the time comes, will you perform your duty as the rightful heir to the throne?"

A feeling of relief washes over her as he offers an escape from the box she trapped herself in. "Always," she answers softly.

The council contemplates her answer.

Councilman Menas is the first to address the members. "I call for a vote on the appointment of Princess Nadira Naram-Sin as heir apparent. All those in favor say 'Aye' and those opposed 'Nay.'" He starts by saying, "Aye."

One by one, ten council members proclaim, "Aye."

When only Quintus remains, he stands and says, "I withhold my support until after the demonstration."

Amon states, "Fair enough." He looks at Nadira and winks.

The demonstration site is an abandoned factory complex containing a five-story concrete building with an outer steel skeleton of catwalks, stairs, and mixing vats. Huge stacks of twisted metal dot the grounds. The council members loiter about, assessing their surroundings and glancing at each other quizzically.

Quintus inquires, "Why did you bring us here?"

Amon innocently smiles. "You asked for a demonstration."

The council members nervously glance at each other, unsure what kind of demonstration Amon has planned for them.

Councilmember Menas asks, "Here?"

Amon expansively stretches his arms. "The perfect place." He looks pointedly at Quintus. "This is the site of a recent Vigile raid capturing a young coven of traitors. Sadly, the leader was killed but not before revealing their maker's name."

Menas asks, "What is the name?"

Amon stares directly at Quintus, who recognizes the implied threat. "Coatl."

A collective rumble of disapproval runs through the council. Amon turns and nods to Nadira, indicating she should begin the demonstration.

Nadira faces the complex with her back to the council members. She raises her arms and commands, *"Casso!"*

The ground shakes, the buildings rock back and forth, and steel twists. The tremor continues for a minute until a loud explosion startles the council, followed by a cloud of dust and debris that pollutes the air. The audience members cover their ears and crouch down to protect themselves from flying shrapnel. The entire area is blanketed with dust, and dirt obscures their vision. Once the cloud dissipates, nothing remains of the complex except for a pile of rubble and melted metal. Picture framed by warped rebar, Nadira stands calmly in front of the demolished factory.

With a flamboyant flourish, Amon addresses the council. "Behold, the phoenix rising from the ashes." He adds scathingly, "Are there any more questions?"

CHAPTER XXVII

HASEEM IS LOST somewhere in the bowels of the underground tunnels. He originally went down to run an errand, got curious, and started to explore. The wall directories helped at first, but he turned down some unlisted tunnels. Now he cannot tell where he is. He admonishes himself—how stupid not to bring a map or cell phone. He turns around and retraces his steps. The faint sound of voices fills him with relief. He follows the voices until he comprehends some words. One word stops him in his tracks: Coatl.

The voices are distinct. "Lord Coatl wants these blueprints immediately."

The sound of footsteps echoes off the walls and makes it difficult to tell from which direction they originate. Haseem freezes and looks for somewhere to hide. The smooth walls offer no refuge. He leaps up and clings to the roof of the tunnel just as two vampires pass below him.

"Trust me, you don't want to keep him waiting. Especially if you want to remain in one piece."

The vampires pick up their pace and quickly move out of sight. Haseem drops to the ground, unsure how to proceed. The princess and Vigiles are searching for Coatl. He should report to them. On the other hand, maybe he could follow the vampires and find Coatl. Haseem chooses the latter.

He keeps well behind the vampires, following them by sound, creeping along, and clinging to the shadows. Their voices are muffled, and he sprints to catch up, turning at a tunnel intersection. He spots an arched opening in the rock wall, tiptoes toward it, and peers inside.

The doorway opens into a cavernous space outfitted with office and electronic equipment. There are a dozen or so vampires inside with headsets, working at the computers or desks. Others gather around a large conference table, their conversations masked by the noise of phones and machines. He sneaks closer to hear better and realizes this is Coatl's secret headquarters.

Coatl studies the blueprints spread out on the table. Councilman Quintus and Aleksei are on the opposite side of him.

"You cannot attack her outright. She is too powerful now. I was at the demonstration," Quintus pleads.

"How was the demonstration?" Coatl's lips curl into a twisted smirk.

"She leveled the complex in less than five minutes." Quintus's eyes widen as though he still can't believe it.

Coatl snarls, "Yes. It was the headquarters of my youngest coven. That Vigile bastard murdered their leader and captured the rest."

Quintus studies Coatl. It is always safer to tread lightly with him. "Why attack your coven?"

Coatl frowns at Quintus as if he is simpleminded. "To teach me a lesson, idiot!" He clenches his fists and then pounds the table. "Damn them!" Coatl curses.

Everyone in the room freezes, holding their breath and waiting for his next move. Coatl glances at his minions and smells their fear. He thinks, *Good. As long as they fear me more than Amon, I can control these morons.* He considers making an example of one of them. However, he needs every follower and can't spare one to kill. He sighs, disappointed.

Quintus nervously asks, "What will you do?"

"Good question," Coatl answers. Coatl ponders his response. *What will I do?* He smiles. "If I cannot attack the head, I will find her blind spot, strike it, and bring her to her knees."

Astonished by Coatl's brashness, Quintus adds, "My lord, you balance on a razor's edge. Make one mistake . . ." He stops speaking when he sees the expression on Coatl's face: a look of utter contempt. He freezes, realizing he crossed the line with his temperamental dictator.

"Do you lack the balls to complete the task?" Coatl studies Quintus.

"Of course I am with you," he says with mock sincerity. Quintus questions his decision to back this maniac. However, he knows better than to show any indecisiveness around Coatl and understands there is no honor among thieves. He asks, "What is your plan?"

"Operation Moonlight. A bit melodramatic, but appropriate." Coatl wears a perverted expression somewhere between pleasure and pain.

Aleksei chimes in. "We have hired mercenaries to carry out the mission. Lord Coatl must not appear to be involved." He points to various areas on the blue prints. "They will breach security here. Gain entrance at this point. Assassinate the target here."

"Who is the target?"

Quintus studies the blueprint. His eyes widen with astonishment and stares at Coatl, who grins back. Coatl begins to answer, but the conversation is interrupted by a scuffle at the doorway as two of his soldiers drag Haseem into the room.

"My lord, we captured this spy eavesdropping outside the door," one of the soldiers reports.

Coatl comes around the table. He inspects the prisoner. Haseem stands solemnly, head upright, and stares Coatl in the eye. Coatl smiles wickedly, thinking, *Good, a new toy to play with, tonight's entertainment.* He licks his lips. "What have we here? A vampire spy?" Coatl asks. Haseem does not answer but continues to stare at Coatl. Coatl drums his fingers on Haseem's face. "Who sent you?"

Haseem silently watches Coatl. Coatl glances around the room. Everyone stares at the intruder and then at Coatl. He grins, walks up to the prisoner, and backhands Haseem. "Speak, dog!" he barks.

Haseem staggers backward, struggles to stand upright, and then resumes studying Coatl. Haseem understands not to show weakness or fear in the face of cruelty, a lesson he learned early in life. Weakness fuels the flames of evil.

Coatl raises his hand to strike Haseem but hesitates. "You look familiar."

Councilman Quintus whispers, "He is Nadira's Abd."

Coatl's eyes light up. "I could not be this fortunate. The princess's personal servant."

Coatl ogles Haseem, barely containing his glee. He slides very close to his prisoner, leaning forward until he's only inches away from Haseem's face.

"What, nothing to say?" He cups his ear, but Haseem remains silent. "I can't hear you!" Haseem's calm demeanor annoys him. "Cat got your tongue?" The anticipated pleasure of torturing Nadira's servant thrills Coatl.

Haseem braces himself for the next blow, which splits his lip. Blood trickles down his chin, but he does not wipe it way. The prickling sensation of terror creeps into his subconscious, but he wrestles it down, reminding himself that this monster feeds on fear.

Coatl contemplates his prisoner and notices the look of pity on Haseem's face. He senses no fear, just resignation. It enrages Coatl that this servant, this nobody, shows him compassion and not respect. He attacks Haseem, grabs him by the neck, and savagely buries his fangs. Haseem struggles until his body goes limp. Coatl tears himself off his victim, dropping him to the floor. A smeared lipstick of blood paints his lips. The occupants of the room are mute witnesses, afraid lest Coatl unleash his wrath on them.

He orders his soldiers, "Take him to my playroom. I will loosen his tongue." He wipes his mouth with the back of his hand and then slowly licks his fingers. "Delicious."

The soldiers hoist Haseem to his feet and drag his sagging body toward the door. Haseem focuses on Coatl. A peaceful smile transforms his face. *"As-salamu alaykum."*

The color drains from Coatl's face. "Take him away."

"What did he say?" Quintus's eyes follow the prisoner.

"'Peace be with you.'"

Disgusted by Coatl's savagery and impulsiveness, Quintus suggests, "My lord, it may be prudent to show mercy and use him as a hostage."

Coatl's eyes smolder. No one is going to rob him of his pleasure. He will vent his hatred on Nadira's servant. "It may be prudent, but I have other plans for him. Mercy is not what I intend," Coatl snarls.

"But he is part of the princess's entourage." Quintus tries to reason with Coatl. "It is too soon to tip your hand. Better to wait."

Coatl slinks up to Quintus. He purposefully licks the last of the blood from his fingers and then runs his tongue over his lips. He rivets Quintus with a vicious look. "Let us understand one another. I am the master here. My word is law. There is no democracy, no debate, no vote. If you do not want to join Nadira's spy in my playroom, you will do as you are told." Coatl leers at him. "Do you understand?"

Quintus knows this is a do-or-die moment. He looks Coatl straight in the eye and replies, "I understand perfectly."

"Good boy," Coatl sneers, and Quintus wrestles down his anger at the barb. "Aleksei, I want Operation Moonlight ready in a fortnight. First, I have to prepare my wedding present for Nadira." Coatl sniggers. "Wedding present. A good pun."

He sweeps out of the room, accompanied by his guards. His Machiavellian laughter echoes down the tunnel.

Aleksei shakes his head, looks down at the blueprints, and remarks, "A fortnight. Who talks like that anymore?"

Quintus stretches out his hands on the blueprints, racking his brain for a way to escape this mad scheme. Coatl has him trapped. Quintus glances up at Aleksei and replies, "A vampire, that's who."

CHAPTER XXVIII

STRIPPED TO THE waist, Gregor and Drostan are practicing with long swords in the arena. They fight with powerful thrusts and skillful parries. Their movements are vampire-fast, muscles bulging with the exertion and torsos slick with sweat

"Fancy footwork. You're good. Where did you learn that move?" Gregor asks.

"My sword master. He taught me that a sword was used for good or evil depending on the hand that wields it." Drostan stops to catch his breath.

"May I?" Gregor indicates Drostan's sword.

Drostan passes it over. Engraved on the blade is part of the one hundred fifteenth Psalm: "Nothing for us, Lord, nothing for us but for the glory of thy name." Other than a leather wrapped grip, the weapon is austere with its lack of embellishment, as befitted a warrior monk. Gregor hefts the sword and swings it in a figure-eight pattern. It's a perfectly balanced weapon, obviously forded by a master bladesmith. He hands it back to its owner.

"My teacher wouldn't allow me to carry a blade until I mastered all the medieval martial arts. Fighting with a wooden sword got old fast. Once I earned my weapon, he forced me to carry it twenty-four hours a day until it became an extension of my arm. It saved my life many a time." Drostan strokes the blade. "It's a shame the gun has replaced it. Any idiot can fire a gun, but a sword is an elegant weapon. The craftsmanship of the bladesmith and the flexibility of the steel combined with the skill of the swordsman fuse together, creating a deadly poetry in motion." Drostan demonstrates this point with several fanciful sword techniques.

Gregor is impressed. "I hear you, brother. That's why the sword is so symbolic."

Drostan nods his agreement and studies his opponent. "Gregor, I never got a chance to properly thank you for protecting Genevieve."

"Damn Coatl, the perverted son of a bitch. I almost beat him to death."

"You should have finished him."

"Nadira asked me to stop. It's strange—all my rage vanished when she spoke."

"Lucky you. I still want to kill him. But Amon commands otherwise. You know, for the first time, I almost disobeyed my sovereign," Drostan replies.

"I don't understand why Amon tolerates him."

"He says Coatl has his uses. I don't know what they are except to stir up trouble. He went berserk after Amon announced Nadira as his successor," Drostan shares.

"Big surprise." Gregor's voice is laced with sarcasm.

"Our intelligence reports revealed his covens plan to disrupt your joining ceremony."

"Shit!"

"Don't worry, brother. I have it covered. The Vigiles will be stationed strategically. Any problems, we'll shut them down," Drostan reassures him.

"I'd hate for him to ruin our special day."

"I have a favor to ask," Drostan says.

"Anything, just ask."

"My duties as the commander have me spread thin. I don't have time to focus on the internal security of the Ordinatio. The recent breach in our defenses exposed our vulnerabilities. Would you consider taking on the role of director of security?"

"I will discuss it with Nadira, but I would be honored." Gregor smiles broadly. *Good, something useful to do.*

"Amon thought you might. He recommended that I speak to you."

Gregor shakes his head. "He is always moving me around like one of his chess pieces."

"Welcome to our world." Drostan slaps him good-naturedly on the back.

Gregor grins. "Now, show me what you can do with that blade, Sword Master."

"Gladly," Drostan answers.

They circle each other, each testing strategies and pushing their physical limits, both equals in strength and speed. They use the sword hilts for close-quarters combat.

Genevieve watches the match, enthralled by the combatants' prowess.

Nadira joins her sister on the sidelines. "Nice scenery," she comments.

"Princess." Genevieve giggles and curtsies.

Nadira wrinkles her nose in disdain. "All this bowing and the formal titles take some getting used to. I am the same Nadira." She frowns at Genevieve, whose lips twitch with mirth.

"Yes, Your Majesty."

Nadira rolls her eyes.

Genevieve asks, "What are you doing here?"

Nadira frowns. "Kashta requested a rematch."

"You *are* a glutton for punishment." Genevieve makes a face.

They watch the men spar, their powerful upper bodies glistening from the strain. Genevieve and Nadira are entranced by their significant others.

Genevieve sighs. "I never get tired of watching Drostan, especially without his shirt on."

"I feel the same about Gregor. The sight of his muscles does wicked things to me," Nadira adds wistfully.

Genevieve glances at Nadira. "You haven't broken that insane vow of chastity?"

Nadira shakes her head. "No, I have tried a few times, but Gregor is adamant. I guess he's waited so long that he wants our first time to be special."

"I respect your control. As for me, give me Drostan any time." Genevieve surveys the sparring men.

Nadira shrugs nonchalantly, covering up her growing frustration with the status of her sex life. They continue to watch the match until Jerry joins them.

"I have some urgent papers for you to sign, Princess."

"I see the classes on etiquette are producing fruit." Genevieve smiles and studies Jerry.

Jerry frowns and adds sarcastically, "I am a quick study. Ayame has me housebroken."

Genevieve raises her eyebrows. "A bit touchy, aren't we?'

Nadira signs the papers and then shoots Genevieve a disparaging look. Genevieve smiles coyly and returns to watching the match.

Gregor gets the advantage over Drostan, knocks him to the mat, and demands, "Do you give quarter?"

"Watch this." Genevieve smiles at Nadira.

Drostan clinches his teeth and answers, "Never." Drostan kicks Gregor off with super vampire strength, vaults high in the air, and lands on his feet. A sheepish grin crosses Drostan's face, the tip of his sword pointed at Gregor's chest.

Startled, Gregor looks down at the sword and laughs. "Okay, Superman. You win."

They slap each other on the back and clasp forearms.

Jerry exclaims, "Badass."

Nadira and Genevieve glance at Jerry, look at each other, and shake their heads.

"Whatever that means. I just know there is way too much testosterone in this room," Nadira says. They all laugh at the idea.

"Do you like martial arts?" Gregor asks Jerry.

"Yes."

The sight of Jerry aggravates Drostan, and he doesn't hide it well. The women's affinity for this human fuels his jealousy, which irritates him even more. The powerful military commander is embarrassed that he's envious of a human and takes out his angst on the hapless human.

He asks, "Ever done martial arts?"

Jerry replies, "I did a little fencing."

"How little?" Drostan asks condescendingly.

Jerry studies Drostan and realizes this vampire dislikes him but hasn't a clue why. He shoots Drostan a challenging look and answers, "I made it into the Olympic games."

Gregor whistles. "He's got you there, Drostan."

Drostan's animosity is not lost on the other vampires.

Genevieve smiles. "Touché. Is your blade as sharp as your tongue?"

The double meaning does not escape Jerry. He is an expert in the flirtation game. He gives her a smoldering look, turns on the charm, and answers her in a husky voice, "Both equally lethal." He dazzles her with a sexy smile.

Genevieve is enthralled. "I understand what Ayame sees in this human."

Drostan does not like the direction of this conversation. His temper is on a slow burn. "Are you flirting with my wife, human?"

"I believe I am, and my name is Jerry. Not human." Jerry's eyes narrow as he sizes up Drostan and decides to take a stand. This vampire could kill him, but it would be better to die a man than to be their mascot forever. He covers his fear with bravado and gives Drostan his most menacing stare, the same overconfident look a Chihuahua gives a Rottweiler.

Drostan, surprised by Jerry's reaction, decides to call his bluff and points his sword at Jerry's throat. "Don't flirt with my wife," Drostan warns and touches the point of the blade to Jerry's skin.

Slowly, Jerry deliberately pushes away the razor sharp blade and accidentally slices his palm. Blood trickles from the gash to the floor, a slow, steady drip that splashes on impact with the hard surface. Jerry skewers Drostan with a foul look and does not attempt to staunch the flow of blood. The air is perfumed with the tantalizing aroma of plasma. All the vampires experience the powerful draw of human hemoglobin. Drostan's eyes look like two ice chips, his jaw clinches, and his lips stretch over his fangs.

Without taking his eyes off Drostan, Jerry raises his palm to his lips and noisily sucks the wound. "Or what?" Jerry taunts.

The tension is unmistakable and the threat is raw, with Drostan clinching and unclenching his fists. Nadira watches the antagonists preparing to face off, weighs her options, and winks at Genevieve.

"Drostan," Genevieve purrs.

He glances at Genevieve. Beguiled by his beautiful wife, he forgets all about Jerry.

She slides over to him and plants a luscious kiss on his sweaty lips. Her sultry voice charms him. "My jealous husband. Don't you know no one can replace you? You own my heart and soul." His anger evaporates with her smile. Genevieve can take the starch out of any man or vampire.

"Shit. Kid, you have balls the size of melons, bleeding in a room full of vampires. A new vampire would be all over you like—what is the phrase—'white on rice.' See, I am learning this slang," Gregor teases.

He claps Jerry on the back, who jumps on contact, his nerves ragged. Jerry gambled that Drostan had enough control not to attack him. He looks at the vampires and realizes he passed some kind of test; bravery is another piece to the vampire puzzle. They respect courage above all.

Gregor changes the subject. "I haven't used a foil since my last duel. That was in the eighteenth century. I am rusty. Would you honor me with an assault?"

Nadira winks at Gregor.

"I would be glad to give you some pointers," Jerry answers, an innocent smile tacked to his face. The vampires laugh at his pun.

Gregor chuckles. "You hit the mark again, kid. Are you any good at darts?" The tension dissipates with Gregor's retort.

"Jerry, do you have the guest list for the ceremony?" Nadira asks.

"No, Haseem has it," Jerry answers.

"Have you seen Haseem? I wanted to give him some notes, but I can't seem to find him," Nadira asks.

"No. Now that you mention it, I haven't seen him for a while." The whereabouts of Nadira's servant is the furthest thing from Jerry's mind. He is just relieved he did not become the flavor of the day.

"No matter. He is probably preparing for Adrian's arrival. Gentleman, if you are done comparing who has the bigger dick, I have other matters to attend to."

Genevieve looks over at Kashta approaching the group. "Nadira, are you ready for your daily beating? Here comes Kashta."

Kashta joins the others, bows, and addresses Nadira. "Princess, are you ready for our match?"

They all stare up at him, each glad they are not in her shoes.

"Excuse me." She follows Kashta out to the central sparring arena.

"I don't think I can watch this." Genevieve looks worried.

Gregor inwardly smiles. "Stay. I think you may want to see this."

Puzzled, they stare at Gregor. He does appear concerned.

Genevieve adds, "I heard about her first match with him. He beat her unconscious. If you can stand to see your true love pummeled, who am I to say no to you!" She shoots him at hateful look.

Jerry watches his boss trail behind the giant. Jerry admits, "She looks so tiny compared to him."

News spreads rapidly regarding the competition between the heir and the Nubian giant. Large groups of vampires enter the arena to watch the match. Off-duty Vigiles wander in, curious to see how the next regent fairs with the "Colossus." Each remembers his defeat at the hands of Kashta.

Nadira and Kashta bow to each other.

Nadira calmly asks, "Would you like padding, Kashta?"

Kashta smiles at the snide remark. The combatants circle each other slowly. Kashta is the first to move. He charges Nadira and grabs her by the waist, flinging her into the air. She tucks her body into a tight somersault and flips backward over his head. Catlike, she lands on her feet behind him, hands on her hips, and taps him on the shoulder.

He glances over his shoulder, reaches backward, pins her arms, and hoists her over his head. Nadira counters by locking her legs around his neck and arching backward. This action has a lever effect on Kashta, who loses his balance and crashes to the floor.

Calmly, Nadira rolls off Kashta, wipes a bead of sweat from her cheek, stretches out her hand, and gestures for him to come to her. Kashta jumps up, pissed off that she dropped him so easily. His anger clouds his reason. He stomps over to her with no subtlety, just brute strength, and advances on his slight opponent. She runs toward him, slides on the floor between his legs, and punches upward. She delivers a crippling blow to his groin. He grabs his crotch and collapses to the floor. The crashing weight causes a tremor followed by a loud thud.

He cradles his aching groin, taking more than a few moments to regain his feet. The giant staggers upright, beads of sweat popping off his forehead, glares at his opponent, and moves cautiously toward her. She waits for him to come to her. Eyes locked on her, he advances in a circular motion until she runs to meet him. Their bodies clash together like two cymbals, a loud clap on impact. The combatants grapple until Kashta vise-grips her shoulders, pushing her backward. She digs in, her feet sliding across the floor, making an irritating fingernails-on-a-chalkboard noise, prompting some of the audience to cover their ears. It looks like he has the advantage and she is doomed.

However, she has one more trick up her sleeve. Her face distorts with a look of extreme concentration as she focuses on his chest. Instantly, Kashta flies across the arena, crashing through the far wall. Everyone looks from Nadira to the hole in the wall.

There is a stunned silence. Drostan and Gregor spring to action and run to the hole just as Kashta climbs through the gap.

He stops, scans the crowd, and glares at Nadira. Everyone waits quietly to see what will happen next. Will he crush her or tear her limb from limb? Face twisted with rage, he marches purposefully toward her, the stuff of nightmares, a huge terrifying monster coming for her. Nadira strides forward to meet her adversary. They face off in the middle arena. Kashta glares down at Nadira, who meets his gaze unflinchingly. A wide grin of pearly teeth stretches his scarred face. What he does next surprises everyone. He sinks to his knees and bows his head.

"Princess, you are ready," he announces.

"Ready for what, Kashta?" Stunned, she studies him.

"To be queen. I told you that one day you would defeat me. Today is that day. I have a boon to ask of you."

"You have but to ask." Nadira continues to peer at his bowed head.

He glances up at her. "I ask to become your bodyguard when you are our queen."

Everyone is staring at the drama unfolding in the center arena. She glimpses the speculative looks on the faces of her future subjects. She notices one beloved face watching her. Her fiancé winks. She focuses on Kashta's shiny head as he waits for his answer. What better bodyguard could she ask for?

She announces her decision. "I grant your boon. You shall be at my side when I take the crown."

He places his fist to his chest, salutes her, stands to his feet, and takes his place by her side. They make an odd pair: the Nubian giant and petite beauty.

Drostan exclaims, "If I hadn't seen it with my own eyes, I would never have believed it." His voice startles everyone from his or her reverie. Each vampire is unnerved by what they witnessed in the arena today. The princess defeated the Colossus.

Gregor is nonchalant. "You haven't seen the half of it."

CHAPTER XXIX

Nadira and Jerry lounge on the sectional in her quarters, papers scattered on the coffee table and over her lap. She thumbs through a sheaf in her hands.

"The event planners have everything under control. If you want any changes, just jot them down," he tells her.

"A vampire joining ceremony is very different than a human wedding," she informs him, scanning the list and scribbling some notes.

Curious, Jerry asks, "How so?"

"First, the participants are vampires." Nadira smiles.

Jerry chuckles. "Duh."

"Second, the attire." She grins.

"Attire? Is it optional?"

"You wish." Nadira laughs.

"Seriously, I noticed under vows it states the ceremony is in the ancient language. Which language?" Jerry asks.

Nadira looks up at him. "Our language."

Jerry's eyes widen. "I didn't know there was one."

She nods. "It's one of the oldest spoken languages."

"Every vampire can speak it?" he asks.

"Yes. During the transformation, the language is assimilated."

Jerry contemplates her answer.

Nadira glances at him and senses there is something on his mind. She puts down her papers and focuses on him. "How are your classes?"

"Illuminating. The history sessions have been an immense help. Now I understand the reluctance of some vampires to trust humans. Both species have been killing each other for centuries. I didn't realize the extent of the animosity."

Nadira enlightens him. "Vampires have hunted humans since our beginning. The tables turned during the Great Persecution, a dark and deadly period for vampires. Condemned by the church, thousands of vampires were burnt or beheaded. I lost my husband to the Inquisition." She stops talking, the painful memories etched on her face, takes a deep breath, and then continues, "The vampire hunter was sanctioned by the church or local authorities and pursued us relentlessly. Stoker's character Van Helsing was based on a particularly loathsome slayer. He became the scourge of our kind until Coatl found him."

Jerry interest is peaked by the mention of Coatl. "The same Coatl? I've heard rumors about him."

She warns him. "Stay away from Coatl. He is old school and views humans as a source of nutrition, nothing more. He regards you as no more than a walking McDonald's Happy Meal. Coatl hunted down many of the slayers, dispatching them in various gruesome ways. At the time, no one questioned his methods, just praised the results." Nadira grows quiet, lost in thought.

Forgotten for the moment, Jerry studies her. Her skin is so taut that her cheekbones protrude, her eyes recede into their sockets, and her lips form a slash of crimson. What was an arresting face has metamorphosed into an eerie mask. She looks very much the stereotypical vampire. It is the first time he has glimpsed her unguarded. The transformation frightens him. It is easy to forget these vibrant beautiful creatures are savage predators.

Jerry whispers, "Not all vampires perished."

Nadira gazes at him with a look that sends a shiver down his spine. "The old ones survived, but the young vampires were massacred. The resentment lingers for many vampires."

"Do you resent us?" he asks.

Her face relaxes. "I did for a long time. You see, vampires feel emotions intensely. It is hard for us to let things go. We hunted humans for a millennium, and eventually, mankind was bound to fight back. For a long time, I fed my hatred. Now I see both sides of the argument."

Jerry wonders what she means by feeding her hatred. "My knowledge of vampires was limited to fiction, pop culture, and movies. In New York, we lived in my world, familiar territory. Here my ignorance abounds." He jokes, "Keeping up with all the titles is mind-boggling. We have no aristocracy in America. I don't know the difference between a lord, a baron, a marquis, or whatever."

Nadira smiles. "Ours is a hierarchical society with a government that hinges on the cumulated wisdom of our elders, personal freedom, and equality among the sexes. A benevolent monarch rules our nation. We developed these guiding principles over centuries, keeping the best and tossing out the rest. The result is a system filled with checks and balances that protects us from disasters and provides for a fluid society. As for the myriad of titles, we retain our noble rank, and a coven may convey the status of lord on its leader, or a vampire can address a higher ranking vampire as 'lord.'"

"It makes my head spin. Ayame is a wealth of knowledge and cleared up many of my misconceptions. Because of her, I realize vampires and humans can coexist." His expression softens when he mentions Ayame.

Nadira notices the subtle change. She scrutinizes Jerry and asks, "How is Ayame?"

Jerry blushes when she catches him daydreaming about his lover. "I could try to cover up my feelings for her with some small talk or dodge your question, but I think honesty would be best." He answers without embellishment, "I love her."

Nadira is surprised. Jerry never lacked for female companionship, but they were causal, brief affairs. Female curiosity prompts her to ask, "Is it love or infatuation?"

"Ayame is different, not because she's a vampire but in spite of it. It's something more." He pauses, reflecting. "I've been with many beautiful women, but not one had the substance that Ayame possesses. I filled my life with causal sex, hollow conservations, and empty words between checking text messages. Ayame rarely speaks about the mundane; her words carry weight. She is a strong woman with a depth of emotion that I would gladly spend my life discovering. But I am a man. She is immortal. What future do we have?" His brow furrows.

"A happy one. Love is a rare and precious gift. Share a life together," Nadira tells him.

"Eighty years together that ends with beautiful Ayame pushing me in a wheelchair. She will resent me or just leave me, her love turned to pity or loathing," he spits out.

"Can't you live for the present and let the future take care of itself?"

"A short-sighted view, in my opinion. I do not want to be a brief interlude between centuries. Ayame said she had lost all taste for life. Her existence was without meaning, but together we are whole. I want to share eternity with her," Jerry tells her.

Humans are so predictable, Nadira thinks. She knows what's coming but asks any way. "What are you telling me?"

"I want to become a vampire." His face reflects his inner turmoil.

Nadira stares at her assistant. It was inevitable from the moment she brought him to the Ordinatio. In her secret heart, she wanted him to join her world. A pivotal part of her life, he fills it with laughter, and leaving him behind was more than she could bear. Not unlike her father, she manipulated events to bring him to this decision. Jerry's liaison with Ayame was an accident. That they fell in love is a happy consequence. She loved a human herself and cannot begrudge him the same joy.

"You cannot undo this transformation. Immorality has a price. Every human you know and love will die. Say goodbye to the sun for the first fifty to one hundred years. Death is a ruthless taskmaster—vampires are enslaved by the thirst for blood. Your main diet will be blood, either human or animal. The thirst is so powerful that you will kill anything to sate it. You will never father any children. The taking of life slowly erodes the last of your humanity."

Jerry bows his head and studies his hands, wrestling with his last vestiges of doubt, and she waits patiently for his decision. "I have no immediate family. My parents died in a plane crash. I do not look good with a tan. I won't have to kill anything because I'll use the blood bank." His response has a flippant hollow sound.

She thinks something else is missing from his declaration. "Have you discussed this with Ayame?" she asks.

"She is against it." His love's repugnance for his decision disturbed him.

"You both must agree about this choice," Nadira adds.

"If I want to proceed, would you do it? Ayame refused." Jerry's desperate eyes plead with Nadira.

Nadira answers, "The bond between a new vampire and his maker is very strong. Ayame refused because she did not want you to mistake this bond for love, the same reason I refuse."

Jerry looks crestfallen.

Her heart goes out to him. A hopeless romantic, she offers a solution for the star-crossed lovers. "If you both decide to move forward, we can ask Gregor. He would be an excellent mentor, and I don't think there will be any danger of you falling in love with him." She offers him an olive branch.

"Thank you." He did not know what to expect when he broached the subject and is relieved that he shared his plans with her.

A knock at the door interrupts them. One of the royal guards enters carrying a large gift-wrapped box. He bows and addresses Nadira. "Princess, a delivery for you."

Nadira points to the table. "Just put it on the table."

He nods and lays the package on the table. "Will there be anything else?" the guard asks.

"Thank you." Nadira shakes her head, and he exits the room.

Jerry stares at the package. "A wedding gift?"

"Unlike human weddings, vampires don't give gifts unless it is a memento of a shared personal experience or talent. We don't register at Tiffany's." Nadira appears uninterested, flipping through papers.

"Do you ever give gifts?" Jerry looks disappointed.

"We view personal possessions and wealth differently than humans. Living for centuries, vampires accumulate wealth, but the idea that the one with the most toys wins is nonsensical. Material possessions are transient at best. We value our intellect, relationships, and accomplishments. These are the things that transcend time." She pauses to scrutinize Jerry and points to a spectacular oil painting on the far wall. "A vampire painted it who apprenticed under da Vinci. We perfect our talents over centuries."

"No birthday presents." Jerry makes a face.

Nadira grins, amused at her assistant's avarice. "Occasionally, we will share a token of affection with another vampire. Something personal that speaks to the recipient." She turns her attention to her work, but Jerry fidgets and keeps glancing at the box. Nadira peeks up at him. "You are like a child. If you want to open it, go ahead."

Jerry leaps up and bounces over to the table.

Nadira shakes her head. "Humans are perpetually impatient," she remarks.

Jerry unties the large bow and opens the box. He pulls out a small card, rips it open with his thumb, and takes a minute to scan the inscription. "I don't understand," he mutters and scratches his head.

Nadira glances at him. "Don't understand what?"

"The message says, 'Your canary would not sing for me, so I took his heart.'" He lifts up an object for her to see. "There's a ring—" He cuts his sentence short because of the look on her face, which is devoid of all color.

Nadira realizes what is in the box. Everything moves in slow motion, the room spins, and time stands still. A sharp pain grips her heart, paralyzing her. She wants to hide, to run away, but it will not alter her new reality. On unsteady legs, she makes her way to Jerry. She takes the ring, closes her fist around it, and cradles it in her hand. She delays looking at the ring because once seen, it will confirm the painful truth. One finger at a time, she opens her fist and exposes a heavy gold ring with the initials *HH* inscribed on it. She recognizes the gift that she gave him in China. "Open the box."

Jerry is perplexed but opens the box. He wonders what has his boss so rattled. He lifts the lid, exposing the contents. They stare into the interior, their facial expressions very different, Jerry's registers shock and Nadira's resignation.

"What is . . . is that?" Jerry stutters.

"A heart. To be exact, Haseem's heart," she whispers.

Jerry drops the lid to the floor and looks away. Nadira's hands quiver as she picks up the lid and replaces it.

Jerry is pale. "Who would do this? He had no enemies."

Nadira runs her hand over the box, closes her fist over the ring, and levels an ice-cold stare at Jerry. "No, but I do. It was Coatl."

Jerry turns green, retches, and runs to the bathroom. The sound of him vomiting echoes in the silent room. Nadira walks to the window and stares out at the view, its beauty unseen, masked by the tears blinding her. Her universe shifts with his murder, ripped from her for no other reason than to inflict pain. She pushes the silent alarm.

Jean-Louis and two guards enter the room, and she points to the box. Jean-Louis lifts the lid, studies the contents, and then re-covers the box.

Nadira meets his eyes. "Haseem."

"We—we were friends," he stammers.

Nadira can't look at him lest she cry. She summons her courage and hands him the note.

He scans it and then gazes at Nadira. "Damn him to hell," Jean-Louis curses.

She glances away, folds inward, and fights to control her conflicting emotions. A teeter-totter of raw feelings rocks her, grief washes over her, and a flame of rage ignites her anger, but she cannot allow emotion to dictate her actions and must remain rational. She can grieve later. Alone. "I want the guards doubled on my father. Guards assigned to Genevieve, Gregor, and Jerry. The bodyguard will never leave Jerry unless he is in Ayame's quarters," she orders him.

Jean-Louis hesitates and glances at the box.

"What are you waiting for? Do it now! Every second counts!" Her commanding tone wills him to action, cracking and stinging like a whip.

He orders the guards in the room, "You, guard the human in the bathroom." He points to the remaining guards. "You and you, find and secure Secretary Genevieve and the baron." The soldiers salute and double-time it.

Drostan enters the room and glances at the soldiers running out the door. The expressions on their faces alert him to trouble. "You activated the security alarm?"

Nadira indicates the box.

Drostan picks up the card and reads it. "Coatl? What's in the box?"

"Haseem."

"You know the message has a hidden meaning. An enemy sends a dead bird as a warning," Drostan adds.

"Yes, of another death in the household. This is not the end. Only the beginning," Nadira replies.

"Where are the guards going?" Drostan asks.

"I sent them to Genevieve and Gregor. I have doubled the guards on Father."

Drostan ponders her answer. "Aren't you being hasty? I can protect my wife, and Gregor can protect himself."

Infuriated by Drostan's comment and the fact he is questioning her directive, she finds it unacceptable and decides to exert her authority. She walks over, picks up the box, carries it to Drostan, and shoves it under his nose. "Haseem would think otherwise. I should have acted sooner, been more cautious, then he might be alive. You have a short memory. Coatl attacked Genevieve and me. He grows too bold and mistakes our inaction for weakness. He is targeting my family. I will not lose another person I love. Your wife will have a bodyguard when she is not with you. *Do you understand?*" she shouts.

He notes the subtle change in the dynamics of their relationship. She is the commander, and he is her subordinate. He glares at her, but her stare is wilting. Her eyes indicate that she will brook no disobedience.

Jean-Louis watches the interplay between the two. Drostan is a strong leader, but Nadira is the ultimate power. He was with her when she cremated a whole town and unleashed her vengeance on her husband's executioners.

Nadira stares unflinchingly at Drostan. He never could dominate her, although he tried many times, which led to the breakup of their affair. She is the stronger vampire, and his pride could not tolerate it. She is his sovereign, and he pledged his obedience. His word is his oath, and he must obey without question.

"Forgive my impertinence, Princess." He bows his head, and his apology takes the sting out of his comment.

"Nerves are frayed and emotions are on edge, it is understandable. Your duty is to find Coatl. Do not kill him." She gives him a wan smile. "Yet."

Jean-Louis takes the box from Nadira. "I will remove this, Princess."

She shakes her head. "I want to save it for Adrian. He arrives tomorrow. We will have a private ceremony for Haseem."

"I will keep it safe." Jean-Louis removes the box.

Jerry emerges from the bathroom looking worse for wear. His bodyguard shadows him.

"Will you be all right?" she asks.

"No, but I'll recover. Why the guard?" Jerry asks.

"Coatl is attacking my family. You are my family. The guard will remain with you unless you are in Ayame's quarters."

Touched by her reference to her family, he is puzzled by her orders.

"Won't Ayame need protection if she is with me?" Jerry asks.

"She is one vampire who doesn't need protection," Drostan says.

Jerry looks to Nadira for clarification.

"Ayame is an assassin. She will protect you with her life." This information rocks him to his very core—his beautiful Ayame a professional killer, but it explains some things he did not understand.

"Becoming a vampire is not for the faint of heart. Still want to join the club?" Nadira watches his reaction and orders the guard, "Take him to his quarters."

Her strength has been sapped by the shock of Haseem's murder, Drostan's outburst, and Jerry's vulnerability. She feels disconnected standing in the midst of the room's occupants, their conversations muffled, and she no longer hears them. She focuses on the doorway, waiting for her knight to rescue her. Gregor strides in and scans the room. Their eyes meet, and her silent plea registers.

He turns to the others and commands, "Leave us."

Drostan, Jean-Louis, and the guards glance at him, bow, and leave the room, closing the door.

Gregor rushes to her. "Are you all right?"

She bursts into tears and slides into his embrace. Her tears stain his crisp white shirt red. She releases the floodgates of her grief. This pressure cooker of events since they arrived at the Ordinatio has taken its toll. She has rushed headlong into challenges, with little time to rest, relax, and recharge. Haseem's murder is the catalyst to an emotional purge.

Gregor picks her up, carries her to the sectional, and cradles her in his lap. His silence gives her time to squelch her inner chaos. Eventually, her sobs diminish to an occasional sniffle.

He lifts her chin and gazes into her distraught face. "Better?"

Comforted in his embrace, she lays her head on his chest and draws strength from him. Her voice empty, she says, "Haseem was special. The title of servant was long forgotten. He was my friend. We were bound together through mutual admiration."

A small sob escapes her control, and Gregor kisses the top of her head and tightens his embrace. She continues, "He had a quiet dignity, a unique vampire who never lost his humanity. He said that humanity separated us from the other predators. He never fed on humans, only animals. His compassion for others was boundless." She raises her face and stares at Gregor. "When I was in China, he nursed me back to health. If it not for Haseem and Amon, I would have perished. A senseless act of violence robbed us of his gentle presence. It is my fault that he is dead," she says.

Gregor takes her face in his hands. "You didn't murder Haseem—Coatl did. Do not waste your energy with guilt. Instead, redirect your anger into action against his murderer. If anything, I should have killed Coatl when I had a chance."

Nadira stares at Gregor's troubled expression. "You only stopped because I asked you to. Beloved, we cannot undo what has been done." Her head droops onto his chest.

"When was the last time you slept? We don't require much rest, but occasionally, we have to sleep," Gregor tells her.

"I don't remember."

Gregor carries her to the bedroom, lays her on the bed, goes in to the bathroom, and comes out with a washcloth. He sits beside her on the side of the bed and washes her face.

"Thank you." Grateful, she graces him with a wistful smile.

"You're welcome." He smiles back and pulls up a chair, placing it by the bed.

"I hoped to lure you to my bed," Nadira teases, offering a half-hearted attempt at flirtation.

"As ravishing as you are with that puffy red face, I'll try to resist. Let us keep our vow until our joining ceremony. Now sleep," he answers good-naturedly and holds her hand.

"Our ceremony is soon." Her eyelids heavy, she drifts off into the dreamless sleep of exhaustion.

Gregor leans back in the chair. He broods about poor Haseem's murder, cut up and put in a box as a warning. *Our extensive security failed him. No telling what else Coatl did to him. He deserved a better death.*

How in the hell can I protect her? he wonders. The magnitude of the task before him seems overwhelming, the dangerous pitfalls numerous, and the chance for success slim. Doubts flood his thoughts. It is a funny thing: the mind can complicate the simplest matter into a complex maze of what-ifs. However, his mind does not hold the answer, but his heart does. The key is love. Their love can conquer all obstacles. His love binds him to her, sitting at her bedside, watching over her until she wakes. He will always be there.

271

CHAPTER XXX

G REGOR ANSWERS GENEVIEVE'S soft rap on the apartment door.

"Remain here," she tells her bodyguard, who stations himself with other guards outside the door. She slides inside. "It looks like an armed camp."

"Nadira insists."

"I came as soon as I heard. How is she?" she asks, her voice subdued in an effort not to disturb her sister.

"Still sleeping."

Preoccupied, she walks to the sectional, sits down, and glances up at Gregor. She hates being the bearer of bad news. "I came to fill you in. Coatl has disappeared. No one seems to know his whereabouts. Drostan is directing an intensive search of the subterranean network for his headquarters, but that could take months, even years."

"I would expect no less," he replies.

She hesitates for a moment, unsure how to proceed with the remaining information.

Gregor sits down next to her and takes her hand in his. "Tell me the truth."

Surprised by his comment, she reveals, "They found Haseem's body. What was left of it." A lump forms in her throat. She'd rather forget what she overheard outside Amon's secret door to his study.

Drostan told Amon that the search team discovered some kind of dungeon. They found the remains of a human and Haseem. She cried when Drostan described Haseem's corpse. Amon remained silent during the whole report. His only statement was "Find him." She waited until Drostan left, slid open the study door, and stepped into the room. Amon's back was to her, standing by his glass display case and hefting the silver dragger. What happened next shocked her. He hurtled the dagger across the room, the throw so forceful that the blade imbedded to the hilt in the wall. "Damn him," Amon cursed. Involuntarily, she gasped. Amon spun around, his countenance so distorted, almost unrecognizable, with blazing red eyes. She had never witnessed her king's anger or rage until then. The sight terrified her. "Leave me!" he bellowed, his voice no longer calm and controlled but guttural and violent. She apologized, bowed, and backed out of the room, so afraid that her legs shook for a half an hour. Amon's wrath was a terrifying sight that she wishes to never to see again.

"Best spare her the details," Gregor says.

Startled, she realizes that he read her thoughts.

No one except Nadira knows that he is able to read minds since the episode on the mountain. He smiles and then asks, "What's next?"

"Coatl has been charged with murder and declared a criminal of the state. A warrant for his arrest has been issued. Drostan is gathering intel about his covens' locations. If anybody can find Coatl, Drostan will." Genevieve looks toward Nadira's closed bedroom door. "She was very close to Haseem. I gave Adrian the box with Haseem's heart and his body. He was despondent but requested a remembrance ceremony." She notices that Gregor looks distracted, continually staring out the window.

His eyes scan the darkness, focusing on something outside. He jumps to his feet. "Someone is outside."

She turns toward the window. It is dark, but her heart sinks when she sees movement. She joins him and gazes out the window.

The windows shatter, making a soft popping noise as shards pelt the room. Gregor turns his back and grabs Genevieve to protect her from the deadly slivers. Twenty-five black-clad assassins sail through the openings with grappling hooks and ropes. Stealthily, they land on their feet, assess the room, and pinpoint their targets, Gregor and Genevieve.

Genevieve is too stunned to move, but Gregor bolts into action and pushes her into the safety of the corner next to the fireplace. The assassins fan out, forming an offensive line between the front door and their victims. Gregor grabs the fireplace poker, welding it like a spear. The assassins are uncertain of their target's strength, but they outnumber him twenty-five to one. Confident that there is strength in numbers, they attack. Genevieve is not their main objective; they ignore her and swarm their primary target, Gregor.

Gregor roars ferociously, impales the first attacker, and slices the head off a second assassin, his blood slickens the wood floor.

Unprepared for the savagery of Gregor's defense, the assassins back off to reorganize. The front door crashes open, and four burly royal guards charge in and join the fray. The guards rally on Gregor and gather into a defensive circle, placing Genevieve in the middle. A guard tosses Gregor a knife, and they shout the Templar battle cry, "Beau Seant," and make their stand. Both sides face off, calculate the other's strength, and fiercely attack. All the vampires fight desperately. It is a life or death struggle for all.

One guard succumbs to an assassin's blade, slit from ear to ear, his blood spraying Genevieve. Gregor hacks at one of his attackers just as he feels the sting of a blade in his side. Blanketed with blood, he continues fighting, desperation spurring him on. If he falters, Genevieve is doomed and Nadira lies unprotected in the next room. Outnumbered, the defenders hold their ground, but the assassins are master killers and turn the tide.

The bedroom doors slide open, and Nadira, clad only in a nightgown, steps into the medley in her quarters. She spots Genevieve trembling in the corner and Gregor and the guards holding off the assassins. Gregor is bleeding from a myriad of wounds and staggers under the weight of numerous assailants, each stabbing him repeatedly.

She strides to the center of the room. Gregor sees her moving in his periphery and attempts to fling off his latest opponent. He wonders, *What is she doing?* The assassins spy the newcomer, regroup, and advance on a more important target, the heir. They surround her. She levels a piercing gaze at the assassins and communicates telepathically with Gregor, Genevieve, and the guards.

"Cover your eyes," her mind tells them.

They obey instantly. She cocks her head to the side and concentrates on the assassins. As she does so, her eyes turn white. A soft light emanates from her, its intensity increasing until a brilliant luminance radiates from her. The intruders cover their eyes and drop their weapons, but their retinas are already fried. Blinded, they stagger around, disoriented. The brilliance increases until nothing is visible in the room. The light's intensity scorches the assassins' skin and incinerates them. Suddenly, the light disappears and nothing remains of the would-be assassins but ashes.

Nadira rushes to Gregor's side and grasps his waist to support him. He sways, unsteady on his feet. Genevieve helps prop him up.

Nadira asks her, "Are you okay?"

Genevieve nods.

Drostan and Jean-Louis rush into the room followed by a heavily armed squad of Vigiles. They fan out, ready to engage the enemy, but find no intruders, just a floor coated with sticky slurry of blood and ashes.

Drostan strides to his wife.

"I am fine," she tells him.

"Help me get him to the bed," Nadira says.

Drostan flings Gregor over his shoulder and carries him to the bedroom. They lower him onto the bed.

Nadira sits down beside him. "Beloved, I must attend to the others. I will return in a moment," she says, and Gregor nods his understanding. She kisses his forehead.

Drostan takes Gregor's hand. "Once again, I have you to thank for my wife's life. This is becoming a habit."

Gregor smiles.

"Stay with him. No one enters without my permission," Nadira orders a Vigile, who takes his station at the door. Reassured Gregor is safe, Nadira leaves the bedroom with Drostan and Jean-Louis.

"How are the others?" she asks.

"We lost two good vampires. The others will recover," Drostan informs her. Genevieve runs to Drostan, who wraps her in the safety of his embrace. "Nadira, I must thank you for your foresight. If you had not assigned the extra guards, the outcome might have been different."

She nods and addresses the injured guards. "Thank you for protecting my family. I will not forget your bravery."

The guards beam with pride.

Nadira takes a minute to contemplate what just happened. She came close to losing both Gregor and her sister. She will not sacrifice another mate as she did with Cristo. This time, she will respond with any force necessary. Her inner resolve is mirrored with the hardening of her face, replacing her soft beauty with a powerful, unyielding presence.

She orders Drostan and Jean-Louis, "All security is to be equipped with side arms."

"Firearms are forbidden in the Ordinatio," Drostan reminds her.

"Not anymore. I want Coatl captured, his covens rounded up and imprisoned, and all vampires involved in this conspiracy charged."

Drostan studies Nadira. "If they resist?"

Nadira's face is devoid of emotion. "Kill them. Kill them all."

Drostan acknowledges her order with a nod.

Unsettled by her sister's orders, Genevieve asks, "What about your father's order not to harm him?"

Nadira impales her sister with caustic look. "Did you enjoy Coatl's bridal shower, or did I miss something? I'll handle my father." Her response is brusque.

Only Jean-Louis is not surprised. He remembers France, where he witnessed firsthand what the princess is capable of. Her supernatural powers are beyond his comprehension. She frightened him then, but this calm, controlled version is infinitely more dangerous. A cold chill grips him.

"Please excuse me. I must attend to my fiancé," Nadira tells them.

Her chilly announcement dismisses them all. They bow and back out of her quarters.

She returns to Gregor's bedside. "You may wait outside. No one is allowed entrance," she instructs the guard.

He salutes and leaves.

Gregor's eyes open when he hears her voice. "I thought I heard you." His cracked lips part in a crooked smile. His swollen eyelids lower to half-mast.

Her handsome knight is bruised and broken. She runs her fingers across his temple and down his bloody cheek.

"That feels good," he murmurs.

She goes to the bathroom, returns with a basin, and washes his face.

He struggles to pry open his eyes, and the effort furrows his brow. "You look different," he says.

She smiles, gently removes his shirt, and methodically continues to wash his wounds. She finishes and sits on the edge of the bed.

"Thank you," he says.

"You did the same for me." She gingerly touches his lip.

He moves his head to see her better and winces with pain. He contemplates the multifaceted woman he loves, soft and yielding one moment, then hard and inflexible the next. He is afraid to ask the extent of his injuries. It will be a week before he is able to move about with some semblance of normality.

She gazes into his bruised eyes. "Not too bad. You still have your limbs," she answers his unspoken question.

"It's fortunate that you can read my mind. It saves me from speaking."

She nods and raises her wrist to her lips.

His eyes widen, and he grabs her wrist. "Don't," he mumbles.

Puzzled, she stops. "My blood will hasten your recovery. Without it, your body will take days to rejuvenate."

"I can wait until our joining ceremony to mingle our blood and share our memories, but not before. When our bodies and blood are united, then we will be truly one." His bloodshot eyes plead with her.

"We will wait," Nadira concedes, and a satisfied smile limps across his face. Nadira lies next to him on the bed, gently lays her head on his chest, and holds his hand. "I cannot live without you, beloved," she whispers.

He has slipped into the bliss of unconsciousness and does not hear her. She listens to his heartbeat. A feeling of déjà vu sweeps over her to another time, another man, so many years ago. She has loved only twice, and she lost one husband to the law. She will do whatever it takes to protect Gregor, no matter the cost. History will not repeat itself.

Damn the law. Damn Coatl.

CHAPTER XXXI

*W*HAT A DISASTER, *the assassins failed to eliminate Gregor. How am I going to tell Lord Coatl?* Aleksei's mind races for a solution. *You never know how Coatl will react to bad news. He is so volatile.* If Aleksei could have found some lackey to deliver the news he would have. However, they are in a short supply now.

Our covens are scattered. Our supporters have fled the Ordinatio like rats fleeing a sinking ship. Our ship is not really sinking, just taking on a lot of water. I will plug all the holes and bail like crazy to keep afloat, he muses.

Aleksei smiles to himself, very pleased he planned for all scenarios. He worked out the kinks in his strategy long ago. His motto is "plan for the worst-case scenario." It is unfortunate that the assassins failed, but it is just a hiccup in the big picture. No plot ever goes as planned.

He implemented their Plan B strategy. The new headquarters will be ready by tomorrow. Logistics will be a nightmare because the place is in the middle of nowhere—very good for security but hard to supply.

The army of the Old Order is training in Mongolia. The generals are en route. In three months, the final delivery of weapons will arrive. Overall, things are going better than he planned, except for the Gregor fiasco. Luckily, the assassins were eliminated, which tied up any loose ends.

"The army of the Old Order" has a nice ring to it. Lord Coatl wanted a more flamboyant moniker, but Aleksei suggested a compromise to appease their more conservative supporters. It's a challenge dealing with his master, a regular Dr. Jekyll and Mr. Hyde who will kill someone one minute and be their friend the next. Alekesi likes the roller coaster ride. Before Coatl, he was a low-level strategist, drowning in the basement level of bureaucracy.

The sound of approaching footsteps catches his attention. He steels himself for the inevitable choleric display, plasters a fake smile on his face, and attempts to control his nervous tics.

He hopes that Coatl has Beydaan with him. She can usually take the sting out of him, and less people die when she is around. Awkward and unattractive, Aleksei is more comfortable dealing with statistics than women, and beautiful ones might as well be aliens from another planet. His usual nervousness disappears around Beydaan. She treats him with respect and values his opinion. He knows she belongs to his master, but he still harbors a secret crush.

Coatl makes his entrance with his paramour draped on his arm.

Aleksei addresses them. "Good evening, my lord." He bows. "Beydaan," he says, and she nods. He does not meet Coatl's gaze, but his eyebrows twitch sporadically.

Coatl studies his advisor—that dancing eyebrow is not a good sign. "What is wrong?" Coatl demands.

Aleksei stalls, and decides to start with the good news. "Recruitment is up for our army. You were right: targeting young humans was the answer. They flock to our cause. It seems being a vampire is badassical." Alekesi grins.

Coatl is confused and looks to Beydaan for clarification.

"Highly exciting. Excellent," she translates.

Coatl nods and then studies his advisor. "Stop procrastinating, Aleksei!" Coatl skewers him with a terrifying look. "You don't want to end up like Renfield, do you?" Coatl asks.

The tone in Coatl's voice makes his skin crawl. He swallows hard. "My lord, the assassins failed."

He drops to his knees and bows his head in a position of subservience, afraid to look his master in the eye. There is dead silence. It is so quiet that Alekesi can hear his own breathing and feel the sweat beading on his upper lip.

Coatl says in a cold, controlled voice, "Tell me."

Beydaan watches Coatl, sensing his rage is barely contained. This is when he is the most exciting and dangerous. He glares down at Alekesi, who cowers pitifully under his scrutiny.

"Master, the plot was executed as planned. Success was within our grasp, but Nadira was in the next room. She interrupted the assassins and destroyed them." Alekesi speaks so fast that he is breathless.

Beydaan stares at Coatl, dumbfounded. "You ordered an assassination on Princess Nadira's consort? Are you insane?" She shakes her head. "There are limits to what even you can do, Coatl."

Alekesi peeks up and then immediately stares at the floor. Coatl's face is distorted, with black eyes bulging and lips twisted over his fangs. His dark face is tattooed with blood where his fangs punctured his lips. His rage bubbles below the surface, about to erupt. Someone is destined to die, but the only ones in the room are Alekesi and Beydaan.

Coatl demanded Gregor's life, payback for the humiliating beating Nadira's fiancé gave him. No vampire has ever bested Coatl in a fight—Gregor beat him senseless. He told no one the truth about the tunnel. Instead, he slunk away like a wounded animal, licked his wounds, and resurfaced when he was recovered.

All his carefully laid plans have gone astray, and someone must pay for this blunder. He sizes up his advisor and Beydaan. Alekesi is necessary for his success, but losing Beydaan stings his heart. Torn between his head and heart, it is a unique position for Coatl, who does not think with either. His reactions are impulsive, with no thought for the consequences.

Beydaan sees Coatl's rabid look and knows what to expect. She knew her relationship with Coatl would end badly. In her profession, a violent death is the norm. Her fate is in Coatl's hands, but poor Alekesi's is in hers. Coatl and Beydaan stare at one another, a test of wills. The sooner he does it, the better. She licks her lips, her eyes glittering and challenging him. If he will not make the first move, she will, so she slaps his face.

"Coward." Her voice is a ragged blade severing his madness.

His rage overpowers him. He grabs her, bares her neck, and plunges his fangs into her carotid. The sacrificial offering, she surrenders herself to his wrath.

Alekesi glances up and sees Coatl draining Beydaan. Blood streams down her neck. Her eyes roll back, her pupils disappear into their sockets, and a sad moan escapes her lips. Tears fill Alekesi's eyes, spilling down his cheeks and flooding his nose. He sobs audibly, relieved that his master did not kill him but terrified for Beydaan. If he were not such a coward, he would save her.

Alekesi's blubbering pierces Coatl's fury, dragging him back to reality. Beydaan is near death. He withdraws his fangs and clutches her in his arms, her body limp and almost lifeless. He raises his head, his mouth awash in blood, and roars like a lion.

"Damn you, Nadira," he curses.

He releases the last of his anger, the power of it shattering the glass bar into pieces and peppering the room with shards. Alekesi ducks into a fetal position to protect himself from harm. Coatl's rage dissipates, allowing him to contemplate his lover's fate. Her heartbeat is so faint that even he can barely hear it. He must turn her or she will die. He eyes Alekesi sniveling and shaking on the floor.

Coatl barks at Alekesi, who visibly jumps at the sound of his voice. "Look at me!" Coatl orders.

Alekesi peeks up at Coatl. The creature hovering over him is not Coatl but the stuff of horror movies. Like the engravings in Dante's *Inferno*, Coatl has transformed himself into the image of Satan, bat wings and all. Alekesi cannot control his shaking and curls into a ball as small as possible. "Yes, master," he croaks.

Coatl commands, "You will stay here. I must attend to Beydaan." Coatl eyes his advisor and sniffs the air, a pungent odor assaulting his nostrils. Alekesi has soiled himself. He smirks. "You may clean yourself, but do not leave the room. Do you understand?" he growls.

"Yes, master." Alekesi continues to hug the floor, too terrified to move.

Coatl hoists her over his shoulder and carries her to the bedroom. He kicks the door shut, dumps her on the bed, and then sits down next to her.

Beydaan's eyes flutter open.

"You're dying. I got carried away," he blurts out.

"Bastard." Even in her weakened state, her spirit is indomitable.

"If you wish to live, you must become a vampire." He glances into her eyes, which defiantly stare back at him.

"Do it," she mumbles.

"Hear it all. Your human body will die and metamorphose into a vampire. This is a painful process," he tells her.

"How bad?" she asks.

"Like a son of a bitch." He smiles.

"Figures."

"That's my girl," Coatl adds. He whips off his shirt and eases back on the bed. He licks the marks on her neck and then slowly penetrates the wounds again. She gasps, and he drains the dregs of her blood. He withdraws his canines, kneels beside her, rakes his fingernail across his chest, and opens a vessel. Blood trickles down his torso. He lifts Beydaan's inert body, placing her mouth on his chest, like a mother suckling her child. "Drink!" he commands her.

Her first attempts are feeble, her lips moving against his flesh, sending a delicious sensation through him. He enfolds her in his arms, holding her tight against his chest. Her eyes fly open when the taste of his blood explodes in her mouth. Her lips and tongue explore the gash, lapping up the life-sustaining liquid. A low moan emanates from Coatl, and his arms constrict around her as her arms encircle his neck. They rock back and forth, her tongue tracing circles on his bare flesh, creating a powerful suction. His eyes flutter shut as his face contorts in ecstasy. She devours him, ravenous for the taste of blood; the sweet pleasure of it is unbearable.

Coatl can stand no more, breaks free, and pushes her away. "Enough!" he shouts.

She falls onto the bed, and her back arches and thrashes about in the throes of a seizure. Only the whites of her eyes are visible, her face monstrous. Wave after wave of convulsions beat her senseless, releasing her body from its human confines.

Coatl climbs out of bed and slowly buttons his shirt, watching her tormented flailing. He brushes a lock of hair from her forehead, and a masochistic smile twists his lips. "I told you it would hurt," he says.

A subdued Alekesi waits patiently on the sofa. Coatl admonishes himself for losing control, especially in front of his advisor. Instilling fear in his subordinates is one thing, but terror is another. Humans do not perform well if they are terrified, and Alekesi is scared senseless. Coatl must handle him carefully.

"Alekesi," he whispers.

Alekesi jumps like a frightened horse.

Coatl speaks softly, gentling him. "Thank you for waiting for me."

Alekesi asks meekly, "Will Beydaan be all right?"

Coatl is taken aback by his advisor's concern for his prostitute. Human compassion, he will never understand it. He contemplates his faithful Alekesi, who has rescued him from more than one plunder, and decides not to toy with him.

"Beydaan is fine, just resting." Coatl waits for him to relax and then continues, "I need to ask a favor."

Alekesi eyes him suspiciously.

"Will you to take Beydaan to my safe house? After the botched assassination, they will be looking for us."

"I have implemented Plan B. The headquarters will be up and running by tomorrow," Alekesi informs him.

"Good. You did well, Alekesi. I must remain behind," Coatl praises him.

"Master, it is not prudent. Drostan and the Vigiles are searching for you."

Gregor is still alive and leaves him no choice but to pursue his other option. Coatl asks, "Will you take Beydaan?"

Alekesi answers, "Yes, of course. But I advise against this course of action."

"There is something that I must do," Coatl says.

Alekesi waits for Coatl to enlighten him, but he doesn't elaborate. Instead, Coatl stares into space, lost in thought.

"Let me inform Beydaan," Coatl says. Coatl leaves Alekesi and returns to the bedroom. Stretched across the bed, she shows no evidence of her prior physical agony. All that remains is a breathtakingly exotic vampire. He slides onto the bed, leans back on his elbow, and studies her. She fixes him with a baleful stare and slaps him across the face. He grabs her hand and kisses it. "Is this foreplay?" he teases.

Lightning fast, she pins him down, straddles him, glares down, and exposes her fangs.

He laughs. "The alley cat has become a tiger." His eyes glitter with pleasure. Rapidly, he flips her over and pins her down. "No time to play. You leave with Alekesi tonight." He gives her a rough kiss, but she shakes him loose.

"You aren't coming?" she asks.

"I will join you later. There is one last thing I must do. Let's rustle something up to dine on. We don't want you eating Alekesi," Coatl tells her.

The evidence of her transmutation peeks beneath her sultry, smiling lips.

CHAPTER XXXII

Beydaan watches Coatl in the Mercedes's rearview mirror. He stares out the car's back window, occasionally glancing up at her. She focuses on the twisting mountain road illuminated by the car's headlights. Twilight escapes, and darkness spreads its blanket of shadows across the mountains. Darkness is her reality for the next fifty or so years. Damn Coatl. He robs her of human life, strips away the sun's rejuvenating warmth, and leads her down an unfamiliar path—a journey not unlike tonight, where her destination is uncertain.

"Where are we going?" she asks.

"I told you," he replies.

She peers at his reflection in the rearview mirror. The moody son of a bitch wants to play games. *It worked when I was a human but not now.*

"No, you didn't. You owe me an explanation. I am not some silly toy for you to play with. Not anymore," she snaps.

"I said I was sorry," he snarls.

"'Sorry' is used for a spilt drink. It doesn't cover killing me."
Her voice is a lash, whipping his meager conscience.

"I warn you. Let it go, Beydaan. Or else." His veiled threat
is not lost on her.

"Or what? You'll kill me? Too late," she whips back.

They glare at each other.

"Watch the road!" Coatl shouts.

Beydaan glances at the road, jerks the steering wheel, and
swerves to avoid hitting a person. She pounds the brakes, and the
car fishtails and comes to a screeching halt further up the asphalt.
Luckily, this lonely stretch of forest road is empty. She glances
backward and realizes she barely missed flattening a hitchhiker.

A college-age kid lugging a huge backpack runs up to the
car. He pokes his head in the window, a concerned expression
riveted to his attractive face. "Damn, you almost hit me."

"Are you hurt?" Coatl asks. His voice is oily sweet.

Beydaan eyes the hitchhiker apprehensively.

Relief floods his face, and he flashes a genuine smile. "I thought
I was a goner for a minute," he jokes, glad to be alive. His pearly
whites shine in the cabin light. He takes a minute to scan the
occupants of the vehicle and cannot believe his luck when he
spies Beydaan, but the guy in the backseat gives him the creeps.

"What are you doing walking in the road this time of
night?" she asks.

"I'm hitching across Europe after college break. I didn't
realize how deserted this highway is and got caught after dark,"
he replies.

"Let us give you a lift. It's the least we can do after almost
running you over," Coatl offers.

Beydaan eyes Coatl suspiciously. He never goes out of his way to help anyone.

The hitchhiker is not convinced but gives Beydaan the once over. He is out of options, and a ride with a beautiful woman in a Mercedes is a perfect ending to a lonely day. "Sure, if you could drop me at the next village, that'd be great." He jogs to the other side of the car, opens the back door, and plops his backpack on the seat beside Coatl. He slams the door and joins Beydaan in the front. He flashes a brilliant smile at her. Coatl haughtily glances from the backpack to the hitchhiker, the embryo of a smile lifting his lips. Beydaan adjusts the rearview mirror and catches Coatl staring at her and then studying the hitchhiker with that rabid vampire look she has come to know so well. She wonders what he is planning in that twisted noodle of his.

"What's your name?" she asks.

"Sam," the hitchhiker answers.

"I'm Beydaan, and the silent fellow in the back is Coatl," she introduces them.

"Yes, let's all be friends," Coatl adds sardonically.

Beydaan shoots him a nasty look in the rearview mirror. "Where are you headed?" she asks.

"No place. Checking out the scenery. I have to be back in Paris in a couple of weeks," he replies.

"Family?" Beydaan asks.

"No family. A girl I met at school," he answers.

"A girlfriend?" she guesses.

"No, but I was hoping she would like the title." They both laugh.

Beydaan glances at the rearview mirror. Coatl's eyes are as hard as obsidian. Without warning, he grabs Sam's shoulders and jerks him across the top of the seat into the back. Sam's flailing feet pummel the windshield, cracking the glass and spiderwebbing it. They knock Beydaan's hands off the steering wheel, causing the car to swerve precariously close to the edge of the road. She struggles to regain control, hits the brakes, and sends the car spinning onto the shoulder. Sam and Coatl struggle in the backseat. The kid lands some brutal blows before Coatl latches onto his neck. Beydaan flings open the car door, bolts to Coatl's side of the car, and jerks open the rear door. Coatl releases Sam's neck, and the kid drops like a lead weight, leaving Coatl, the rear seats, and windows blood-splattered.

"What the hell are you doing?" she demands.

"Securing your dinner," Coatl answers, offering a toothy grin, blood dripping from his fangs. He grabs Sam's arm, offering him to Beydaan, and she stares at Coatl, flabbergasted. A moan escapes from Sam. "He is quite tasty," Coatl boasts.

The sight of so much human plasma overwhelms the new vampire. Her bloodlust wanes, quickly replaced by disgust over Coatl's brutality and amazement at his lack of discretion.

Coatl mistakes her blank stare for inexperience. "Here, I will show you how," he says. He grasps Sam's neck and rips open his carotid. Blood sprays them both crimson.

Beydaan covers her mouth, runs to the side of the road, drops to her knees, and retches. Her empty stomach rebels, but with nothing to expel, her dry heaves subside. Eventually, she is able to stand up.

Coatl drops his victim and strides to her. "You are overwrought. Come, you must finish him," he says.

"Is this your idea of teaching me to be a vampire?" she asks.

He grabs her arm and pulls her toward the backseat slaughterhouse.

"No." She jerks her arm free.

"You must. You are a vampire. This is how it's done," he tells her.

"I will not." She glares at him.

"Yes, you will." He slaps her face but realizes too late that he pushed her too far. Her eyes are hooded slits and her fangs bared, the look of a predator ready to defend itself. She rakes his face with her nails, opening four parallel gashes on his cheek that ooze blood. They glare at each other in a standoff. "You don't own me. You took my life. Our contract is null and void."

"What life? The life of a whore?" he asks.

"It was my life to give or keep, not yours to take."

"But I gave you so much more. Immortality. Powers you have yet to explore. A fair trade, I think," he says.

"You must be joking. Our relationship has never been about fairness. You bought me and manipulated me with sex and death. No more," she tells him.

"What do you mean?" Coatl asks.

"You control me no more."

"I can kill you," he threatens.

"We both know you won't. From now on, I decide my destiny."

"Are you leaving me?" Coatl asks, his voice strained and uncertain, so atypical for him. A shadow creeps into his eyes, an expression on his face she has never seen before.

She studies her maker. Her puzzlement gives way to an epiphany. "You love me." She hazards a guess.

"Love I do not remember, but with you, I have peace and a vague recollection of happiness. My inner voices are silenced when you are beside me. You accept me as I am," he explains. The confession confuses and unsettles Coatl. It is easier to hate than love and destroy rather than create. A vampire of profound extremes, he wrestles with the simple concepts of joy and affection.

Beydaan ponders his revelation. She does not love him but is bound to him, her maker and lover. Her sexual appetites threatened to consume her until he extinguished the fire. "I will stay with you but on my terms," she tells him.

"Terms?"

"Sexually, we are well matched, but outside the bedroom, we are very different people. I will not become a murderer to please you," she says.

"You are a vampire. Blood is essential to your survival."

"I understand, but I won't kill humans," she tells him.

"Feeding on animals is degrading. You might as well be a dog."

"Maybe so. But I don't have to commit murder to share human blood."

"Bottled blood is an abomination!" Coatl spits out.

"It is this or nothing."

"When I am king, these choices will be outlawed."

"Then it is good you are not king. Nadira is heir. Give up your pipe dream. We can build a life on our rocky foundation," she offers.

"You do not understand me at all. I am sick of hearing about Amon the great vampire king. Nadira has no claim to the throne. I will be king. You will be my queen," he tells her.

"I have no desire to be queen. These ideas drive you insane and push you to violence. The consequences of failure are catastrophic. Give up this madness," she pleads.

"Never. It is my destiny to be king." His frustration pushes him over the edge of reason. He knocks her down, strides to the car, reaches inside, and tosses Sam into the brush. He slides into the driver's seat, grips the wheel, and shouts, "You will see! I will be king!" He stomps on the gas. The tires spin, kicking up clumps of sod, and the car launches forward into the darkness, abandoning her in the middle of a deserted mountain road with a corpse at her feet.

She stares at the car's taillights vanishing down the road and wonders what it says about her that someone so messed up loves her, but no answer comes to mind. She peers down at the hitchhiker, and matters that are more practical prevail. She kneels down, feels for Sam's pulse, finds none, and rifles through his backpack. She finds his cell phone and scans its contents for more information; it is packed with selfies of its owner and a pretty redhead—kissing, carefree, and happy. In his backpack, she finds his wallet, books, and a small box. His nondescript wallet houses a student ID, a driver's license, and a folded scrap of paper tucked away in a tiny compartment. She pulls it out. It is a note with a simple love poem scribbled on it. She opens the small box, and it contains an Irish Claddagh ring, the kind you give a sweetheart. She sits down beside Sam's body, her intense emotions suffocating her.

So, this is the thrill of the hunt and the pleasure of killing that Coatl raves about. Her heart contracts with pain. She can add "murderer" to the list of her other sins. A drop of water mars the scrap of paper, smearing the ink, followed by another, staining the paper pink. She touches her eyes and peers at her fingers tinged with blood: vampire tears. Cramming his things in the backpack, she tosses it over her shoulder, gingerly lifts Sam in her arms, and carries him into the woods. She wanders deep into the forest until she finds an isolated glen of tall trees with a beautiful view. Then, she lays him down, drops the backpack, brushes off the carpet of leaves, and scrapes the hard soil with her bare hands. She digs a shallow grave until her fingernails break and her fingers are raw and bleeding.

Once the hole is deep enough, she gently lowers Sam in it. She pulls out his cell phone, smashes it with a rock, and drops it and the backpack into the grave. She retrieves his love poem and the ring. She unfolds the poem, puts it over his heart, and places the ring on his pinkie. She pushes the loose dirt into the grave, her broken fingers plastered with mud and blood, evidence of her villainy.

She studies her handiwork and glances up at the full moon, her beautiful face tormented with sadness and streaked with tears and grime. The opal orb's glow illuminates the proof of her crime. This is a vampire's life: death and regret. *Forever is going to be a very long time.*

CHAPTER XXXIII

Distracted, Nadira drums her fingers on the chessboard. With two days until the joining ceremony, she has the attention span of a gnat. Normally, she enjoys the mental sparring with Amon. Chess games are their special time, debating philosophy or sharing confidences, but not today.

He makes his move. "Knight to G7."

Nadira frowns; his move is aggressive and blocks her escape. She ponders the board.

"What is the latest on Coatl?" he asks.

Nadira stares at the board, picks up the knight, and fingers the smooth ivory. Carved to resemble a medieval crusader, the ivory has aged to a golden patina—a pretty figure but not the right move. She advances her queen. "Queen to D8." She grins, knowing she has limited his possible countermoves. "Drostan found Coatl's secret headquarters, but it was abandoned, hidden deep in the labyrinth of tunnels. His covens are scattered. It looks like he has been planning this for some time."

Amon concentrates on the chessboard. "Go on."

She adds, "Gregor is questioning the followers who didn't escape."

He peers at Nadira. "Is he up to the task?"

"He is almost fully recovered," she lies.

Gregor is not yet one hundred percent. His body healed rapidly, but his psyche remains bruised. The sting of the assassins' blades was nothing compared to the insult to his pride. He continues to berate himself for being caught off guard, frequently brooding alone at their secret place on the rooftop. Her reassurances, her support, and the task of interrogating the prisoners lessened his angst. She remembers holding his hand the night of the attack. A smile lifts the corners of her lips at Gregor's bravery.

Amon peers at his daughter, who radiates a joy he has not seen in centuries. "The joining ceremony draws near." He slides his chess piece forward. "King to F6." He offers this advice, "The threat is stronger than the execution."

Damn, he caught me daydreaming. She stares at Amon. "Are we discussing chess or Coatl?"

Amon is impressed she understood his meaning. He hesitates before answering for added impact. "They are one in the same," he replies.

Nadira looks up from the board to Amon. *He never ceases to amaze me with his insight. He must have anticipated a possible assassination attempt.* Another piece of his strategy becomes clear to her.

He mentions nonchalantly, "I am interviewing someone myself later."

"Father, why bother yourself? Gregor can handle the interrogations."

"Thank you, Daughter, but this interview requires my specials skills." He guards his thoughts; she mustn't uncover his secret, not yet.

"You are not being forthright. Your mind is closed to me." She wonders what he is hiding and then moves her knight. "Knight to F6," she says, tickled with herself—she has him trapped.

"You have not been totally frank. Drostan told me of your order to kill any of the conspirators if they resisted. You know my wishes regarding Coatl, yet you disobey me," he admonishes her. She is stubborn and not an easy hand to manipulate, so his voice is accusatorial, a useful ploy to coerce her rebuttal. He must force her to choose.

Nadira does not flinch but instead glares at him. "During the council interview, you asked if I would do the right thing for our people. Yes, Father, I will. Even if it means disobeying you." She pauses, trying to read him, but his face is a mask and his mind a sealed vault. Without any paternal direction, she forges ahead. "Coatl murdered Haseem. He has slaughtered vampires and humans indiscriminately. These crimes are punishable by death. He flaunts our laws and encourages others to do the same. His influence is corrupting. The right thing is to protect my family and my people. I will show him no quarter," she says.

Amon contemplates his daughter. "If I ask for mercy?"

The two stare at each other across the chessboard, a battle of wills with only one winner. She knows this is another test, but this time, she must follow her head rather than her heart. Although painful, she severs the emotional umbilical cord to her father. "No. I cannot allow my love for you to override what is best for my people."

"Be careful you do not allow destructive emotions to rule your life. Rage, hatred, greed, and jealousy are insidious but powerful and pave a path of destruction. Remember your lessons after France," he tells her.

Amon has a faraway look in his eyes. She realizes he is talking about someone else and wonders who, but she respects his privacy and does not ask. She fails to see his next move.

"Bishop to E7. Checkmate," Amon says.

She stares incredulously at the board and glares at Amon. "You defeated me in twenty-three moves!" she exclaims.

"Yes. You were distracted. I saw the advantage and took it." He waits for her response, but her silence prompts him to add, "This is just a game of chess, but life is the true contest. The stakes are too high to fall to chance. As sovereign, you cannot afford to be distracted or you will fail. If you err, all is lost."

She picks up the bishop and examines it: the piece is carved out of ebony, aged over centuries. The wood is strong and almost indestructible. She appreciates the similarities between her father and the chess piece. "You defeated me on purpose?" Nadira asks.

"To expose how easily you can be outmaneuvered. In any game, in order to play, you must make a move. Regimes are no different. Your regime will be birthed in blood. You must be prepared to spill it. Remember, every new life begins with blood and pain—with us and humans."

A chill runs down her spine. She searches his face for any clues to his prophesy. The familiar face has lost its tranquility, replaced with an impregnable stillness. His eyes are black bottomless portals to another dimension, a thin veil separating the present from the future. She drags her gaze away, fearful lest she be swept into the vortex. A knock at the door interrupts them.

Amon answers, "Enter."

Councilman Quintus enters the room, escorted by two Vigiles. His eyes are downcast, and his manacled hands shake. Nadira glances from him to Amon, whose face is impassive. Puzzled, she waits for Amon to explain, but he answers with silence. Amon takes her arm and casually escorts her to the door. She peers at him, bewildered and unsure if she should stay or go.

"Thank you for coming, Daughter. The councilman and I have important matters to discuss," Amon tells her.

"Father?" Nadira implores.

He caresses her face and strokes her hair. "Daughter, everything is as it should be. I am master of the game. You are my student. Only the master can do some things. Time will reveal all." He turns to the guards. "You may leave us."

Nadira glances at her father but follows the guards out the door. Amon shuts it behind them. The guards take their stations on either side of the doorway. Nadira is perplexed. *My father did not want me in the room with Quintus. Why?* She leans against the door. A loud male scream emanates from the other side of the door. It startles her, raising the hairs on her neck, but the guards stare impassively ahead. Another blood-curdling scream reverberates through the walls, followed by a series of jumbled pleas.

She recognizes the voice. It is Councilman Quintus's.

CHAPTER XXXIV

T HE SANCTUARY ROOM is lit with hundreds of candles. Amon, clad in his priestly garb, prepares for the joining ceremony. He opens a massive ancient leather volume. Instead of studying the ancient verse, his mind wanders to two vastly different ceremonies centuries ago. Both began in happiness and ended in tragedy. However, this ceremony will be different. He picks up the leather jewelry case from the table. It holds his wedding gift to his daughter. He flips it open, the candlelight reflects what is inside, and a smile animates his usually tranquil countenance. He snaps the lid closed.

Nadira sweeps into the room, resplendent in a deep red gown with a long train, the blood-red color making her eyes glow, showcasing her pristine beauty. She greets her father with a kiss.

He steps back to admire her. "*Magnifico*. Red, the symbol of life," he exclaims.

Nadira joyfully twirls for his inspection, aware that she has never looked better.

Amon taps his finger and makes a face. "Something is missing." He retrieves the jewelry case and hands it to Nadira. "For my daughter, the queen of the vampires."

Nadira opens the case, and her eyes light up. She lifts out a magnificent ruby and diamond necklace, the mate to the earrings she is wearing. She whispers, *"La Linea de Sangre."*

"The Bloodline necklace, passed down to every vampire monarch since the beginning of time. It is one of a kind, ancient, and priceless . . . like my daughter. A rare gem." He takes the necklace from her and fastens it around her neck. The jewels sparkle against the alabaster of her breasts. Amon exclaims, "Perfection."

Nadira glows, rewarding him with a radiant smile.

"Gregor is a fortunate vampire," he tells her.

"Father, I wish you could share this happiness, love someone as I love Gregor."

Amon smiles. "Do you think you are the only woman in my life? My true love has lasted a lifetime."

She is surprised. He has never spoken of his mystery love. "Who is she?"

Amon stares past the flickering candles, his mind racing through the millennium to another place and time. "Her name was Hathor. She was my maker. I gave myself to her freely and withheld nothing." He pauses, a whisper of happiness softening his face. "She loved my brother more, so I gave her up. The two vampires I loved the most . . . together."

Stunned, she does not know what to say. Her father in love with Hathor? Who was she? A brother? He has never spoken of a brother. She wants to know more. "What happened?"

His happiness takes flight, quickly replaced by sadness. "She was murdered."

She gasps. "And your brother?"

"The brother I loved died." Hardness creeps into his eyes, and he says no more.

She embraces him and kisses his cheek. "I am sorry, Father. It was thoughtless of me to speak of the past and open old wounds," she apologizes.

"How could you know? It was a very long time ago."

They hear the music begin to play in the adjoining room.

Amon smiles at her. "Are you ready to face the firing squad?" he asks.

Nadira takes a deep breath.

Amon kisses her forehead and winks. "Your husband awaits," he tells her.

The doors open, and the glow of thousands of candles bathe them with light. The candles line the nave of this Norman-style limestone cathedral, part of an ancient monastery. Its interior is grandiose, with stone vaults soaring to the heavens. The church was built in the twelfth century, abandoned after a religious purge, and moved stone by stone to this mountain fortress. The stained-glass windows warmed by the candlelight flood the guests in a spectrum of colors. The song "Vide Cor Meum" whispers its ethereal spell. The ambiance is romantic, but the effect is gothic drama.

Vampires and humans cram the aisles, scrambling for a glimpse of the wedding of the century and the union of their future leaders. The dramatic setting is eclipsed by the guests' appearances, the vampires' attire pulled from various periods in their eternal lives. The ethnic mix is eclectic, flamboyant, and a wild kaleidoscope of color and textures. A royal mishmash of styles—Chinese robes, Elizabethan gowns, kimonos, hooped skirts, and medieval garb—populate the room. The younger vampires wearing black are in stark contrast to their seasoned counterparts. The humans pale in comparison.

Nadira floats in on Amon's arm. The elegant pair proceeds down the nave toward the choir. Their graceful procession marches past the bystanders, who peek around the church's silvered buttresses for a better view. The regal majesty of the king and future queen inspires awe in their subjects, and a hush falls over the guests. They pass Jerry and Ayame. He casually waves at Nadira. She grants him an indulgent smile.

Handsome in his knightly raiment, Gregor waits for her at the altar, sword at his side. He looks like a character from the pages of *The Canterbury Tales*. Drostan, draped in Templar splendor, stands stoic beside him. Genevieve, enticingly delicious in a low-cut black gown, waits impatiently for her sister.

Nadira and Amon formally ascend the altar. Amon kisses Nadira's cheek and then places her hand into her future husband's. Amon takes his place behind the podium, glances up at the audience, and closes the ancient leather volume.

"With respect to the mortals present, the ceremony will not be recited in the ancient tongue." He pauses for effect and then continues, "We gather on this day to witness the joining pledge of Princess Nadira Naram-Sin, my daughter and beloved acolyte, to Baron Gregor Lackovic."

Nadira and Gregor come together. Gregor is spellbound, unable to take his eyes off Nadira. Always strikingly beautiful, she borders on the divine today. She is captivated by his look as it warms her heart, which threatens to burst with happiness. To lessen the tension, he winks at her. She offers a nervous smile.

Amon turns to Gregor. "Pledge your oath."

"I, Gregor Lackovic, take Princess Nadira Naram-Sin to be my mate. I pledge that your name will always be the name I cry aloud in the dead of night. Our love is never ending. We remain, forevermore, equals," Gregor declares.

Amon addresses Nadira. "Pledge your oath."

"I, Nadira Naram-Sin, take Baron Gregor Lackovic to be my mate. I pledge that your name will always be the name I cry aloud in the dead of night. Our love is never ending. We remain, forevermore, equals." Her eyes are brimming with tears.

Drostan steps up and hands Gregor a gold ring that he slips on Nadira's right hand above her engagement ring.

"A life without beginning and without end," Gregor pledges.

Genevieve hands Nadira a man's gold ring that she slides on Gregor's right hand.

"A life without beginning and without end," Nadira repeats.

Amon steps from behind the podium. He ties Gregor and Nadira's hands together with an embroidered silk cloth. "Gregor and Nadira are one. They share one life and one heart as husband and wife forever," Amon declares.

Each has waited an eternity for this moment. Their eyes communicate silently until Gregor takes her in his arms and seals their union with a long kiss.

A chant drags them from their private world. *"Regis Filia."* The chant is contagious. The audience picks it up, accompanied by a barrage of clapping and cheers.

"Regis Filia. Regis Filia. Regis Filia."

Jerry leans over to Ayame and whispers, "What does that mean?"

"It's Latin for 'daughter of the king,'" Ayame answers.

Nadira and Gregor lock hands, a symbol of their unity. Amon places gold diadems on their heads as symbols of their royal destiny. Amon lifts their entwined hands. The audience members jump to their feet and cheer wildly. Gregor sweeps his new bride into his arms and boldly kisses her sweet mouth.

One bystander is not cheering. He slinks into a dark corner of the balcony and stares down at the happy couple. His face is twisted into a sneer, his fangs are exposed, and his eyes are deadly daggers. Coatl plays the voyeur to his enemy's joy. His eyes shift to Amon, who is staring back at him. Amon taunts the hapless wretch, deliberately places his fist to his chest, and salutes the couple, which elicits a new wave of chanting from the guests. Coatl's rage clearly etched on his sharp features, he takes one last look at the beaming newlyweds until he can stand it no more, pledges his vengeance, and disappears into the darkness.

Amon watches the shadowy figure storm out of the church. He thinks, *The die is cast, and the next move belongs to Coatl. My work here is almost complete. My daughter is safely joined to Gregor. I have one more thing to do and it is finished.* He smiles and whispers, "Check."

CHAPTER XXXV

GREGOR LEADS NADIRA by the hand to their bedroom, pauses outside the door, and raises her hand to his lips. "Alone at last," he whispers. His smoldering eyes and beguiling smile promise much, making her heart race in anticipation of the pleasures to come. He scoops her up in his arms, and a nervous giggle slips between her lips as he prods the door open with his foot.

The soft glow of a thousand candles lights the room. Gardenias blanket the interior, releasing their sensual fragrance. The windows' sheer curtains are drawn back to allow the moonlight to caress the red silk-laden bed. The chandelier's pendants tinkle with each vagrant breeze.

Nadira looks at Gregor. "You did this for me?"

His eyes smile, pleased that he surprised her.

Captivated by the look in his eyes, her body responds with a delicious tingling in her stomach.

"Your story about the loss your virginity touched me. I wanted tonight to be your first time with love and tenderness," he promises, watching for her reaction.

She is overwhelmed. No one has done anything like this for her, not even Cristo. She snuggles closer, burying her face in his chest and breathing deeply of his scent that reminds her of the Scottish Highlands, earthy and windswept. She offers him her soft ripe lips.

He accepts her gift and covers her mouth with his, playing a game of hide and seek with their tongues.

Her arms embrace his neck, pulling him closer. "Let me down, Husband."

Reluctantly, he releases her from their embrace. She pulls the comb from her hair, allowing it to cascade down her back. He caresses its silky texture, his fingers tracing the curve of her cheek and neck. Blissful, her eyes close and a soft moan escapes her lips. When she opens her eyes, he is staring at her.

"Beloved, you have bewitched me body and soul. We will have many passion-filled days together. Let us make tonight the standard we measure them all by," he tells her. He showers her face with kisses and runs his tongue over her neck, tasting and teasing her senses. Her breath quickens. He moves behind her, inches the gown off her shoulders, and kisses her naked flesh. "I have waited so long," he groans. His tongue tickles the curve of her throat, his lips slide across the satiny skin of her shoulder, and his fangs penetrate her soft flesh. A trickle of blood escapes his lips and undulates across her breast.

Unprepared for the power and force of her blood, his eyes fly open. Over four thousand years of memories flood his psyche. Her memories appear as flashes of bizarre rituals, pharaohs, Cristo, burning pyres, uncontrollable rage, shame, and then a vast emptiness. Her memories play like a schizophrenic video in his brain. Her strongest emotion is loneliness followed by a yearning for love. He sees himself as she sees him, the key to her happiness.

The steady beat of her heart rings in his ears and reverberates in his veins, growing stronger by the minute, the sheer power of it threatening to engulf him. He withdraws his fangs, breaks the connection, and staggers backward. He struggles to catch his breath and overcome his sense of disorientation. It takes a few minutes to return to reality. He inspects the puncture marks on her shoulder, but they've already disappeared.

"I should have warned you that my blood is potent," she tells him.

"What a rush." An expression of astonishment is affixed to his face.

She kisses him, and it deepens and grows in intensity until both grasp for air.

"Husband, let us remove your knightly arraignment," she suggests.

"*Husband*—I like the sound of that. Wife, do you remember how?" he teases.

"It's been a few centuries, but I have a long memory. I am pleased you did not include the armor," she teases.

"It always scratched in the most unseemly of places." He looks at her knowingly.

She smiles coyly. "Now, we can't have that, can we?"

Methodically, she reaches around his waist and unbuckles his scabbard and sword. She carefully lays them to the side, kisses him, and continues with his surcoat and doublet, dropping each to the floor. He kicks off his boots. All that remains are his linen undershirt and pants. He smiles and whips the undershirt over his head. She grins and runs her hand over his bare chest. Her touch is electric, sending goosebumps over them both.

"Delicious," she purrs with sweet pleasure.

She reaches behind her back and fumbles with the gown's laces. Gregor spins her around, unlaces her gown with practiced hands, and peels it open. He lavishes her back with kisses. In a slow motion striptease, she edges the gown downward, exposing her breasts and waist, wiggling the gown pass her hips and slender legs to slide to the floor in a heap, her lush body exposed.

His eyes devour her. "Much better."

She steps into his arms, feeling his desire. They gaze into each other's eyes. The flame of passion burns brightly between them. Patience exhausted, he scoops her up in his arms, kisses her roughly, and carries her to the bed.

He lays her on the crimson silk, stares down at her, and drinks in the sight of her sculpted-marble body. Her skin seems to glow, burning hotter, and her eyes capture him in their embrace. He drops his pants, and her eyes widen at the sight of him, which sends a thrill from his heart to his loins.

She reaches up, beckoning him. He climbs into her embrace. Theirs becomes a duet of kisses, sighs, and embraces. They explore each mound and crevice, tasting, teasing, and tantalizingly moving closer to a physical junction.

Her tongue traces past his manhood to his inner thigh. His artery pulses beneath her lips. She impales it and samples his blood. His memories are a collage of great battles, a horrific attack, rejection, aching hunger, loneliness, and then only of her, as though he did not exist until they met. The magnitude of his devotion and love overwhelms her. She releases her hold on his artery. "I didn't know," she whispers.

He kisses her and tastes the salty tang of his own blood. Their duet of passion reaches its zenith. Slowly, he joins himself to her and watches her shimmering eyes darken with pleasure. Their bodies are linked in a blissful coupling, moving together and matching pace and rhythm toward the ultimate rapture. His thrusts build intensity into a climactic merger of body and soul, a final cataclysmic release of life and death.

Spent, they collapse into each other's arms. Breath returns, and her head lolls on his chest as his hand tangles her hair. Sated, they savor the afterglow.

"Words cannot describe how I feel," she languidly murmurs.

"Then don't use them," Gregor smiles, self-satisfied.

She rises on her elbow to see his face. Their minds interweave and whisper their souls' secrets, their hearts' treasures communicated without speech because words are inadequate. A shared kiss becomes the stamp that delivers their silent message.

They rest with their bodies intertwined in a sweet lassitude, listening to their hearts beat in unison. One flesh—together at last.

CHAPTER XXXVI

COATL CREEPS INTO Amon's study through the secret door. He scans the room and spots Amon at the chessboard, gazing out the window. Coatl slinks forward.

"You have come for me, Brother?" Amon asks.

Startled, the element of surprise lost, Coatl drops all pretenses. "Yes, Big Brother," Coatl answers.

Amon rises, walks over to Coatl, embraces him, and kisses his cheeks, arousing Coatl's suspicion. "Do not be afraid. I will do you no harm," Amon reassures his brother.

"You knew I would come?" Coatl asks.

"Yes, Little Brother. I always knew you would." A forlorn smile crosses Amon's face.

"I should be heir," Coatl reminds Amon.

Pity for his brother etched on his face, Amon replies, "Yes. I hoped to rule beside you. You were the best and brightest of us. However, you embraced our dark nature. Crazed megalomania rotted your soul. Death and destruction are your constant companions. Your kingdom would be one of chaos."

"The darkness has made me powerful," Coatl disagrees.

Amon shakes his head. "You delude yourself, Brother. You are strong but not powerful. Absolute power corrupts and vanquishes integrity. It is easier to follow base desires than master control and obtain true power. Your perverse appetites weaken you. They are the strings I use to manipulate you. The light is always stronger than the dark," Amon tells him.

Coatl cocks his head. "Manipulate me?"

Amon glances toward his desk. The Qayin dagger lies exposed and ready. Coatl eyes the weapon and ponders his brother's motive.

Amon dares him. "If you want to rule, it is the only way."

Coatl hesitates. "We could still rule together."

"'The light shines in the darkness, and the darkness comprehends it not.'" Amon studies his brother's puzzled expression. "Still you do not understand this scripture." He shakes his head sadly and says, "The time for that dream has passed. We do not share the same vision. Mine is a world where humans and vampires coexist to the betterment of both species. Your vision is twisted and corrupted with the subjugation of humanity for our pleasure. I won't allow it."

Coatl is incensed. "Will not allow it? Who are you to dictate to me? I have lived in your shadow for centuries, stealing the scraps from your table like a mongrel dog. My followers do not share your vision of assimilation with humans. Coexistence is an abomination. We will fight any movement in that direction, even if it means war."

Amon watches his brother work himself up into a frenzy. He fuels the fire with his next comment. "Without assimilation, we will perish. The fate of our people is uncertain. There is no place for you and your followers in our new world. I have protected you for the last time."

Coatl cackles. "Protected me?"

"At first, I could deny you nothing, but the brother I loved died. Only the creature Coatl remains, and he leaves a wake of slaughter and carnage. How many humans have died at your hands? Tens of thousands? How many vampires? Even one is too many. I protected you when justice demanded death for your crimes. Eventually, the good of the many outweighs the needs of a lost brother. Gregor would have killed you that day if Nadira had not stopped him. Do you know why you were powerless against him, Brother?" Amon derides his brother.

Coatl snaps back, "Instruct me, Big Brother."

"Love. His love makes him powerful. Their love makes them indestructible," Amon answers.

"Love is sentimental nonsense. It cannot stand against tanks or guns. Wars are won in the real world, not the pages of poetry," Coatl spits the words out.

Amon disagrees. "It was not nonsense with Hathor."

Coatl shakes his head. "You promised never to mention her name again. We both loved her, but she died."

He rebukes his brother. "She did not just die. You murdered her in a fit of jealous rage. You can deceive yourself but not me. My love died with her, and the last vestige of good deserted you. You have become the twisted monster that stands before me."

"You lie. She was unfaithful. You were lovers!" Coatl shrieks.

Amon studies his brother, who teeters on the brink of sanity. His brother's capacity for self-deception is limitless. Amon knows he must nudge Coatl to the edge of madness. He calmly states, "You were wrong about us, and you are wrong now. You are not fit to be a king."

Coatl's control snaps. He lunges to the desk, grasps the dagger, and advances on his brother. There is no mistaking the murderous expression riveted to his face. Amon waits patiently for his brother and the inevitable outcome to their quarrel. Coatl, blinded by rage, does not see his brother but the impediment to his success. He grasps Amon by the shoulder and plunges the dagger into his heart.

"Now I am king," he rants.

Amon covers Coatl's hands with his and buries the dagger into his chest to the hilt. A look of relief floods Amon's face. He smiles and looks his brother in the eye. "Checkmate. I sacrifice my bishop to win the game," Amon declares. His poor brother was never good at games of strategy.

Coatl, shocked by Amon's statement, stares at his bloody hands and releases Amon, who sinks to his knees, struggling to remain upright. Coatl crouches down and awkwardly cradles his brother. The brothers stare at each other.

"I spared you all these years for this very moment. You completed what my daughter would not. Her love prevented her from conducting the ascension ceremony. She sacrificed the crown for love, something you will never understand. Your lust for power drives you to fratricide. You finished the ritual for her," Amon reveals.

Comprehension registers on Coatl's face quickly replaced by horror. His rage vanishes on a tide of self-castigation.

"You killed me and thus sealed your doom. Nadira will hunt you down and wipe any evidence of you from our history," Amon warns.

"Brother, what have I done?" Tears slip down Coatl's face.

"Hathor prophesied you would be my Cain. Cain slew his brother, and then God cursed him. So it shall be with you. The cycle of life and death complete." Amon grabs Coatl hand.

"What will I do?" Coatl asks.

"Run," Amon answers. Amon raises his eyes to Coatl's face and searches for some vestige of the younger brother of his childhood. "I will remember a beautiful, golden boy full of life and laughter."

Coatl sobs and clutches his brother's hand.

Shouts and knocks on the study doors interrupt them. "Your Majesty, are you all right? Please, sire, open the doors! Coatl is in the building." Drostan pounds on the outer doors.

"Father! Open the doors!" Nadira shouts. Concern gives way to alarm and she orders, "Break them down!"

Amon peers at his brother. "Your time is at an end."

The brothers share one last moment. Coatl gently props Amon against a chair, an obscene sight with the dagger jutting from his chest. Amon watches his brother flee while his life ebbs into a morbid pool on the carpet.

Coatl escapes through the secret door just as the study doors crash open. A squad of heavily armed Vigiles floods the room. They scan the area for danger.

One shouts, "Clear!"

Nadira rushes past them to Amon's side. She cradles him in her lap. Blood blankets him, soaking her clothes and hands. Amon raises his hand to her face marking it his blood.

"Father!" she sobs.

"Daughter." He smiles weakly.

"Let me help you." She bites her wrist, but he grabs it in a vise like grip.

"No!" he exclaims.

She is surprised at the ferocity of his hold and his adamant denial. She pleads, "My blood can revive you."

He shakes his head. "It is my time."

Nadira hugs him to her breast, rocking him back and forth, tears streaming down her face. Gregor and Genevieve kneel beside them. Genevieve clutches his hand tightly and sobs uncontrollably. He offers her the ghost of a smile. He gazes up at Drostan. "My loyal knight and protector of the realm."

Drostan kneels. "Sire." Drostan's face hardens as he wrestles to control of his emotions. His fury cries for release, but his strict discipline wins out.

Amon studies him and lays his hand on his bowed head. "It was Coatl," Amon says.

Drostan salutes his dying monarch and signals the Vigiles to start the search for Coatl. A number of them exit the room double-time. The remaining soldiers guard their king.

Nadira utters a heart-wrenching moan. Gregor wraps his arm around her shoulders; they lock arms and cradle Amon.

"Gentle Genevieve, please instruct Shen regarding the ascension ceremony. There must be no gap in leadership."

Genevieve nods as tears streak her cheeks.

He tells Drostan, "Protect your wife. Coatl covets her."

Drostan nods, his anguish threatening to crack his brave outer shell.

Amon gazes into Nadira's eyes and communicates in their special way. He reminds her of their discussion in the mediation room. "It is your time. My time is finite. We must complete the Enlightenment," he tells her.

"I'm afraid."

"Do not be." Amon weakly turns his head, exposing his neck.

Reluctantly, Nadira cradles his head and punctures his jugular. The Enlightenment is a ritual so secret that it has only been witnessed by sovereigns. The occupants of the room are not sure what is happening.

Amon's blood explodes into Nadira's subconscious. His memories are a kaleidoscope of experiences back to the beginning of time, flooding her senses and obliterating reality. She can barely absorb the images. A whirlwind of people, places, and knowledge sweeps the recesses of her mind until she reaches a black void and peers into the abyss. Fear creeps into her psyche until Amon telepathically communicates with her.

In her trance, Amon stands before her, cloaked in white, radiant, with no evidence of the savage attack. *Daughter,* he says.

"How can this be?" She touches his chest.

"Come with me." He takes her hand.

She feels herself rising above the room. Apprehensive, she peeks down and sees her dying father cradled in her arms and surrounded by people. This out-of-body experience is disturbing and unsettling.

"Do not look backward." He beckons her.

She follows him, higher and higher, to a strange place bereft of a sky, the sun, or clouds. There is no context to identify where they are. An utter silence and eerie stillness occupies this vacuum as though robbed of organic life. She looks to her father. *"Where are we?"* she asks.

He answers with a puzzle. *"Nowhere and everywhere."*

"Is this real?"

"As real as anything your mind perceives. Slip off the chains of certainty and allow your consciousness to expand. This is the dimension where thought and energy intersect," he answers.

"I don't understand." She steps closer to him, loses her footing, and reaches out to grab her father's hand, but he seems far away.

He watches her grasping at the empty space between them. *"It's time to go: you to your destiny . . . me to mine."* His statement is cryptic and his face enigmatic.

Her troubled mind tumbles back to earth and plunges into the recesses of her conscious. She gasps, releases his vein, and breaks the bond. Her unfocused eyes stare blankly into space, and her mind spins like a carousel.

"Now you understand the power of the mind," Amon says.

She is rocked to the core by her experience, tears bathing her cheeks as her head bobs her acknowledgement.

Amon pleads with Gregor, "Take care of my precious daughter."

"Always," he promises and kisses Amon's hand.

Nadira clutches Amon. "Father, don't leave me!"

"We are one blood—connected by love. I am with you always." He strokes her hair. "Release me. Let me join Hathor and the others. Allow me the peace I have earned," he pleads. He gazes at his family, their familiar faces stricken with grief. He raises his hand. "I place the fate of our people into your capable hands, Queen Nadira." The others watch the tragic passing of leadership.

A serene expression transfixes his face. He releases the bonds of this life and slips into the next plane of existence.

Nadira utters a loud wail, the cry of a dying animal. It sends chills down their spines.

A powerful tremor rocks the building, followed by another. The residents of the Ordinatio scurry about for shelter. The occupants of the study scramble to secure their surroundings. The tremors rhythmically pummel the foundation until the windows crack. Gregor realizes Nadira's anguish is spiraling out of control.

He says softly, "Beloved," and she concentrates on the sound of his voice. "You must stop. You are terrifying your subjects." Gregor slowly pries her fingers from Amon's body. "You must release him." Gregor hugs Nadira and indicates to Drostan to assist with Amon's body.

Drostan's shaking hands extract the dagger from Amon's chest, and he ceremoniously hands it to Genevieve, who clutches it to her breast, the blood of their king staining her dress.

"Rest in Hathor's embrace," Nadira whispers, bending down to kiss him.

Mystified, Gregor, Drostan, and Genevieve look at each other, unfamiliar with the name Hathor. Drostan embraces his wife, who buries her sobbing face in his chest. Gregor watches Nadira clutching Amon's hand. Glancing around the room at the shattered faces, he realizes Nadira must assume her new role with little time for mourning.

"The people await their new queen," Gregor tells her and shelves his sorrow until a later date. He stands and stretches out his hand.

She studies her husband and knows everything will be all right with him at her side. Her sense of duty replaces the excruciating pain. She looks up at him, grasps his hand, and stands up, but her knees shake, and he shifts his hand to steady her. She clings to him for dear life.

The occupants of the room watch her expectantly before kneeling and pledging, "Long rule Queen Nadira."

Nadira regains her composure, moves toward the door, but pauses by Drostan. She commands him, "Do not kill him. I want Coatl for myself." Her eyes are fearsome.

Drostan replies, "Yes, Your Majesty." Her wish is his command.

"Take your king. Prepare him for his funeral," she commands the Vigiles.

Drostan and the guards gather around Amon's body. They lift it to their shoulders and silently proceed out the door. Nadira steps outside the sanctuary of the study. Jean-Louis and a detachment of royal guards stride to her, stop, and kneel. "Your Majesty. We are at your service." They rise and fall into position around the royal couple.

Dazed, Nadira instinctively heads for her quarters. She knows her bravado will not last long. News of their sovereign's assassination spreads like wild fire. Leaderless for the first time in centuries, fear and trepidation grip the residents of the Ordinatio. Vampires and humans mill about aimlessly and congregate in the reception hall. Nadira comes face to face with her subjects, whose apprehension she can taste. She affixes a strained smile of confidence onto her face and addresses them.

"Today, our sovereign was assassinated by the criminal Coatl. We have all lost a great leader. I have lost my beloved father. Our nation will observe the customary mourning period and perform the rite of transition to honor him. I promise that justice will be swift. My regime, although birthed with blood, will be built on hope for a brighter future for all of us," she announces.

The people in the crowd, in a wave-like motion, drop to their knees, bow their heads, and proclaim, "Long rule Queen Nadira."

The agony of Amon's death robs her of any pleasure from this sign of allegiance. Her consuming thought is of her duty. She puts her mind on autopilot and glances at Gregor, who knows her so well that she does not have to communicate her need for privacy. She acknowledges each group of subjects that offers condolences. Her face aches from the effort. She continues the gauntlet that seems to drag on endlessly. The distance to their quarters becomes a mirage. Gregor sees the toll it is taking on her and pats her hand. He is the rock supporting her crumbling foundation.

Kashta approaches the group. In her weakened emotional state, she knows that if he kneels, it will crack her last vestige of emotional control. Kashta falls in beside Nadira. He nods. "Your Majesty." She is grateful there are no outward displays of alliance.

"Kashta," she says.

The party continues until they reach the private hallway to her quarters. Nadira's knees buckle, and Gregor scoops her up in his arms and trots to the door. The security detachment trails behind them.

"No interruptions without my permission," he orders.

Kashta enters the room, locks the door behind them, and takes his new post. Gregor carries Nadira to the bedroom and lays her on the bed. This bed, home to her recent pleasure, will now be home to her present sorrow. He embraces her and feels the racking shudder of her shoulders.

"Gregor, what will I do without Amon?" Nadira tearfully asks.

"I do not know, my love. Do what he wanted you to do. Live." He brushes back her hair and asks, "Do you want to be alone?"

"For a little while, please," she answers.

He kisses her forehead. "If you need anything, I'll be right outside the door." He gets up and leaves the room.

His absence leaves a vacuum in the room. She realizes asking him to leave might have been a mistake, just as Amon's death leaves a vacuum in her life. Her father was constantly supporting, loving, and teaching her. Always manipulating and strategizing, he played life out on a chessboard. *His loved ones were his chest pieces, and he moved us about until he won—we were unaware of his manipulation. Chess is a game played by two. Amon was a solitary gamemaster. He told me chess was like ruling, that it was a lonely profession.*

Amon manipulated Gregor until I was aware of what was obvious to everyone else. All the years of unhappiness wasted when love was staring me in the face. My father knew I needed Gregor as much as he needed me. Together, we are complete. I am so stubborn that sometimes I miss the obvious.

My father is gone. Who will fill this void? Does someone need to, or was his goal my own self-sufficiency and ability to function independently?

An intriguing concept grips Nadira, and her mind races dangerously close to an epiphany. *Is Amon interconnected with me even after his death?* Nadira goes to the dresser and retrieves the jewelry case. She sits on the edge of the bed, opens it, and ponders the Bloodline necklace. *I will wear it to my ascension, just as Hathor wore it at hers. Coatl murdered his wife and brother. Why would he do that?*

Until the Enlightenment, she knew very little about her father's past. Now she realizes there is still more to learn. His death clarified that she loved him above all things.

Reunited with Hathor, he is free of the confines of a physical body and the duties of a king. Ancient vampires do not just die, and rulers do not just step down. Amon planned his transcendence to this next plane of existence. It was the only way to purchase his freedom. He groomed me to rule, secured for me a worthy husband, and surrounded me with loyal friends. Amon even tricked his brother into executing him. Everything I would need to secure the throne.

She glances down at the necklace. *I am part of an ancient tradition of rulers, the first female vampire in millennia to rule, and in the rare position to alter the face of vampire and human relationships. I am the one vampire who can bring Amon's vision to fruition. Amon was right when he presented me with this necklace. I am one of a kind. I am the key.*

Exhausted, she lies down on the bed, clutching Amon's parting gift to her. Her last thoughts before drifting off to sleep are of Amon, Gregor, and Hathor.

Gregor steps softly into the bedroom to check on his wife. She is sprawled asleep, a small smile on her face and the jewelry case clutched in her hand. He bends over, kisses her, takes the case, and places it on the dresser. He covers her with a blanket, lies down beside her, and watches her sleep, wishing his queen sweet, peaceful dreams.

CHAPTER XXXVII

THE GLASS-ROOFED ROTUNDA of the Ordinatio offers a commanding view of the mountain's deep chasm, an impressive venue for a public ceremony. Amon rests atop a central dais, laid out in his Egyptian priestly attire and draped in a leopard robe. The silence in the rotunda, punctuated by the occasional sob, unsettles Nadira, making the pounding of her heart deafening. She is a living statue with cold flesh draped in white mourning, her face devoid of color except for a slash of red lips and the sparkle of the Bloodline earrings. The strain of viewing her father's corpse is reflected in her desolate eyes. Her sole comfort is that the ceremony affords Amon the respect he deserves, but the thoughts of so many threaten to disrupt her dignified façade.

She filters out their sorrow and glances toward the sky, seeing a falcon hovering overhead and observing the funeral. Is this the messenger of Horus, the Egyptian god of the sun? It circles twice and then flies out of view.

She glances at the mourners, wishing she could fly away like the falcon and escape all this death. She remains steadfast, standing adjacent to Amon and surrounded by her family. Gregor and Drostan are clad as pallbearers in red robes. A procession of somber mourners dressed in white, symbolizing rebirth, snake around the deceased. Once the rotunda fills to overflowing, she addresses the crowd.

"We gather today to honor a singularly great ruler among many rulers: Amon, the Hidden One, Sovereign of the Ancient Gods, who united us, preserved us during tribulation, and built our strong nation. My father was a visionary who could see beyond our differences and prejudices to the promising future for vampires. I glimpsed the future through his eyes. Now it stands before me"—Nadira spreads her hands and gestures—"in the faces of vampires and humans united in their grief for him." She studies her subjects. "I promise you all that I will fulfill my father's dream. No longer will we hide in the shadows, spectators of history, but we will be participants of this world and make it a better place because of vampires and humans."

Nadira scans the many faces watching her expectantly, all filled with the same expression: hope. It is the one thing she can give her people and her legacy to her father. She signals Gregor and Drostan, who take their position around Amon's burial platform along with the other red-robed pallbearers. In unison, they lift Amon's coffin, placing it on their shoulders, and begin the long journey to the site of transition. The vampires take up a low methodical chant as the procession inches its way out of the rotunda. Nadira, flanked by Kashta, Genevieve, and the royal household, falls in behind the pallbearers, followed by the mourning vampires. Once the last vampire exits the area, a detachment of Vigiles blocks the humans, who are forbidden to participate in the rest of the ceremony.

The ancestral lair of vampires is the site of Amon's rite of transition, a singular honor for ancient vampires. Its location is a guarded secret, a cave deep within the granite bedrock; isolated and protected, it has served as sanctuary during the Great Persecution, a repository for the ancient ceremonies, and a place sacred to all vampires. Nadira's ceremony of succession will be here.

The cave contains a massive central cavern, festooned with stalagmites and stalactites. A waterfall overflows into a pool at the rear of the cavern, and mid-chamber, a low, sloping ramp is the only access in or out. The area is illuminated with torches as no modern intrusion is permitted in this sanctuary—it has been thus for centuries. The exquisitely carved walls have high reliefs that depict vampire history. Scenes of horrific battles, great victories, vampires burned at the stake, and Vigiles slaying the vampire hunters decorate the walls. Sculptures of the great vampire kings and queens proudly stand at attention among the carvings. Nadira pauses at the statue of Amon. The stone has aged a golden ochre color, capturing Amon's skin tone, and combined with the artist's realistic rendering, the likeness is startling. She touches its face—the stone is as cold as death—and withdraws her hand.

The procession winds down the ramp into the cavern, the way illuminated by torchbearers. The vampires' haunting funerary chant reverberates against the cavern walls. Its melancholic ancient lyrics weave a tapestry of mournful gloominess. The pallbearers carry their precious cargo to a large wooden pyre in the center of the cavern. They hold Amon's coffin aloft, chanting, and lower it on top of the pyre. Nadira, Genevieve, and the other mourners follow behind and slowly fill the cavern. Each mourner tosses a sprig of wolf's bane on the coffin. Gregor and Drostan take their respective places beside their wives.

A tall red-haired vampire waits beside a podium carved out of a massive crystalline stalagmite. He is an imposing presence, with wild hair and intense green eyes that hint at incredible power. A Druid with a past shrouded in the mists of time and rumored to be the wizard Merlin, this is Oengus, the spiritual leader of the vampires.

Oengus studies the mourners, the consummate performer waiting for the perfect moment to begin the ceremony. The chanting dies, the torchlight casts its antiquated glow, the atmosphere drowns in sorrow, and the air is pregnant with grief.

"Viva enim mortuorum in memoria vivorum est posita." Oengus's baritone voice shatters the stillness, setting the stage for Amon's eulogy. "'The life of the dead is retained in the living.' Our sovereign Amon will indeed live in our nation's consciousness. He was fluidity itself—a politician when diplomacy was necessary, a decisive commander during a crisis, and always a strategist, manipulating and striving for the betterment of his people. He rescued us from extinction and dragged us kicking and screaming into the new millennium. His reign was cut short by treachery, but evil does not divide us; instead, it empowers and unites us." Oengus's speech resonates with the listeners, who nod their encouragement.

Nadira steps up to the podium. "My father believed in the united strength of humans and vampires. His favorite saying was *Dum inter hominis sumus, colamus humanitaten.* 'As long as we are among humans, let us be humane.' He believed vampires had evolved beyond our human origins and beyond our predatory instincts. There is nothing we cannot achieve with humanity." Her voice cracks.

Oengus declares, "*Vita mutator, nun tollitor.* 'Life is changed, not taken away.'"

He signals Gregor and Drostan, who pick up torches, carry them to the pyre, and await the signal. Nadira hesitates, loathe to give up her father. Her courage flees, and tears slip past her downcast lashes. Finally, she nods her consent. Gregor touches his torch to the pyre, and Drostan repeats the action. The flames seize the wood and steal across the pyre.

Nadira grasps Genevieve, clings to her, and sobs without reservation. The mourners watch as the pyre is transformed into an inferno. Gregor and Drostan embrace their wives, and everyone stares at the blaze. Once the fire reaches Amon's coffin, the flames change to bright blue, whirling and twisting into a humanoid shape. It hovers on top of the pyre. The mourners gasp when the figure wavers, undulates, and stretches out what appears to be a limb toward Nadira.

"Father." She reaches toward the figure.

All eyes are transfixed on the pyre. The blue flames drift, waver, and then shoot through the cavern ceiling, soaring to the heavens and disappearing. A sigh escapes the mourners mesmerized by the fire and astonished by what they witnessed. The pyre continues to burn, collapses on itself, and crumbles to the ground. Nadira, racked with grief, buries her face in Gregor's chest.

Oengus completes the ceremony as it began—in Latin. "*Consummatum est.*"

CHAPTER XXXVIII

NADIRA STARES OUT the windows of Amon's study—now her study. She turns toward the closed doors. "Come in," she says.

Drostan steps inside. "Your Majesty," Drostan says.

Nadira frowns. "Please do not call me that. Every time I hear 'Your Majesty,' I look around and to see to whom they are speaking. Just Nadira." She smiles at him.

Drostan humors her. "Yes, Your Majesty. Excuse me, Nadira. I will do so in private."

She nods, accepting his small concession. He notices Kashta standing quietly in the corner. Her shadow, he never leaves her side except when she is with Gregor. He blends so seamlessly into her life that Drostan frequently forgets Kashta is present, a clever trick for a vampire so massive.

"I did not knock. How did you know I was at the door?" he asks, and she smiles knowingly. "Your father did the same thing all the time. Sometimes, he'd answer my questions before I asked."

Her eyes bore into his. "You don't have anything to hide from me, do you, Drostan?"

"No," he answers. Embarrassed, he looks away. He cannot look her in the eye lest she know what is in his true heart; his love for her exposed would destroy those they both love. He changes subjects. "Coatl escaped. The slippery bastard got away."

Nadira studies him. He is hiding something of a personal nature regarding a woman he loves. His thoughts are unclear, but she assumes he must be concerned about Genevieve. Amon's death has been a strain on everyone. "Do not punish yourself about his escape. Coatl is cunning and obviously planned his escape well," she says.

Drostan nods. "The High Council indicted Councilman Quintus for treason. He stands trial next month and is a wealth of information. He confessed to foreknowledge of the attempt on you, Haseem, and Gregor, but he denies knowledge of Coatl's plan to assassinate Amon."

Nadira adds, "Trying to save his own skin."

"Agreed."

Nadira contemplates him. "Drostan, what I am about to tell you cannot leave this room."

The seriousness of her tone catches him off guard. "You have my word," he swears.

"I need the Vigiles ready for war."

He is not surprised. Amon realized that war between the factions opposing human integration was inevitable and his death would be the catalyst for both sides. "We'll be operational in three months. Amon had a contingency plan for years," he reports. "Why do you think he insisted on all the tactical, weapon, and physical training for you? He feared that he would not survive the transition and wanted you ready. It is why he pushed you so hard. *Exercitus sine doce corpus est sine spirtu*," he tells her.

"'An army without a leader is a body without spirit,'" she translates. "I intend to make the announcement at my national address." Nadira glances toward the door just as Genevieve enters the room. Genevieve saunters over to Drostan and plants a kiss on his cheek. He grins at her. Nadira studies the two of them. *Everything looks fine between them . . . maybe I misread Drostan.*

"I am here to help you practice your speech for the ascension ceremony. You have to get the enunciation perfect. The ancient language can be tricky," Genevieve advises Nadira.

"Good, there are a few words that I am not sure of the pronunciation. I haven't used them in centuries," Nadira answers and looks up when Jerry enters the room.

"Your Majesty, your clothing for this evening is ready and in your quarters," he says.

Gregor strolls into the room. "It looks like Grand Central Station." His observation elicits a round of laughter.

Nadira stands and addresses them. "May I have a few minutes with my husband, please? Genevieve, please come back in about thirty minutes. I want to discuss all the particulars regarding the ambassadors and magistrates arriving for my first council session."

"Are you sure that is enough time?" she adds saucily with a wink.

Drostan chuckles and playfully swats her butt. "Troublemaker!"

Gregor grins at Nadira. "Not nearly enough." They all leave and close the door. He sweeps Nadira in his arms. "Time for a quickie?" He kisses her, but she shakes her head.

"Never a quickie. You are like a fine wine to be savored slowly, the first taste as sweet as the last. I love you, my king." Those three little words make his heart leap for joy and his loins swell.

"I love you, my queen. I waited centuries to tell you." He stares at her with those marvelous eyes that melt her knees.

"I waited centuries to hear you," she purrs.

"My love, I am truly sorry we failed to protect Amon." He takes her hand in his. His apology is heartfelt.

"Beloved, there was nothing you could do. Amon wanted Coatl to slay him."

Gregor is puzzled. "I don't follow."

Nadira explains that during the Enlightenment, she was able to unravel the mystery of how a powerful vampire like Amon was caught unaware. "Amon knew I would never execute him and ascend the throne. So, he manipulated Coatl into killing him, thus bringing all the loose ends together." She does not include the revelation that Coatl is Amon's brother.

"A brilliant solution to the problem." Gregor ponders her statement and notices the ring on her left finger. "You are wearing Haseem's ring."

"As a reminder of true loyalty and devotion"—she lifts her right hand and indicates her engagement ring—"and this one the enduring power of love." She kisses him.

"Whoa. If we get started, we will never stop." He kisses her nose and then adds, "See you before the ceremony."

She grins. "Give me a few minutes alone, and then send in Genevieve."

He kisses her hand and leaves.

Nadira watches him go. Alone in Amon's study and surrounded by his things, she feels his presence. She walks to Amon's chessboard, contemplates the chess pieces, and remembers all the lessons she learned on it. She picks up the black bishop, pressing it to her heart. "Father, you sacrificed yourself for your people and for me. I give you my oath that your sacrifice will not be in vain." She gazes down at the board. The white queen moves diagonally across the board. Nadira smiles, sets the bishop down, and takes her place on the opposite side of the chessboard. "Let us begin."

The End . . . or the Beginning

G.A. Stratton is an award-winning author of numerous screenplays and works of fiction. *Shadow of Life* started as a feature script, but her readers loved the characters and asked for a novel. She lives with her family in the film capital of the south, Atlanta, Georgia, where she is at work on her next book, *Shadow of War*. For more information, visit www.gastratton.com.